ANCIENT HISTORY

A SOUTH ROCK HIGH NOVEL

A.J. TRUMAN

Cover by Bailey McGinn

Proofreading by Heather Caryn

❀ Created with Vellum

1

AMOS

Hamlet pondered to be or not to be. Tina Turner asked what's love got to do with it. And this morning, I got stuck with my own eternal, soul-bursting question.

Is Hutch Hawkins back?

I was gabbing with my fellow teachers in the faculty lounge during my off period, gossiping about some high school drama that we should've been too mature to care about, and through the window of the door, the familiar waves of auburn hair and chiseled profile of Hutch Hawkins flashed for a second as someone walked by with Principal Aguilar.

Was that someone Hutch?

Now perhaps I drank my morning coffee too fast or inhaled too much chalk dust. It'd been a long-ass time since I last saw him. A freaking decade. By design. He was the reason Britney Spears invented the word toxic. He was the reason why people willingly cried along to Adele songs.

Not me, of course.

Not for a long time anyway.

But the thing was, a guy like Hutch was impossible to forget.

He was etched into my brain and my soul. And there was a Hutch-shaped hole from when I extracted him from my heart a decade ago.

But now he was back?

"Uh, Mr. Bright?" Rosalee, my star student of fourth period, stared at me from the front row of class.

In fact, twenty-four sets of unblinking eyes stared at me. It was like that nightmare that people had about being in front of class naked. Except I wasn't naked, but it was just as embarrassing.

"Yeah?"

"You were talking about the Middle Ages and then you trailed off." She grit her teeth as if she were watching a car wreck in slow motion. Being a teacher was like performing a one-man show every day without any intermission.

"I did." I felt the chalk heavy in my hand.

"Are you having a stroke?" Dale, a should-be-playing-basketball tall student who occasionally reeked of pot, leaned forward in his chair. "Can you feel both sides of your face?"

"I can."

"Maybe you should put your hands on your face just to be sure." He massaged his own cheeks to demonstrate.

"I'm not having a stroke, Dale. I just lost my train of thought for a second."

"I can call an ambulance," said Reyansh in the front row, destined to be one of those slick corporate raiders who makes his living finding efficiencies and redundancies in companies. He held up his cell, the latest iPhone model.

While it would've been nice to have students care this much about their teacher, I recognized this as a ploy to turn the rest of class into free time.

"I'm fine. Thank you for your concern," I said with a healthy dose of sarcasm. "Why don't y'all read the rest of the chapter to yourselves for a moment? I'm just going to get a drink of water.

And put away your cell, Reyansh. Remember school policy. No cell phones in class."

I texted the group chat as soon as I left my classroom.

Amos: I think I saw Hutch Hawkins today?

Amos: Or a guy who looks like him.

Amos: Have you heard anything about him being back in town?

Chase: Are you texting during your own class?

Amos: I'm not in class.

Everett: You abandoned your class?

Amos: Why are y'all on **your** cell phones?

Julian: Chase and I have off this period. Everett?

Julian: And I haven't heard anything about Hutch.

Chase: Same.

Chase: And when did you start using y'all? You've never been south of Maryland.

Amos: Y'all isn't just for southerners. Everett, have you seen Hutch?

Everett: I'm showing my class TED Talks on YouTube to improve their public speaking skills.

Amos: Slacker.

Everett: :)

Everett: And same. No sign of him.

Okay, that settled that. I was going crazy. Maybe I *was* having a stroke. I made sure the hall was empty before feeling my face like Dale suggested.

"The feudal system!" I yelled when I returned to class, making some of my students jump. They all had their books open, which was a better outcome than I expected.

Except for Tommy, my twenty-fifth pupil, and the one who was angling for an award for Most Disinterested Student. He was doing a bad job at hiding his phone in his lap.

"Tommy. Please put your phone away."

He thought the rules didn't apply to him because he was some kind of athlete. Not in my class.

The front of the class was my stage, and I happily took up the space. I was a great teacher. And Hutch Hawkins was nowhere to be found at South Rock High.

"Now can someone tell me what brought the downturn of the feudal system?"

I pointed at Rosalee and her raised hand.

"Industrialization."

"And what did industrialization bring?"

I searched for another hand. Dale held up two fingers like he was signaling for the check.

"People moving to the cities for work?"

"Correct! Instead of being siloed on farms, people were now coming together, interacting. Cultures mixing. Knowledge being shared. Which led to innovations in technology and medicine and led us out of the so-called Dark Ages." I raised a triumphant fist for humanity. One of the many things I loved about history was that it was one long story. The present was confusing and made no sense. Only when we looked back did we see the narrative logic of our lives.

Hutch returning and roaming the halls of our alma mater would defy every iota of narrative logic.

"Why are we learning about this?" Tommy called from the back of class, slouched so low in his chair I could only make out hair. "Who cares?"

"I beg your pardon?"

Students traded looks, preparing for a fight. As a teacher, I had to stand my ground. Class was a power struggle. I'd seen other teachers who caved to their students and were essentially door-mats the rest of the school year.

"Who cares about this? It was hundreds of years ago. Who's going to use any of this in the real world?" Tommy asked in that disaffected tone that I was certain straight guys developed at birth.

I held back from laughing. As if any of these kids really knew the real world. Sourwood was home to two pet spas and a bougie supermarket.

"Why do we think it's important to learn about the past?" I asked the class.

Crickets. Rosalee seemed tempted to raise her hand but stopped herself.

"Anyone?" They were too young to have a past.

Dale, ordering another drink, "Because, like, history repeats itself?"

"Exactly. History can repeat itself if we aren't careful. Those who don't study history are doomed to repeat it. The same conflicts, the same short-sightedness, the same mistakes."

I heaved out a short breath. A brief thought about the person who I wasn't thinking about flitted in my mind. Still. After all these years, after how things ended, after how he hurt me, he still lived rent-free in there.

"But if we study our past, really study it, we can break the cycle," I said with full conviction. "So, who wants to tell me about the benefits of the vassal system?"

When the bell rang, students gathered up their books and shuffled out, some wishing me a good day. And it was going to be a good day.

Because there was no Hutch Hawkins in my school.

Or in my town.

Or anywhere within the Sourwood area.

The last I heard (or, read online), he was in Nashville kicking balls into nets for a living. He was living out his high school dream.

The halls outside my classroom bustled with students mingling and walking. I made some notes on how to liven up the lesson on the feudal system for my later periods before entering the hallway fray.

Fortunately, I was on the tall side. A good chunk of the student population was still going through puberty and thus hadn't had full growth spurts. So that enabled me to peer over the tops of students' heads.

And at the end of the hallway, just before the turn to the science corridor, I realized that I had been given a false sense of security by my friends. My eyes had not gaslit me earlier.

It was decidedly not going to be a good day.

I never knew what people were talking about when they spoke of outer body experiences. I only saw things from my point of view. And when my two eyes fixed on Hutch Hawkins—and it was *definitely* Hutch Hawkins—well, all the oxygen left my body like it was running for cover.

Hollow, that was how I felt.

Watching him talk with Principal Aguilar sapped me of all energy. I was in fight or flight mode, but my feet were glued to the floor. Maybe I wanted a fight.

The universe was a nasty ass bitch who loved to mess with me. Because not only was Hutch here, but he was still freaking gorgeous. Still with the homecoming king glow that he had in high school. His dark hair hung over his electric blue eyes, and his defined jaw was brushed with stubble. And even from this distance, the perfect, innocent-but-not-that-innocent way his lips curled into a smile sent shockwaves pummeling through my body. His lone dimple on his left cheek still sent a wave of warm-and-fuzzies through me.

How was this possible?

Time was supposed to heal all wounds. Yet ten-year-old scars had instantly transformed into fresh bruises.

He shook his hair out of his eyes, like he'd done when we were in high school. I swooned for a millisecond.

Time stopped. Every student in the space between us stopped moving, frozen, as Hutch tilted his head and we locked eyes. His smile dropped and made way for a slight *oh shit* reaction.

I could be mature. I was an adult. I was almost thirty. Hell, I had a mortgage. People with mortgages could handle being around people who'd seen them naked.

I marched through the crowds of awkward teens, feeling like one of them. "Hutch," I said with all the stern confidence I could muster.

I held out my hand to shake.

"Famous Amos."

Gaaah, he used my nickname. Hearing my name in his voice made me equal parts enraged and melt like a stick of butter.

"It's Mr. Bright now."

"Amos teaches Ancient History here." Principal Aguilar smiled between us, completely unaware that he'd lodged himself in a sticky situation.

Aguilar used to be a bit of a hard ass, as prickly as his cactus collection, until he fell into schmoopy love with a parent last year. After a year, he remained in a love haze that made him clueless at times. Like now. When he was oblivious to the obvious tension in front of him.

"Ancient History, huh?" Hutch's eyebrows jumped on his creased forehead. I hated how much time I could spend staring at him. "Like cavemen?"

"We start with cavemen and go all the way to the Renaissance."

"Sounds like quite a journey."

Oh, we were all on our journeys. Mine seemed to keep going.

"Amos also runs the History Club after school."

My face turned red. Aguilar was making me sound like a huge nerd.

"We just talk about...historical stuff." Historical stuff? My brain had obviously ducked out for an early lunch.

"Cool." Hutch had trouble meeting my eyes. He smoothed out wrinkles in his shirt, bringing attention to his trim physique.

"Did you two overlap at South Rock as students?" Aguilar asked.

We overlapped a metric fuckton.

Hutch and I were co-valedictorians of the graduating class of Awkward High.

"What are you doing here?" I winced at the sharpness of my question, but inquiring minds wanted to know. "Are you giving a talk?"

He shook his head and laughed. Red burned on his cheeks, and he cut his eyes to Aguilar to answer for him.

"Even better," said the principal. My, how I envied his obliviousness. "Hutch is returning to South Rock to coach our soccer team this season."

Shock, anger, disgust, (and joy?) twisted in me. The entire cast of *Inside Out* was having a field day in my head. Coaching meant he would be here regularly. And through the immutable laws of space and time, I would see him regularly.

But instead of unleashing my true thoughts on the matter, I answered with a soft "Oh."

"Yep," Hutch said.

"What a treat! Having South Rock's former soccer superstar come back to coach. Soccer superstar. Try saying that five times fast. Soccersuperstar. Soccersuperstar."

"We get it," I said. Aguilar was way too jolly to work in public education. But I had bigger things to deal with. I turned to Hutch. "The soccer team has a lot of games in a season."

"That they do."

"So you'll just come here after school then?"

"Incorrectamundo!" Aguilar was so excited he looked about to piss himself. "He's joining the faculty. He'll be teaching Phys Ed during school and then coaching."

"Oh."

"Let's bring you back to the office so you can fill out more paperwork. I'll also fill you in on my cactus collection. You wouldn't think they could grow cacti in New York State, but they can, Hutch. They really can."

Aguilar motioned for Hutch to follow him. I would've had pity on Hutch for having to listen to Aguilar drone on about his cacti, but pity was never something I could feel for Hutch Hawkins.

"Maybe we could grab a drink sometime and catch up," Hutch offered.

"Can't. Busy," I immediately shot back. He might've stumbled from the impact.

"Okay." Hutch smiled awkwardly. I used to press my finger in his dimple like it was a button.

"You should go. Paperwork. Cacti. All that jazz." My throat went thick with emotions struggling to come up. Aguilar could add one more prick to his cacti collection.

"Yeah." Hutch backed away slowly. "I'll, uh, see you around."

And unfortunately for me, that wasn't just a saying. It was a promise.

Amos: Hutch ducking Hawkins is back!

Amos: *ducking

Amos: ahhhh fucking

Amos: HUTCH FUCKING HAWKINS

Everett: Holy duck

Julian: Drinks tonight?

Chase: Multiple drinks.

Amos: YESSSSSSSSS

2

AMOS

I had a few hours to kill before meeting up with my friends for happy hour. High school got out at two-fifteen, and we were too old for day drinking.

Somehow, I managed to get through the rest of the school day after my encounter with Hutch. I think being gay had given me the superpower of compartmentalization. Instead of using it to lead a double life, I used my powers for teaching the awesomeness of history while keeping Hutch in a very small box in my head.

After school, I met with the History Club. Each marking period, we voted on a new historical period to deep dive on. Currently, we were discussing the French Revolution and how a shortage of bread led to overthrowing the government. What could I say? People love carbs. The club was full of nerds like myself, but we had a good time. I'd rather these nerds geek out over history than channel that energy into 4chan message boards.

With a few hours to spare, I continued to keep Hutch-related thoughts at bay while segueing to my post-after school jobs. I did one-on-one SAT verbal tutoring at kids' houses, and I shoveled mulch for an elderly couple who lived in a cute cottage near the school. I had to take two showers to get the smell off my skin, but it was worth it. I was able to help people and make a little extra cash for the travel fund. As a history buff, there were so many places I wanted to visit. The rooms where it happened. The sites of ancient civilizations.

Unlike some of the wealthier families in Sourwood, the ones who paid their grown kids' rent and car payments, I didn't have parents who sent me checks or took me on family vacations. They moved down to New Orleans to be closer to my sister and their grandkids. I preferred not having parents all up in my business. Whatever life threw at me, I could handle on my own. And for anything I couldn't handle, I had my friends.

Seeing my ex-boyfriend, who was now my new co-worker, fell into this latter category.

My friends and I went to the local pub, Stone's Throw Tavern, for happy hour. It was situated on a quiet side street in downtown Sourwood with a stunning view of the Hudson River, about an hour north of Manhattan. And despite its hole-in-the-wall vibe, it was a nice, spacious place with high ceilings and large windows that overlooked the water.

Everett picked me up so I wouldn't drink and drive. Because, honey, I planned to drink.

My friend and former roommate Charlie was bartending that night, an increasingly rare occurrence since he'd gotten promoted to assistant manager.

"It's the ass man!" I cheered when Charlie brought over round number two of beers. Blood alcohol wise, I was barely buzzed, but the drama of today had weakened my tolerance.

"Need any appetizers so you're not drinking on an empty stomach?" Charlie was short but jacked, which made him a hot combo with his lumberjackian bear of a husband Mitch, Stone's Throw

Tavern's owner. They originally met when Charlie used to date Mitch's daughter in college, which was equal parts awkward and freaking hot.

Julian scanned the menu. "We'll take some loaded fries."

"Coming right up."

"Thank you, ass man!" I called out.

"Man, were you pre-gaming at school?" Charlie clapped me on the shoulder.

"He's fine," Everett said. "He's just going through a lot. Blast from the past."

I gave Charlie the come hither curled finger to bring him close. "H-squared is back."

"Seriously?"

"Very seriously. As serious as the bubonic plague, which in part destroyed the feudal system of medieval Europe. He's the new soccer coach and gym teacher." I snickered, both at the situation and at the memory of a student last year earnestly believing the bubonic plague made women flat chested.

"Dang. That sucks. The fries are on me then."

The guys and I thanked him loudly. Charlie returned to the bar.

Everett, Chase, and Julian all taught at South Rock High School. We started on the same day, and that helped forge our bond. That, and all four of us being out teachers at school. I liked to think our presence helped open the door for South Rock becoming more inclusive and much sassier.

I drained the last of my beer, needing a refill. "The brightside is that my recent dating history has given me lots of experience navigating awkward experiences. Working with Hutch should be a cakewalk."

Awkward was an understatement. I hadn't had the best luck dating-wise. The most recent guy I dated tried to fake an orgasm when I was going down on him. I had to break the news that only worked with women.

"Didn't you tell us Hutch was playing professional soccer?" Julian was a sweet, cuddly bear of a French teacher, his extra weight making him soft and huggable. He'd grown a beard to fully own his bear-sona.

"I thought he was." I made a promise to myself to never check up on him, flexing incredible restraint in the age of social media.

"Maybe he's retired. Don't professional athletes retire at like twenty-five?" Chase, who taught Chemistry, was the most inquisitive of us, every social situation a quadratic equation to him. He adjusted his thick-framed glasses, which played well against his combed blond hair and boyish face. He was really going for that 1950s NASA scientist vibe.

We all traded looks. We were nerds. None of us knew sportsball.

"Maybe he wants to give back to his community." Chase shrugged.

Charlie came back with loaded fries and a fresh round of beers. It was perfect timing as my stomach began to growl.

Everett leaned forward in our booth. His pale skin popped against his fiery thatches of red hair. "I was doing some research today, and by research I mean gossiping among fellow teachers, and I got some intel on why he's back."

We all leaned in, afraid for others to hear.

"Yeah?" I gestured for him to stop being his dramatic self and spit it out.

"I heard..." Everett paused for dramatic effect, fitting since he was a drama teacher. "He busted his knee and had to leave the league."

"Oh my gosh." My hand instinctively went over my heart. I was crushed for Hutch. Despite how I felt about him (which was its own TBD), I always admired his skill on the soccer field. Watching him weave through opponents with ease was like watching the hand of God. Or the feet of God? Did God have hands and feet, or was he an omniscient blob with a white beard?

Julian raised a finger. "That's not what I heard."

Heads whipped his way like a courtroom in shock.

"I heard he got kicked off the team because of drugs, and he had to go to rehab." Julian swept his flowing locks behind his ear. All his years of teaching French had given him a refined European quality.

"That's terrible," I said. My hand returned to clutch my heart.

"Which is it, though?" Chase asked.

"Huh?" Julian raised his eyebrows.

"You've presented two hypotheses. Everett said he suffered a physical injury. Julian proffered the theory that he was in rehab."

"Rumors and gossip don't really lend themselves to the scientific method, bud," Everett said. "I think my story is right. Julian's sounds like a Very Special Episode of a sitcom."

"Well, Everett's story is riddled with cliches," Julian countered and crossed his arms in defiance. "Something a drama teacher should be aware of."

"How do you say 'kiss my ass' in French?"

"I've already told you. Several times."

"Guys!" I tapped my beer bottle on the table like a gavel. Hearing Hutch talked about like a tabloid object didn't sit right with me. I hated that I couldn't fully hate him. "It doesn't matter what brought him here. He's here."

I heaved out a breath, the reality settling in. After all these years of actively working to not think about Hutch, I'd almost succeeded. Now I was back at zero.

"What happened between you two?" Julian asked.

"You never heard the story?" Everett raised his eyebrows.

"Just that Amos and Hutch dated in high school and then broke up."

"That's the story I heard, too," Chase added.

"They were closeted star-crossed lovers," Everett said with flourish. "Amos was the pale, meek nerd at the bottom of the social totem pole."

"I was shy, not meek."

Everett held up a hand. "Please. I'm telling this story." He cleared his throat. "Hutch was the uber-popular jock. Both were closeted, but they found each other, against all odds. For two years, they dated in secret. For two years, they communicated in secret through a complex network of stealth notes and backseat blow jobs."

Lord. I slumped down in the booth. Was there a hole I could crawl into?

"Until one day, Hutch was all 'No thanks' and ditched Amos for a large-breasted cheerleader." Everett cut his eyes to me. "How'd I do?"

Everett's flair for the dramatic knew no bounds.

"Her breasts were average, but aside from that...you hit the major beats." I shrugged, trying to stay cool about my heartbreak being given the Broadway treatment. Tale as old as time, right?

Gay nerd falls for closeted jock.

Jock wedges himself into the nerd's heart...and other body parts.

Nerd stupidly thinks that this wonderful, incredible thing they have is love.

Nerd is so wrong it hurts.

Cue tears.

"I'm sorry, Amos." Julian rubbed my forearm. "You never forget your first love."

"Or your first locker combination."

We all looked at Chase.

"It's true. They've done studies. But I can see how that's not helpful to bring up." Chase shoved a loaded fry into his mouth. His non-sequitur brought a needed smile to my lips. I loved my weird, nerdy friends.

"Did he look the same?" Julian asked. "From what you remember?"

"Yeah, about the same."

Kidding. He looked hotter. Goddamn him and his more mature body. Taller, broader, stubblier. He was heftier now, more muscle versus his lean self in high school. He looked like a man. A man I could climb.

I didn't want Chase to chime in with his scientific theorems on this one. "He's still...conventionally attractive."

"That's a diplomatic way of saying fuckable." Everett's sharp tongue had no boundaries.

And now I was thinking of his fuckableness.

Fuck.

"It doesn't matter what he looks like." It was on the inside that counted, and at his core, I knew what kind of guy Hutch was. Hutch was a guy who left. "I'm not going down that path."

I put my beer bottle to my lips like I was a baby in desperate need of being fed. The rank taste of the alcohol helped wash away any ambivalent feelings about Hutch.

It didn't matter that he was still hot. It didn't matter that we were working together.

I nudged the fries to the center of the table. I didn't like being the friend who was falling apart, but I supposed it was my turn. We'd all dealt with our share of drama, from bad boyfriends to family issues to nightmare students. We could vent about anything to each other.

"You know what the brightside is here? When Hutch dumped me back in high school, I was all alone. I hadn't told a soul about us, so I grieved by myself, which was not fun. Watching *You've Got*

Mail can only cheer a person up so much. But I'm not alone anymore. I have you guys."

We tended not to get schmaltzy with each other, covering our love for each other under barbs. But sometimes, schmaltz was needed. These guys were the greatest.

"I may or may not knee him in the groin when I see him." Everett strummed his fingers on the table. "Fuck him. Not literally. You know what I mean."

"Forget him." I liked the sound of that better.

"Exactly. Forget him," Everett said with surprising seriousness. "You have a great life now. You're an awesome teacher. You have a great condo, kick-ass friends i-m-h-o. Just because you two are working in the same building, doesn't mean you have to interact. He'll stay busy on the soccer field, and you can continue to do your thing in the classroom. It'll be like he's not there."

I nodded and hoped that scenario could play out. "Consider him forgotten."

———

AN HOUR LATER, I was home, sitting on the floor of my bedroom, high school yearbook open in my lap, Hutch's grin staring me in the face.

I didn't save anything from our relationship. I purged every note and every picture. The only evidence that we ever floated in each other's orbit was a single yearbook picture where we happened to be in the same frame.

Hutch was mugging for the camera, owning it like he did every frame. I stared back at him, willing myself to keep it together.

To paraphrase the old lady Rose in *Titanic*, Hutch Hawkins wrecked me in all the ways a person could be wrecked.

We started out like a typical high school cliche. He was the super-popular star captain of the soccer team. I was the nerdy closeted gay kid who secretly crushed on, and masturbated to, the thought of said super-popular star captain.

I was satisfied to pine from afar...until sophomore year when we finally had a history class together. I tempted fate every day by sneaking peeks at him one row over, his rumpled jeans hugging his strong thighs. I pretty much cataloged an inventory of all his sweaters. And mostly, I became the only kid in the world excited about history class.

Hutch would lean over and ask me questions when he was lost, which motivated me to become the star student of history. It was like this warm spotlight when he talked to me. I raised my hand and spoke more there than any other class solely so he'd look at me, and I'd have a chance to glance back at him.

My crush on Hutch took over my brain. By spring, I finagled an invite to a party hosted by the jock older brother of a quiz bowl teammate. We were nerds who'd snuck into enemy territory. I made myself a screwdriver that was mostly orange juice. Hutch gave me this big, welcoming smile when he spotted me and bragged to his friends about knowing this insane history buff.

I got permission to use the upstairs bathroom later that night. (Yes, I asked the host, revealing how inept I was at cool people parties.) My bladder went shy in highly public areas and word was that two girls had puked on the floor. When I exited, Hutch was standing in the upstairs hall, a glassy smile on his red lips. He *looked* at me, and for the first time, I felt like somebody worth being looked at.

He put a hand on my chest—even now, I could feel its determined heat—and pushed me back into the bathroom where he proceeded to give me my first kiss.

And what a kiss. Earthquakes. Fireworks. Hallelujah chorus. All of it. His warm lips met mine in a perfect harmony. I was floating, ascending into heaven. I didn't know how I could go on with my life after that kiss.

As I said, wrecked.

At first, dating in secret was exhilarating. Hooking up with the hottest jock in school? That was the gay dream.

Hutch left me secret notes in my locker, and I reciprocated. I pictured him sneaking off to write them, or drafting them while pretending to take notes in other classes, like I had.

And the sex? Wrecked.

The man was a natural born sex god. He was gentle but firm, letting us fumble through it together while being the one in charge.

But by senior year, the excitement of being his dirty little secret had faded. Other kids at South Rock had come out to an accepting student body. There was even an out, same sex couple. Why couldn't that be us? There came a point when a secret curdled from intoxicating to just plain toxic. Each secret note and stolen glance was another paper cut.

Whenever I mentioned coming out, Hutch said he wasn't ready. He needed to get through soccer season. He had to stay sharp for scouts. He didn't want to lose his friends, who wouldn't be accepting.

I didn't want to push him, but it became all about his needs, his wants. Maybe Hutch could live this double life forever, but I couldn't.

That was when we came up with the plan: Go to prom together. Walk in holding hands. Slow dance. Live happily ever after.

I was a jittery sack of pins and needles for the weeks leading up to prom. Soon, we wouldn't have to wait until after school to hold hands. We wouldn't have to crane our necks like dual periscopes to ensure the halls were empty for a quick kiss. It was this weight that had slowly built up until I finally recognized it was suffocating us.

The night before prom, Hutch texted to tell me that he realized he was actually straight, and we couldn't see each other anymore.

Excuse me, *what*?

I got that sexuality lived on a spectrum, but this was some Kinsey-six bullshit.

Even now, I had to shake my head, still unable to comprehend the 180 he did. How could he flirt and kiss and have all the sex with me for two years and then suddenly realize he was actually into women?

He and the average-breasted cheerleader were crowned Prom King and Queen. I spent prom night in my room, watching videos posted on social media of them getting crowned and slow dancing. He gazed at her just like he did with me.

Was he a good faker?

Was I a total chump?

It didn't matter because either way, my heart was broken. Ripped, smashed, put in a blender on the highest setting. Wrecked, in the worst way possible.

There was inherent loneliness in being gay. You had to face the world by yourself and slowly find allies. Hutch rescued me from that loneliness, until he ditched me, and left me feeling more alone than ever. I had to come out alone. I had to suffer in heart-break alone. Even though I was furious with Hutch, I didn't want to out him, so I couldn't even tell my friends at the time what happened.

I promised myself I'd scrub him from my memory. No looking him up online. No asking about him. I'd tried landing a teaching job somewhere else, but it wasn't like there was a dire shortage of history teachers. It was tough at first, working in the space with my past memories.

Yet it actually wound up helping me get over him. With each year I taught at South Rock, I made new friends and built new memories, pushing out the old high school experiences until they were distant memories.

I sat on my bedroom floor, the final lingering buzz of happy hour leaving my system. I clapped my yearbook shut, finding a tiny bit of solace in the satisfying sound.

No, I would not be meeting him for a drink. No, I did not want to talk about what happened. I was there. So was he.

Hutch Hawkins broke my heart once. I wasn't going to let him do it again.

3

HUTCH

It was a strange feeling waking up in my childhood bedroom. Same cracks on the ceiling. Same furniture. Same twin-sized bed. Same sense of panic about being late to school.

It was also an eerily perfect metaphor for my life that, ten years on from high school, I was in the same bedroom and going to the same school. Full circle had never felt like such a kick in the pants.

At least one thing had changed: I had officially outgrown my bed. In my old apartment, I slept on a queen-sized bed. Now I had to slum it on a twin bed. Every time I turned, I nearly fell off. I debated whether I should get myself a new one. On the one hand, my body could no longer fit. But doing so would mean that I was for sure staying here. And that was majorly TBD.

The familiar beeps of my alarm clock blared, sharp knives in my ears. Fortunately, I remembered where the off button was and could reach it without having to open my eyes.

Old posters of bands and athletes lined my walls. Back then, it'd been hard to track down posters for professional soccer players who weren't named David Beckham. I was pumped when they'd come in the mail. I used to stare at them every night and pray that'd be me one day.

Now they stared back at me, taunting me, reminding me of a dream that I watched slip through my fingers in real time. I peeled one of them off the wall, flecks of paint coming off with the tape. I rolled it up and shoved it in my closet, which was stuffed with random shit from the past.

"Hutch, you up?" Pop rapped his fist at my door. Some things never changed. "You're gonna be late for your first day of school."

"It's not school. It's work," I called back, rubbing sleep from my eyes.

"You *work* at *school.*"

"But I'm not going to school. I'm going to work. It's different."

I could practically hear him scratching his head, putting on that twisted face of confusion like I was talking gibberish. I saw that face a lot as a teenager.

"You're going to be late for your first day of work at school."

I fell back on my bed and threw a pillow over my face.

Technically, he was right, but also ughhhh. I was a twenty-eight-year-old guy living at home and working at my old high school. WTF didn't even cover it. I'd worked so hard to get out of this town and make something of myself. That backfired, to say the least.

I pulled up some high school jams on my phone. If I was going to be stuck in the past, then I might as well make it a party. Eminem and Rihanna's "Love the Way You Lie" pulsed through my speakers. I rapped along, remembering more of the lyrics than I expected.

I bristled at the slight limp in my leg as I shuffled to the bathroom to shower and shave. Four years on from surgery, my knee was ninety percent back to normal, but there were those moments, like getting up in the morning, when pain flared up. I made peace with the fact that it'd never be one hundred percent again. I would forever be oh-so-close, but never quite there.

I pulled out the can of shaving cream from the medicine cabinet. Was that the same one I used in high school?

When I opened the cap and saw the rust on the nozzle, I got my answer.

"Pop, do you have any shaving cream?" I yelled as I went into his bathroom. Our house wasn't big, which I felt self-conscious about as a kid but appreciated now that I was slightly less mobile.

I'd forgotten how tiny his bathroom was. Barely enough room to sit down and take a shit. Crowding the corner of the counter were orange pill bottles, making my heart sink. When I was young, Pop was stronger than Superman. He could hold me on his forearms as I pretended to be an airplane. I might've walked into my past, but the pills were a grave reminder that time only marched forward.

After getting myself clean and purdy, I came back to my room to get dressed. I'd unpacked all my clothes into my closet already; for being a small closet, it had surprising depth. It went back so far I thought I'd wind up in Narnia or some shit. Boxes lined the floor and were stacked behind the rack, cardboard reminders of my past lives.

While procrastinating on picking the right first day of work-at-school outfit, I opened the box at my feet. Senior Year. There was my yearbook, pages crinkled with signatures. Old posters people had made for our soccer games. Underneath those, something caught the light. I fished out the crown from senior prom.

My insides crumbled like a glacier falling into the ocean.

I couldn't take back the past, but I could still hate myself for it. My fists curled around the ridges of the crown. I squeezed, willing it to shatter in my hands. This fucker was stronger than I thought, not the five-cent plastic crap.

Maybe it was for the best that I didn't break it. It'd be a reminder of past mistakes.

I didn't know what to expect when I saw Amos at school. I hadn't looked Amos up on social media; I never wanted to intrude on his life since I'd already caused enough damage. Everything happened so fast with me coming back home and taking the coaching job that I didn't have time to come up with a game plan for possibly running into my ex-boyfriend.

Amos was even more devastatingly cute ten years later. He'd filled out some since we were teenagers, but his sweet smile, playful mop of curls, and fiery green eyes hadn't changed. His face was ridiculously expressive, so full of life and curiosity when the rest of the world seemed to exist on autopilot. He had the power to turn this tough jock into a cuddle slut. I loved the way he felt in my arms, holding onto me like I was a shield.

Having him stare at me the other day like I was a monster was deserved, but brutal. As if my confidence wasn't already diminished, his refusal to talk was a shotgun blast through my heart. He had no idea that a day didn't go by when I thought about him, when some random thing would spark an Amos memory. Hell, just passing by a vending machine with Famous Amos cookies was enough to conjure the memory of him.

I fucked up so bad. I knew that. He'd moved on, and rightfully so. I was no longer the popular star athlete of our youth. What could I bring to the table?

Downstairs, Pop read the paper while eating his heart healthy Cheerios. A second bowl was set up at my seat ready for eating. Light reflected off his bald head. His back had a weary hunch to it, but a hearty twinkle sparkled in his Frank Sinatra blue eyes.

"Hey." I kissed his chrome dome and took my seat.

"You're gonna miss the bus."

"Funny." I pulled the milk from the fridge and joined him at the table. I rubbed my hands together. "Breakfast of champions."

"I can make more if you want."

"Nah, I'm good." When I was playing soccer, my breakfast was like a mini-buffet of cereal, toast, omelet, and fruit. Since I wasn't burning all the calories anymore, I had to reign it in.

I drenched my Cheerios in milk.

"Nervous?" he asked.

"Nope." I was never nervous about the first day of school. I was one of those weirdos who liked high school. It was the place where I could hang out with my friends and chat with my favorite teachers and play the greatest sport in the world. Learning stuff was merely the cost of doing business.

School was also the place where I had gotten to see Amos five days a week.

"You're going to whip those guys into shape."

"I'm following in hallowed footsteps. Coach was a legend. He taught me everything I know."

"Now you're the coach, and you'll do the same for your team."

Coach Legrand retired last year. He taught physical education as well as coached the soccer team to multiple champions. Originally, he was going to come back to coach part-time in the spring, but after a winter down in Florida, he and his wife loved it so much they decided to move down permanently. He was the one who put me up for this job, yet another time he'd given me a chance.

"I want to do right by him. I don't want to be one of those coaches who comes in and can't earn the respect of the players and can't keep up the cohesive unit."

"The players are going to respect how much you care. If they see you give a shit, then they will, too."

"South Rock has a good team thanks to Coach Legrand, so if we blow it this season, it's on me."

"What'd we use to say when you played?"

I exhaled my nerves. "Take it one game at a time."

Each game was a test that uncovered our strengths and weaknesses. It was never the final say.

I dug into my cereal, surprisingly hungry. Since I was nearing thirty, I had to be more careful with what I ate. Though I still had muscle, I was filling out a little in the middle from my teenage days. Across the table, Pop ate in peace. His breaths were more labored.

"Did you take your pills?" I asked.

"What pills?" He kept his eyes fixed on the morning paper.

"Pop..."

"I took them." He got that impudent frustration in his voice. Who was the kid now?

I went to the kitchen counter and grabbed the Day of the Week pill container. I flipped open the compartment for Monday. Three pills stared back at me.

"Pop?" I shook the container to emphasize my point.

"I'll take them later today."

"The doctor said you need to take these every morning."

He bristled when I put them on the table. I'd forgotten what a stubborn son of a bitch he could be. Too bad for him, I was just as stubborn.

"I'm healthy! I don't need all these pills. I have an active job." Pop was the facilities manager for the Arden MacArthur Community Center in town, home to a gym, spaces for classes, and a theater. He could fix anything in that place, the handiest of handymen. After thirty years on the job, Bud Hawkins was synonymous with the MacArthur Center, and they put up a plaque in the lobby in his honor for his twenty-fifth anniversary.

"If you want to stay active, then you need to take your medicine."

"What happened to eating well and getting a good night's sleep?"

I understood his frustration. He wasn't that old, just turned sixty. He'd always been the strongest guy I knew. I wished I could eat well and sleep soundly and have my leg suddenly get better.

"An apple a day can't solve everything. That's why we have doctors and science. C'mon. Take your pills, Pop." I mixed them into some applesauce like he used to do for me. Yeah, it was juvenile, but it always did the trick. I mixed in the pills well and handed over the bowl.

"This looks familiar." He heaved out a deep, rumbly laugh.

"I don't know what you're talking about? It's just applesauce."

He cocked an eyebrow. That tomfoolery might've worked on my six-year-old self, but his sixty-year-old ass wasn't playing along. He gave me a skeptical eye as he spooned his applesauce into his mouth.

Next, I took the blood pressure device from the cabinet above the fridge.

"My blood pressure is fine," he scoffed.

"Pop. The doctor wants us to measure your blood pressure daily."

"Why? I'm fine."

"Then how come you passed out on the job?" I stared into his eyes, trying to convey all my care and concern. We could joke about this now, but when I got that call that Pop was in the hospital, I swore my body stopped functioning. Panic and terror rattled my bones so deep that I still felt it, weeks later. They weren't sure what caused his "incident," as the doctor called it. He didn't have a heart attack, but his heart slowed down. It was having trouble pumping blood, which made him prone to dizziness and fainting. He fell off a ladder at work hanging a banner. It left him with a banged-up leg and a nasty bump on his forehead.

Since he lived alone, it wasn't a question that I would come home to help him recuperate. Not like I had much keeping me in Nashville.

I stared him down, angry dude on the outside but a little boy on the inside scared shitless for my Pop.

He was smart enough not to put up too much of a fight. He held out his arm. I wrapped the patch around. He was in good shape for his age, his arms thick with muscle, his tattoo of my birth date wiggling around on his bicep.

After a month, I'd become a pro at working these blood pressure checkers. I pumped it and monitored the tightness and numbers.

"Have you heard of an app called Milkman?" he asked me.

"How do you know what Milkman is?"

"I heard some gentlemen talking about it at the center."

"Gentlemen." I snorted. Such a classy term for a group of gays scouring a hookup app.

"Have you used it?"

"Pop." My blood pressure was about to spike. Good thing I wasn't the one being monitored.

"No judgment here. There are a lot of good-looking gentlemen on the app. Although for the life of me, I don't get why there are so many pictures of their ding-a-lings. Wouldn't you want to leave some things to the imagination?"

I ripped off the blood pressure patch and recorded his numbers in a notebook that we brought to the doctor for our appointments. My face was on fire.

"Pop, why are you on Milkman?"

I added that to the list of questions I never thought I would ask Pop.

"Do guys find that appealing? Pictures of each other's ding-a-lings? Are there pictures of your ding-a-ling online?"

"No," I said firmly, willing this conversation to end. "Why are you on a gay dating app? When you passed out, did you wake up gay?"

"That doesn't happen. You're born gay." He pointed at the little rainbow flag in the middle of the table, something he grabbed from a pride event years ago. "Baby, you are born this way. That Lady Gaga, she's one smart cookie. She has such a lovely voice. Why does she have to cock it up with all those getups?"

I snorted. Pop could always make me laugh, especially when he wasn't trying.

"How were my numbers?" he asked.

"Answer my question first. Why are you on Milkman?"

"For you." His forehead crinkled as he leaned forward to muss up my hair, which I'd spent a significant amount of time fixing this morning. "I was trying to find a nice guy for you to date now that you're home."

"I don't need help."

"Are you even out? I'm confused on your status."

"My status?" Had Pop been reading *The Advocate* and *Queerty* in my absence? "I'm out to you, and if people ask, I'm not going to lie. But it doesn't come up."

Pop's face called bullshit.

"What am I supposed to do? Introduce myself like 'Hey I'm Hutch, and I'm gay.' to every person I meet?"

"Why not?"

Pop made it sound so easy. Straight people didn't have to announce they were straight. The people that knew me knew the truth. Though, in fairness, not that many people knew me. In Nashville, I kept a low profile. And when I played pro soccer, I never wanted my sexuality to overshadow my game.

Fine, *technically*, I supposed I was still in the closet.

"I'm setting up an account for you." Pop's thumbs moved around his screen with the focus of a gopher digging a tunnel.

"Stop." I tried to grab the phone away, but I was too slow.

"What are you afraid of?"

"I don't know. I guess I don't want people looking differently at me."

"Fuck 'em."

"Easy for you to say, you flaming heterosexual." It was like a cloud following me around. Except for a few random, horrifically cringeworthy, down low occurrences, I hadn't been with anyone since Amos. He'd turned my world upside down, but life was lived right side up.

"I saved it, but I haven't set it to go live. I'll leave that up to you. Hutch, life only moves in one direction."

I nodded tersely.

"I've never once heard about a boyfriend. I'd like to be a grandfather one day."

He'd make an outstanding grandpa. He would have a brand new audience for all of his corny jokes. But I would not be bearing that fruit. "Pop, why don't I get you a cat instead?"

"Why don't you want to date? What else are you going to do here?" He held up his hand before I could answer. "And don't say take care of me. I don't need twenty-four-hour care. You're not going to stay this good-looking forever."

"I'll think about it."

He seemed as convinced by that bullshit answer as I was.

"There do seem to be nice guys on the app." He cleared his throat and took a suspicious sip of his now-decaf coffee. "Amos is on there."

My heart did a flip against my better judgment. Whatever feelings cracked open, I pushed them down.

"Good for him."

There was a reason Pop was the only person I'd come out to since Amos. He'd cleaned up my room when I originally moved out and found pictures of Amos and me that we'd taken in a photo booth. In half the pictures, we were kissing; the other half were kiss-free, but just as obvious that we were a couple. It was what prompted me to finally come clean to him about Amos, and it strengthened our relationship ultimately. I did things opposite: I was out to my dad, but never told any of my friends.

Except one.

The downside, though, to being out and proud to your dad was that he wouldn't stop asking if you had a boyfriend.

"Might be worth giving Amos a call."

I shook my head. "You know how it ended between us. He hasn't forgotten. He wants nothing to do with me."

That was crystal clear by the way Amos glared at me the other day. If his eyes were lasers, I'd be dead.

"Did you ever tell him the truth?"

"It wouldn't make a difference."

"Yes, it would. That asshole bullied you into dumping him!"

Ten years on, and the memory still made my stomach cramp up in terror. Picture this: closeted jock and closeted nerd date in secret bliss. Jock has never been happier. They make a plan to come out together at prom. Then jock's homophobic teammate Seth Collins finds his text messages to the nerd, makes some threats, and convinces the jock to ditch the nerd, which he does via one half-assed text message. Tale as old as time, right?

According to Seth, if I came out, I could kiss my friends and my pro soccer dreams goodbye, and Amos and Pop would become town pariahs. I couldn't let the two people I care about most become outcasts.

I still remember the chilling tone of his voice, how it shifted between concerned and threatening. He'd been vocally disgusted by the other students who'd come out during our time. Last I checked, Seth was married with four kids and wrote for a far-right blog.

I figured it was best to stop talking to my teammates and friends cold turkey after graduation. What if they had the same reaction?

A lot has changed in ten years culturally and politically, but I always wondered if Seth would've been right.

"It doesn't matter if what Seth said was true, Pop. That doesn't make what I did right. I texted Amos and told him that I was actually straight and didn't want to see him again." I snorted, not because it was funny but because I was stupid enough to send a text like that. "I still feel terrible. He doesn't want to talk to me."

"You two were great together."

"How do you know? You didn't even know we were dating."

"I saw the pictures when I cleaned your room. They were full of love. And love is love is love."

I could feel myself turn red. Those mementos were intimate, and it left me feeling a different kind of exposed.

If only I was strong enough to follow through and wash Amos out of my system.

"Pop." I placed a hand over his wrinkly, rough skin. I didn't have the energy to fight him on this. I was surprised at his excitement over my dating life. Was I that much of a guy in need? "I'm not looking to date. I need to focus on the Huskies winning the championship. I need to get my shit together." I exhaled a tired breath. "Although if I were to have a boyfriend, I can guarantee you, it wouldn't be Amos."

4

HUTCH

High school memories flooded my mind on my drive to school. I knew the way by heart, still remembered to go down Berman Street to avoid making that impossible left into South Rock High. The building hadn't changed, but there were jarring updates that moved it into the present. The front sign was slick and new, electronic messages now instead of plastic letters slid into rows (and humorously re-arranged by rabble rousers who didn't include me). Two trees in front were chopped down, making way for a pair of benches and cell phone charging station.

I pulled into my usual spot in the parking lot. Students buzzed around me. It was spring and warmth had finally arrived. Kids hung out by each other's cars, sitting on trunks, chatting and sharing things on their phones. I got out of my car, the same beast from high school, and nodded at the girls parked next to me. One was copying something from the other's notebook, which they slapped shut when we made eye contact.

"Hey," I said. Did I still sound cool?

"Uh, hey," said the alleged homework copier.

"I'm the new men's soccer coach. Hu–Mr. Hawkins."

They traded looks with each other, those conspiratorial teenage looks that instantly made me feel like I had gum in my hair or something.

I still had it. I was Hutch Hawkins. South Rock High was my playground.

"I'll see you inside."

"Uh, Mr. Hawkins?" said one of the girls.

Now I got why people said shit like *Mr. Hawkins is my father. Call me Hutch.* Because it's freaking weird to be called mister. When did I get old enough to be a mister?

"Yeah?" I asked back, hands in pockets. Not trying to be cool, but also not not trying?

"You're in the student lot. The teacher lot is behind the school."

"Oh." A true kick to the balls if there ever was one.

I was a teacher. I was an adult. An adult who went by mister.

They shared another look and held in their laughter, which I supposed was deserved. I was giving off major Josie Grossie vibes, not Mr. Coolson ones. (Thank you Amos for making us watch *Never Been Kissed*.)

"All right then. Catch you on the flip side."

Did I really just say that? Did anyone say that? Someone should give me a walker. The ones with tennis balls on the legs.

And then because I hadn't proven just how uncool I was, I gave them not one, but two thumbs up.

Oof. This was officially my worst first day of high school in history.

———

THE TEACHER'S lot was much more my speed. It was quiet and calm, two qualities I didn't know I wanted in my life. The teachers were a mix of my contemporaries, middle-aged lifers, and the relics. I recognized a few from my days as a student. I couldn't wait to catch up with them. Yeah, I was one of those guys who liked chatting with his teachers.

I rolled down the row until I found an open spot. It was a tight squeeze at the end, butting up against some thorny bushes. I made a note to get here earlier tomorrow so I'd land a better space.

The idiot parked next to me didn't look when he opened his door. I nearly took his door off as I pulled in.

I screeched to a stop.

"What are you doing?" I asked myself. I paused before continuing to pull in.

And the guy opened his door again! I was inches away from having an accident. We were like two people who couldn't pass each other in the hall.

This time, he got out and slammed his door shut. Amos glared at me through the windshield. He looked *fine* in slim cut jeans, fitted plaid shirt, and knit tie. But I was in no position to ogle him.

He walked past me. I managed a half-wave and a weak "what are the odds" smile. He didn't respond to either.

I finished my parking job, maneuvering my car as far away as possible from Amos's. When I got out, he was standing on the curb, checking something on his phone. That was a good sign.

The complete lack of friendly smile on his face was not.

"Hey. Sorry about that," I said.

"It's fine." He had a leather messenger bag slung diagonally, which did wonders for showing off his chest. I used my old backpack, frayed on the bottom.

"I thought you were waiting for me to pull in. Looks like we got our wires crossed."

"I think it's customary for the driver to let the other person get out of their car first."

"Actually, I think the other driver waits until the car pulls in to get out."

A tight smile barely hung on his lips. "Agree to disagree."

It might've been spring, but there was a heavy cold front this morning.

"Sorry about that. You heading inside?" I gestured to the school, where other teachers filtered in.

Mrs. Tomski, my old history teacher, walked up to us. She was old when I was a student; her white hair and liver-spotted hands made her seem ancient.

"Hutch, I heard you were coming back. It's lovely to see you! You've turned into a strapping young man." She patted my arm in that good job way that grandmas did so well.

"Mrs. Tomski! It's great to see you. We're colleagues now. Isn't that wild?"

"Coach Legrand said wonderful things about you." She looked between Amos and me, seemingly oblivious to the underlying tension. "Weren't you and Amos both in my class? I could've sworn I once caught you passing notes."

"I have to get inside." Amos looked down at the sidewalk and marched into the building.

My heart lifted as I thought about those times in class when we'd sneak looks at each other, or when I got to watch his ass as he walked up to the board.

Kinda like how I was watching his ass now as he walked away.

I NEVER REALLY VIBED WITH the expression to know something like the back of my hand. I knew my palm better. I once had a palm reader explain the meaning behind the creases and how it told my fortune. I forgot what she said, but I'm assuming it came true.

Even though it'd been a minute since I was last here, I found my way through the halls of South Rock High like they were the palm of my hand. Memories burst out of the walls, the waxed-floor smells, the familiar sounds of creaky lockers and din of students buzzing around. While there'd been cosmetic changes here and there, like new bulletin boards and signage, the bones hadn't changed.

But I had no time to reminisce with myself. I wanted to catch up to Amos and start to lay the groundwork to be on friendly terms. Maybe I could get us to the point where he'd be open to talking.

I fucked things up royally back in the day. There was no previous chapter button for our DVD. Honestly, I still cared for Amos. Those familiar feelings sprang back to life when I glimpsed him in the hall the other day. But they'd have to chill next to my dreams of playing major league soccer again.

I wasn't looking to get back with Amos. That ship had sailed, sprung a leak, and lay at the bottom of the ocean. But maybe we could learn to be colleagues, possibly acquaintances?

My heart did a little somersault when I reached the hall of history classrooms on the second floor. Amos stood outside his class chatting with a pair of female students, laughing along with him like the cool teacher he was.

I approached slowly, a soldier entering enemy territory.

His beautiful face went devoid of emotion when our eyes met.

"We'll definitely continue this convo in second period. But no spoilers. I'm only on episode four," he said to the girls, his smile turned on. He waved to them as they trotted off.

I was on. "Hey, Famous Amos."

"Hi." A greeting had never sounded less friendly. Amos didn't shoo me away, but it didn't take my powers of deduction to know that he wanted me to fuck off, a fact which was a dick punch to the heart.

My brain went blank. Whatever grand plan lay in my head scurried off.

"I thought things would be different. But not much has changed around here. Looks pretty much the same."

"Yep. Same old South Rock." Amos had a lead balloon of interest in his voice. The row of freckles tracked across his face, but I couldn't run my finger along them this time.

"How long have you been teaching here?"

"Three years."

"Nice. You loved high school so much you had to come back."

His jaw tightened. "I like teaching history. I wanted to teach at the high school level. South Rock was hiring."

"Cool. It's meant to be."

"Home room is starting soon. Do you have classes here or are you just coaching?"

Translation: Are you gonna be here every day, all day?

"I'm teaching gym and coaching. I'm technically a substitute teacher for the rest of the year."

Amos nodded. It looked like the conversational burden would rest solely with me. It was so weird getting stonewalled by him when I knew how bubbly and chatty he could be.

"So, are the kids assholes like we were? Well, not us. We were good kids. Some kids in our grade were nightmares." Where the hell was I going with this? Damn him and his luscious green eyes getting me all nervous. "Do you remember Lance Parham and how he'd start singing in the back of class?"

He gave the barest of acknowledgement nods.

"And Melissa Rodriguez who always talked back to teachers and threatened to have her lawyer dad come in to talk to the principal." She dated one of the guys on the soccer team, and I had to suffer through hearing stories in her high-pitched voice throughout junior year.

A teeny tiny slight smile of recognition started to emerge on his still, one thousand percent kissable lips.

"Don't forget Peter Simkins," he said.

"Simkins! He was always on his phone. The teachers would confiscate his phone, but then he'd always have another. He was dealing drugs, right? That's what was happening with all those phone calls?"

"I heard he had six girlfriends scattered across the state." Amos raised an eyebrow. It sounded just plausible enough. "A different cell phone for each."

"Simkins the string bean? Props to him."

It felt like old times for a quick second. I got lost in his voice and brushed my finger through his light forearm hair.

He yanked his arm back, his eyes bulging at the contact. Whatever progress I'd made in the past sixty seconds was reversed. The stonewall was back up, stronger than ever.

"I need to get to my classroom." He turned and started walking at a breakneck pace, one level below making a run for it.

I tried catching up to him, forcing my legs to keep up. He made a sharp right into a hallway that housed the basketball team's trophy-less trophy case. There was a reason why they were tucked away up here and not in the front entrance like football and soccer.

I couldn't pivot turn like I used to, and the quick twist to follow him brought out a fresh lance of pain in my left knee. A sledgehammer ache ran up my leg. I bit back a scream of agony.

"Amos." His name came out somewhere between a whisper and a grunt.

He stopped and spun around. His eyes traveled down to my left knee, which I tried to rub inconspicuously. I managed a smile as I put weight back on it to show everything was hunky dory.

I didn't want that kind of attention. I hated that one little tear in my knee could overpower me like this. No matter how strong the rest of me was, I couldn't fix this.

"You're faster than I remember," I said with a laugh, willing the concern to fade from his face. "I'm not used to running in dress shoes."

"Coach Hawkins, there you are!" Principal Aguilar slapped me on the back with jolly force. "I wanted to make sure you weren't lost. There's a few more forms we need you to fill out. A W-something or other."

"Sure thing." I prayed to every god across every religion that my knee would be cool so Amos wouldn't have to see me limp.

"I see Mr. Bright is helping you find your way around."

Amos's cheeks blushed.

"No, he was—I could find my way around just fine. Not much has changed at South Rock."

"I don't know if that's a good thing or bad thing." I wish I had Aguilar's positive attitude. Would he be so sunshiney if he was face-to-face with his ex?

"Good. All good," I said.

Aguilar pointed to me, then to Amos, then back and forth one more time. "I don't think I ever got an answer from you guys the other day, but did you two know each other as students?"

A heavy silence hung between us. It was a game of chicken. Who would answer first? Amos was frozen, so I spoke up.

"Yeah, we were friends."

Amos's eyes bulged at me, two big, green ABORT buttons.

"No, we weren't friends," I said.

He made another panicked, yet inscrutable face at me. We were playing telepathic charades. I sucked at regular charades.

"We were kind of friends. Friendly. We had a class together where we passed notes."

ABORT ABORT said his eyes.

"Uh, we didn't pass notes. I copied off his test once without his knowledge." That was true. Amos and Aguilar were equally shocked. I had to stop myself before more secrets came out. "We knew of each other. Saw each other around here and there."

NAKED. WE SAW EACH OTHER NAKED. A LOT. "Not friends. But we knew each other existed."

I lost the ability to speak proper English. All I thought about was how good Amos looked naked.

"You know, I heard that professional soccer can be a rough contact sport," Aguilar said, head cocked in concern. "Did you ever get checked out for anything?"

Great. I was going to lose this job for supposed brain damage. "I'm fine. I promise. Just a little nervous about my first day of work at school."

"Nothing to be nervous about, Coach Hawkins! I'll leave you two to chat about old South Rock memories. Make sure to get down to the front office sometime this morning." Aguilar walked backwards, his voice booming to stay with us. "Oh, and I'm working on scheduling you for cafeteria duty shifts."

"What's cafeteria duty?" That was new since I'd been gone.

He jogged back and leaned in for a whisper so surrounding students couldn't hear. "We assign teachers to eat lunch in the cafeteria and keep an eye on students. We say that it helps teachers strengthen bonds with the students. But really, it's because there was a conflict that escalated into a messy food fight last year. Our janitorial staff almost quit in protest during cleanup."

Thank goodness I wasn't a teacher then, though no lie, it would've been fun to participate as a student.

"Sounds good! Keep me posted." I gave him a thumbs up. He returned the gesture, then disappeared into the crush of students.

It was back to Amos and me.

And a thick layer of awkwardness that I'd specifically tried to avoid.

"So, I..." Before I could think of what to say, Aguilar was back, jolly as ever.

"I had a great idea. Why don't you and Amos team up for caf

duty?" His face lit up with so much excitement you'd think he screamed "Eureka" in the bathtub. "Amos's old partner just went on maternity leave. You can shadow him, and it'll give you both time to catch up and reminisce about old South Rock memories."

Aguilar had a master's degree in Not Reading the Room. Judging by Amos's whitening face, he'd rather eat glass.

"I don't think that's a good idea," Amos said.

"Why not?" Aguilar asked back. He looked between me and Amos, completely oblivious.

"It's...well..." Amos bit the corner of his lip when he got flustered. After two years of having a down low relationship, our skill at hiding our feelings in plain sight was still strong as ever.

Why not indeed? Neither of us could answer that without getting into a whole bunch of stuff we were both dying not to get into.

"It's settled then. You can show Hutch the ropes. Gentlemen." Aguilar nodded at us and returned back to the busy hall where he came from.

Amos didn't waste any time leaving in the opposite direction, walking with determination to get away from me.

"Hey, Amos," I called out.

Once again, he faced me. Any warmth there'd been for me was long gone.

How can I get you to smile at me again?

"Yeah?"

I shrugged my shoulders up to my ears. I felt so out of place for so many reasons that in my nervous haste, I said the *absolute* worst thing. "So, we're cool, right?"

Fuuuuck. It was like my brain was actively trying to sabotage me.

Amos's mouth hung open for a second before he regained his resting stone face. "Look, Hutch. What happened between us is in the distant past. It's not worth dredging up. If you have a question pertaining to work or you need help with the coffee maker in the lounge, I'll help you. We're colleagues, and that's it. So in that respect, sure. I guess we're cool."

He turned on his heel and kept on walking, leaving me to recover from the brute impact.

I gave a thumbs up to his back like an idiot.

"See you at lunch," I muttered under my breath.

5

AMOS

Jesus assfucking Christ.

Scratch that. If there really was an assfucking Jesus, then he'd understand the cringey complexity of gay relationships, and he wouldn't have stuck me with Hutch as my cafeteria duty partner. Also, with his flowing hair, eight pack, and carpentry skills, Jesus would totally be a catch in the gay community, like an HGTV renovation show host.

I had a good thing going with my old caf duty partner Mrs. Jin. When we weren't making our rounds around the caf looking for shenanigans, we'd chat about our weekends and TV shows for a few minutes, then do our own thing in comfortable silence.

With Hutch, there would be silence, but it wouldn't be comfortable.

I was not born for drama. Putting up an icy exterior around him was exhausting, like how a real air conditioner would feel at the height of summer.

Clipped responses and stoic facial expressions were not my jam, but that's what I had to do to keep sane and stop myself from feeling things. Hutch was dangerously easy to talk to and be around. He was comfortable like a favorite sweater. His lazy smile and inquisitive eyes threatened to make me forget what he did.

And when he put his hand on my arm? I had a full-body erotic response which I fought like hell to suppress. Damn him for still having that effect on me.

If I didn't watch myself, my old feelings for him could shoot right to the surface, and then I'd be fucked. There was nothing worse than re-falling for the guy who broke your heart.

Ten years ago, he declared in no uncertain terms that he didn't want to be with me. Those feelings hadn't changed. He was being nice to me because we were now colleagues, and he didn't want things to be awkward. That was all.

I thought I'd only have to nod if we passed each other in the hall, not spend every lunch period eating across from him.

But I could be cordial. Cordial as fuck.

Hutch and I passed each other in the hall between first and second period, and then second and third period. I gave a perfunctory head nod each time. It was difficult because he had a face that was meant to be looked at. The horniest of the Greek gods cultivated that face. Catching glimpses of Hutch in the halls got my closeted ass through high school.

Fuck him and his smoldering, matinee idol looks.

Amos: Hutch and I are caf duty partners. [five crying face emojis]

Julian: What?????

Everett: Shut the fucking fuck up.

Chase: How'd that happen?

Amos: Aguilar put us together because he thought it was cool we were classmates. [five more crying face emojis]

Everett: You'd think our gay principal would be able to sniff out gay drama between two ex-lovers.

Chase: Studies have shown that humans can smell disgust. Perhaps Aguilar's allergies were getting in the way?

Everett: Or maybe he just wants to stir the pot.

Julian: It won't be so bad. Lunch will fly by. You two can talk about safe topics like the weather.

Amos: Sure. I can ask Hutch if it was cloudy out the day he dumped me.

My third period class was the most engaged. I led an invigorating discussion on fiefdoms and serfdoms and how they related to subcultures in America today. The zealot henchmen of aristocracy would be right at home yelling on cable news shows. It was incredible, and scary, how much of history repeated itself.

I wouldn't let Hutch and I repeat anything. I would be more vigilant.

Third period turned to fourth, and still no pulse on the group chat. I got to stay in my classroom. My problem student Tommy doodled in the back of class, but I let him be. I didn't have the energy to get him to participate.

One more period closer to lunch.

After fourth period came fifth: lunchtime.

There were two cafeterias at South Rock. The large one for freshmen and sophomores, and the smaller one for juniors and seniors, though mostly juniors since seniors were allowed to eat off campus, and most did. Who'd settle for cafeteria food when you could have delicious CJ's Pizza?

By the grace of some higher administrative power, I was assigned to the smaller cafeteria. The upperclassmen were more chill. Monitoring a huge room of underclassmen—highly hormonal and barely mature—sounded like torture.

For cafeteria duty, the two teachers assigned each quarter would do a walk around the room every ten minutes like prison guards. When we weren't patrolling, we were eating together at a small table by one of the doors.

Hutch strolled up to our table, and I got a good look at him.

His South Rock-branded polo stretched over his arms and chest, faint wisps of chest hair peeking out.

Dammit. Why couldn't he have grown a beer gut like other former high school athletes?

Lunch was going to be a first class ticket on Awkward Airlines, wasn't it?

"Hey." Hutch hovered over the table, giving me a sweet view of his crotch. I knew what lay behind the denim. Ugh, I missed it.

"Is it cool if I sit down?"

"Yeah. It's your table, too."

"Cool." He sat down, then hopped right back up. "I should probably get some lunch. Do teachers have any special privileges in the food line?"

"Nope."

"Rats." He snapped his fingers to emphasize his aw-shucks reaction that made his cheek dimple.

Ugh, I missed that dimple, too.

"Has the food gotten any better?"

"They're trying to add more vegan and gluten free options."

"Is any of it good?" He waited for the real answer. God, he could be so charming. I didn't know somebody could exist without neuroses. It was infuriating and impossible to withstand.

"I don't know. I brought my own lunch." I pointed to my black, insulated lunch bag.

"That's right. You never ate cafeteria food."

When I was a student, I didn't have the money to indulge in buying my own lunch. My family wasn't poor, but my parents let it be known that I couldn't luxuriate in eating out every day.

"I can make a better sandwich than what's available. How did you know I brought my own lunch? We never sat together."

"Doesn't mean I never noticed." His blue eyes flecked with an ocean of memories as they looked down at the table. A warm glow fuzzed in my chest.

My resolve to resist the charms of Hutch Hawkins kicked in the backup generators.

I bit off half my sandwich. Stuffing my mouth with food would keep me from my natural inclination for chitchat.

"You should get in line now before it gets really long," I said through my mouthful.

I focused my attention on my sandwich, waiting for him to go. After a few bites, I commenced my rotation. I ambled around the cafeteria, on the lookout for any suspicious, food fighty behavior. Fortunately, it was a quiet day.

On the lunch line, my eyes didn't deceive me. Hutch winced when he made a sharp turn to the register. He gave his left knee a clandestine rub before slapping on a smile for the cashier.

By the time I returned to the lunch table, Hutch was midway through his rosemary chicken and roasted potatoes, the savory scent nearly making me chuck my sandwich. His left leg was sticking out straight, poking out from under the table.

I asked a nearby table of girls for their spare chair and dragged it over.

"What's that for?" he asked.

"You can prop your leg on it. That's not allowed for students, but we can abuse our teacher privilege."

"You didn't have to do that." Gratitude and embarrassment waged war on his face. He didn't touch the chair. "I'm fine, though."

"Are you..."

"Yeah." He pulled his leg back under the table, away from view. "I slept on it weird last night, so it's a little tight. It'll be better by morning."

I wasn't sure how someone slept on their leg funny. My mind went to odd sex positions, and the less I traveled down that path, the better.

"Thanks," he said. "Want some?"

He ripped open the bag of Skittles laying at the edge of his tray.

In ancient cultures, the sharing of food was symbolic of unification. And in modern times, Skittles were delicious.

"Do you still only eat the greens and yellows?" I asked. When we secretly dated, he'd sneak a bag of Skittles in my locker with only the red, orange, and purples. I used to think we were meant to be because our Skittles tastes complemented each other perfectly. Then I grew up and realized that candy was never an accurate barometer of relationship strength.

"I've expanded my palette," he said while munching on a handful of Skittles. Why did I find him chewing attractive? "Want some?"

He held out the bag to me, but I held my ground. It would trigger all those times when we shared candy in the past, the sweetness lingering on his tongue as we made out.

Hutch got up a few minutes later to do his rounds, presumably once his knee felt better. All was quiet on the cafeteria front, and at our table, too. When he returned to the table, he didn't come up with any more questions, comments, jokes, or sly observations. He said nothing.

We spent the rest of the period in silence, two colleagues and nothing more. No charm. No dimples.

Everything was going according to plan then. Hutch got the message to keep his distance.

I heaved out a sigh.

Swell.

6

HUTCH

It was weird eating lunch in silence. I was so close to Amos, yet so far. I missed how easily we could talk to each other. We weren't that high school couple who only fooled around, though we did plenty of that. We could talk about anything and make it feel like everything.

But after two days of caf duty and our no talking rule, I was starting to get used to it, though I still hated it.

Amos walked around the cafeteria stopping now and then to chat with students. I respected his boundaries and didn't check out his ass. Though his fitted pants made it a challenge.

The kids loved him. *Hey Mr. Bright! Mr. Bright, check this out!* While teachers were removed from student social standings, he was definitely more popular now than in high school. No more cute wallflower. It was wonderful to watch. His joy at being a teacher shined through. He loved it here, and I didn't want to ruin that. I didn't want him to feel uncomfortable in what was obviously his happy place.

If he wanted us to be only colleagues, then only colleagues we would be, even if it was a cold fist around my heart.

Aside from school-related questions, we didn't talk. Not even mindless chit chat about the weather. I actually did need help with the coffee maker in the faculty lounge during seventh period, but I asked another teacher.

Whenever we passed each other in the halls, I only gave him a terse nod of acknowledgement, which he reciprocated. It was like when we were secretly together, only this time, there'd be no feverish making out in my car during free periods.

After school, I called my first meeting with the soccer team. Things hadn't changed since I was a Husky. Freshly painted lines over freshly cut grass with large goals at both ends adorned the soccer field. I ran my hand over the goalpost, the familiar grooves of the paint sending me back in time.

This was my happy place.

I inherited a solid lineup from Coach Legrand. He briefed me on the players, their strengths and weaknesses, so I wasn't going in cold. They sat on the grass, looking up at me, the man who was supposed to have the plan.

"Gents, I'm Coach Hawkins. I used to be sitting where you are right now. Ten years ago, I was a Husky. I learned everything I know from Coach Legrand. Whatever happened last year is in the past. Missed shots, missed saves, all of it. Leave it on the field. It's a new season."

I had everyone go around and introduce themselves, then we broke off into drills. It felt good getting back to soccer. The guys raced back and forth across the green, the ball gliding in smooth passes and tap-tap-tapping on their knees. I watched every player closely, cataloging their skills and what needed to be improved. I pulled players to the side for fly-by coaching, giving them pointers on their dribble or defensive strategies.

Soccer was my zone, a game filled with the uncomplicated mission to get a ball into a net.

Practice was cut short by a sudden rain shower, the kind that comes over the mountains in a rush. We hightailed it to the men's locker room.

As soon as I entered, the rank stank hit me in the face like a warm hug from a gross uncle. I was home. It was here in the Huskies locker room that I bonded with teammates and celebrated victories, and I wanted to create the same environment for the guys.

I thought about my old teammates and the shenanigans we got up to here. Except for Seth, I wondered what they were up to. Some had reached out over the years, but I felt so uncomfortable about what happened with Seth, that I figured it was best to keep a healthy distance.

The locker room had gotten an upgrade in the past decade. Rusty lockers were replaced, new floors put down to match the school colors. But the odor of dozens of teenage boys sweating would live on forever.

And then there it was, the Coach's office. I would come visit Coach Legrand all the time, for advice on my dribbling, for advice on life. It was a shame we couldn't work together, but he was only a phone call away if I needed him. I planned to let the guy enjoy his retirement.

His office (or rather, the soccer coach's office) was a windowed room with two chairs and a metal desk. This room was mine for the rest of the season. Crazy to think. Different coaches shared the office depending on the season, so the walls were filled with a mix of schedules and posters for soccer, basketball, bowling, and hockey. It was its own organized chaos, and now it was mine.

I plopped into the wheely chair, which squeaked for dear life when I leaned back. Another sound that transported me back a decade.

"Knock knock," said a tall, Nordic blond guy before he knocked twice on my door.

I sat up straight, as if I'd gotten busted or something. "Hey. Come on in."

"Hutch, right?"

"Guilty as charged."

He stepped forward, and I suddenly felt very small. With his thick blond hair and strapping chest, he could've played the rich kid villain in some 80s movie. He even had a cocky smile to match.

"Raleigh Marshall. Football coach and fellow gym teacher. Looks like we'll be working together."

"Hutch Hawkins." We shook hands, each trying to make the other guy wince.

"Our new men's soccer coach." He studied me. Not sure what he was looking for. "You look like your picture. Shorter in person, though."

"Uh, thank you?"

"I Googled you. Two years with the Nashville Troubadours. Top scorer in your first year. Impressive."

"Thanks, man."

"You decided to call it quits?"

"Wasn't my choice." Heat crept up my neck. I wished I had the power to scrub the internet. I kept my legs under the desk, out of sight.

Raleigh nodded gotcha and sat in the chair across from me. He kicked his legs up on my desk. "So what brings you back to Sourwood?"

"Coach Legrand was a mentor to me. We kept in touch over the years, and when he told me he was retiring, I thought about the chance to come back and coach the team I'd led to back-to-back victories as a player." No harm in a little bragging. Something told me this guy did it often.

Raleigh took it in stride. "Surprised you wanted to leave the pro life behind entirely."

I couldn't tell if he was ragging on me or not. "You ever try going pro with football?"

He let out a deep laugh. "I didn't have the goods. I got an invite to an open tryout, got the wind knocked out of me on the first play. It was then that I had an epiphany. I should get into coaching!"

I didn't expect humility from him. His laughter filled the room and welcomed me to join in.

"Welcome aboard. Excited to work with you." He held out his fist for a bump.

I breathed a sigh of relief. At least I didn't have to deal with a dickhead co-worker.

"Have you met Chris Bergstrom yet?"

"We did a phone interview before I was offered the job." Bergstrom was the athletics director for the Sourwood school district, overseeing all sports programs.

"He's cool. He mostly stays out of your hair unless you make it to the regional playoffs. Then he gets more involved. I have a suspicion he gets a bonus if a Sourwood team wins a championship."

"Do we?"

Raleigh let out a roar of laughter. "Oh, man. You're funny. I'm gonna like working with you."

The feeling appeared to be mutual. He seemed like a guy who liked to take the piss out of someone as a sign of friendship. And considering the other teacher I knew well at this school hated my guts, I could use all the friends I could get.

———

RALEIGH and I fell into a conversation rabbit hole while my players got dressed and left for the day. We shit-talked other schools we'd be playing, traded thoughts on different coaches in the area. Apparently, his ex-girlfriend ran off with the coach at our big football rival North Point High, so he went *off* on that guy and his franchise. Raleigh was a master of shit-talking. I laughed so hard my stomach tightened in glorious pain. When I looked at the clock, an hour had passed.

I was going to have a good time working with him.

He convinced me to grab a happy hour drink. He drove us in his big Jeep to Stone's Throw Tavern. I tried using a fake ID there in high school, but the owner, this huge bear of a man, sniffed me out in a second. Nearly caused me to piss my pants.

I glanced at the upstairs loft in the bar, and the scary bear boss man was there working at the desk. I averted my gaze and hoped he didn't remember me.

We grabbed a table by the window. A pretty waitress our age with heavy eyeliner, dirty blonde hair, and a don't-fuck-with-me attitude took our drink orders.

"So any tips for teaching gym?" I asked jokingly.

"I know people like to shit on gym teachers, but we do help kids. There's value in teaching kids how to compete, how to handle winning and losing."

Huh. I didn't give much thought to teaching gym, but he was making me reconsider.

Raleigh leaned closer, his eyes alive with opinions. "There are teachers at South Rock who think that sports are evil and anyone who likes sports is an idiot. I won't name names, but stay away from the drama classroom." He rolled his eyes as he sipped his beer. "But I believe athletics teaches kids self-confidence, discipline, and the value of betting on yourself.

"One of my favorite memories of teaching gym was this scrawny, short kid I had a while back. It was the baseball unit. He dreaded going up to bat. He faked being sick to get out of gym class. But I told him, I said 'Jerry, you let me help you and you take this seriously, I guarantee you're going to hit a home run by the end of the quarter.'

"I worked with him, gave him feedback on his swings. I kept telling him he could do this. He just had to keep working at it. Eventually, he'd be by the dugout, practicing swings by himself, or watching his teammates' stances. He started to believe in himself. And do you know what happened?"

"He hit a home run?"

Raleigh held up three fingers. "Three of 'em. I told Coach Shablanski about him, and he's now on the baseball team."

He slammed his hand on his table, his excitement unable to be contained with words.

"That is fucking awesome." I clinked my beer bottle against his. I was pumped to teach gym almost as much as I was to coach soccer. Hell, I was pumped for both! "That's what I love about coaching. It's like we have special powers to see the potential of every player, but they can't see it yet, and it's our job to bring it out."

"Right on." Raleigh had an easy way about him, like he was born popular and knew it. "Are you going to get your certification in physical education?"

"What certification?"

"You haven't looked into getting certified to teach? Right now, you can substitute teach with a Bachelor's Degree. But you need to take the certification exam to be a full-time teacher on staff and get all the benefits. Then you have 5 years to get your Master's degree once you're hired."

"That's a lot of school." Currently, I was paid like a temp: less money and no insurance. I wasn't sure I wanted to teach. Originally, I thought about coaching on the side and getting another job during the school day. That hadn't panned out yet, and I was unsure what I'd do. After I left pro soccer, I drifted between different jobs, none of them a career. I thought my career was going to be a pro athlete signing multi-million dollar contracts. I hadn't found my Plan B yet.

Raleigh waved his empty beer bottle at the waitress, and a minute later, she came back with two fresh ones for us.

"Thanks, Natasha," he said, reading her nametag. "You're the best."

"I do what I can," she deadpanned.

Raleigh checked her out as she walked away. "She's cute."

Here it came. Whether it was at a bar or in the locker room, there'd inevitably come the discussion about which girls were hot. I would nod and play along while trying to steer us to a new conversation topic.

He looked at me wondering what I thought.

"Yeah. She's cute." I could feel Pop rolling his eyes.

And I saw a vision of Amos from high school, looking at me with the same heartbreak subsuming his eyes.

"I have a girlfriend, but you should ask her out." Raleigh cocked an eyebrow at me.

I shrugged it off with a grunt non-answer.

When I got home, I joined Pop on the couch to watch TV, but I felt restless. I went up to my room and shut the door, pacing in the small space.

I didn't know why I was still semi in the closet. I didn't want my players to look at me differently. I didn't want my new friend Raleigh to either. There'd been some progress made in sports, but not a lot. The homophobic jokes teammates cracked in locker rooms in high school, college, and Nashville were seared into my brain.

Once Amos and I broke up, it was like I stopped being gay. I didn't date. Were it not for the porn I occasionally watched, nobody would be able to tell.

After what happened with Amos, I couldn't bring myself to risk hurting another person. And I couldn't risk hurting myself. I might've been the one who mucked things up with Amos, but my heart broke, too. I put on a smile at prom for all to see, but when I got home, I sobbed on my bed until the sun came up the next morning. I didn't know it was possible to miss somebody this hard, like every cell in my body ached.

Maybe it was time to tiptoe outside the closet. Amos had moved on. He was out, presumably dating, living his life in the present, not the past. I opened the Milkman app and officially activated the profile Pop had created for me.

It was both one small step and one giant leap for Hutch Hawkins.

7

AMOS

For the rest of the week, things went exactly as I intended. Hutch and I were cordial, but not friendly, and definitely not flirty. We didn't talk to each other unless it was work-related. We ate in mundane silence at lunch. He called me Mr. Bright.

I didn't like it.

It was like some messed-up version of foreplay. How long could we go without having a real conversation? It pulled me back to my high school days when I would gaze at Hutch from afar.

Currently, he was at his most devastatingly handsome. He wore South Rock branded polos and shorts that stretched across his chest and ass, respectively. And on cooler days, since we were still in the quixotic throws of spring, he wore cute crew-neck sweaters and jeans which also stretched across his chest and ass. They were the same outfits he wore in high school! Way to be economical, but also...it was a key bump of nostalgia that scrambled my brain.

And that trademarked Hutch smile and laugh were still on display. But with other people, joking around with students. He was their new favorite teacher.

How did I wind up in a situation where I was quasi-pining for a guy I'd instructed not to talk to me? As I left school on Thursday, passing Hutch for the umpteenth time that week, I was left with another question: why was it so easy for him to keep his distance?

There was a part of me that hoped this would be torture for him, as it was for me. But he handled it just fine. Whatever torch I secretly wished Hutch carried for me had long been extinguished. When he dumped me all those years ago, he meant it.

I treated myself to an adult-sized glass of wine and graded tests Thursday night. Judging from the answers, it seemed several of my students were as distracted as me. The red pen would get an active workout tonight.

After an hour, I took a break through watching the thing that always lifted my spirits: videos of cats and dogs being friends. One of the great ironies of my life was that I knew a ton about cats, and gave off Crazy Cat Lady energy, but I was allergic to felines.

A tabby cat and pitbull mix conspired to break into their owner's treat drawer. Consider my heart melted.

I limited the number of videos I watched so that I didn't run out. My thoughts returned to Hutch. This would not do.

I hadn't had much luck on Milkman, but I decided to fire it up. Hope springs eternal and all that. There had to be a guy on there who could keep me from thinking of the past. I refused to believe in soulmates. There was only one person out there? Sure, but what if they didn't want to be with me? What then?

I scrolled through profiles of indistinctive six pack shots and pics of underwear bulges and guys proclaiming that even though they were on a gay hookup app, they didn't want anyone who acted gay.

And then, perhaps my brain broke because I imagined I saw a profile for Hutch.

Wait. It was a profile for Hutch.

Hutch was on Milkman?

Throwing a guy like Hutch on a dating app was like throwing an opened can of tuna into a room of cats.

Hutch's profile was oddly wholesome. The carousel of pictures were ones a parent would pick out to brag about their child, not ones used for attracting sexual partners: Hutch and his dad posing over a grill. Hutch playing soccer. Hutch visiting The Gateway Arch in St. Louis. Hutch as a ten-year-old holding up a fish.

SoccerStar was his profile name, something so basic it sounded like something my mom would choose. The profile was dorky and cool at the same time, confident in its earnestness.

I'm Hutch. I love playing and coaching soccer, spending time with my family, and outdoors activities including any and all water sports.

Huh?

The Hutch I knew got pee shy in public restrooms.

For purely anthropological reasons, I messaged him on the app.

Mr. Brightside: Hey, you might want to remove the part in your profile about water sports. Unless you're into that.

I left my phone on the couch cushion and retreated to the kitchen to make a bag of microwave popcorn, my go-to wine snack. Two minutes and twenty seconds later, I returned to the couch to find a Milkman notification on my home screen.

Breathe, Amos. It could just be a dick pic from a random guy.

My phone buzzed and slid off the couch. I picked it up and despite my better judgment, cracked a smile.

SoccerStar: Hey.

SoccerStar: I like water skiing and water polo, so...

Mr. Brightside: Go to Urban Dictionary and look up the definition for Water Sports.

SoccerStar: Oh shit!

SoccerStar: I meant water skiing and water polo.

Mr. Brightside: You might want to be clearer in your profile.

SoccerStar: That explains all the weird messages I've been getting.

Mr. Brightside: Now, now. Don't kink shame.

SoccerStar: True. To each his own.

SoccerStar: Deleting now.

SoccerStar: I'm going to have a talk with my dad. I should've reviewed what he wrote. My bad.

That explained so much about the profile, but opened up more questions.

Mr. Brightside: Your dad is your wingman?

SoccerStar: Trying to be. He set this up for me.

Mr. Brightside: He needs a crash course in gay dating apps. If someone mentions NSA, they're not referring to the National Security Agency.

SoccerStar: Of course. That means they support local businesses and never shop Amazon.

Mr. Brightside: It means they're down for dinner because they have a normal supper appetite.

SoccerStar: And just because they say they're a daddy doesn't mean they have kids and wear their cell phone clipped to their belt, right?

Mr. Brightside: You're getting the hang of this online dating thing. And RN means right now, not registered nurse.

SoccerStar: Why can't they be both?

Mr. Brightside: You never know.

Mr. Brightside: They'd be a real unicorn.

SoccerStar: According to the internet, a unicorn in gay dating language means a single person who joins a couple. I thought it had to do with being horny.

SoccerStar: Because of the horns.

SoccerStar: Horn.

Mr. Brightside: Why can't they be both?

SoccerStar: Thanks for looking out for me, Famous Amos.

I stared at his message, a warm feeling filling me up. Was I breaking my rule engaging with Hutch? Technically, I was engaging with SoccerStar, who could be catfishing me with Hutch pictures for all I knew. I'd better keep talking to him to be sure.

Mr. Brightside: You're lucky.

SoccerStar: Why's that?

Mr. Brightside: Sounds like you haven't had to use apps. You've been able to pick up guys the old-fashioned way.

SoccerStar: Can I be honest?

Mr. Brightside: I'd prefer you lie to me. Jk

Mr. Brightside: That means just kidding.

SoccerStar: Not join kickball?

Mr. Brightside: Nope.

I sat up straight, awaiting his honest-filled response. What was it about the faux anonymity of screen names that made it easier to share?

SoccerStar: I haven't dated anyone since you.

SoccerStar: How about you?

Mr. Brightside: No one worth mentioning.

Mr. Brightside: It's hard out there. [shrug emoji]

SoccerStar: It shouldn't be for someone like you.

Heat seeped into my cheeks, but that could've been the wine. No, it wasn't the wine. This conversation needed to take a sharp turn before I bared my soul.

Mr. Brightside: Why did you leave Nashville?

SoccerStar: I was cut from the team.

Mr. Brightside: Because of your knee?

SoccerStar: I tore my ACL during practice. Most ACL graft operations are successful. Mine was for the most part. I can walk on it and do some light jogging. But it wasn't one hundred percent, and only people with fully functioning legs can play professional soccer.

Mr. Brightside: Can't they make an exception and let you use your hands?

SoccerStar: Sadly, no.

SoccerStar: I'm not good with making sharp turns, like when I need to chase after someone in a corridor. :)

Mr. Brightside: Shit. My bad.

I sunk deeper into my couch, a flash of anger at myself as I recalled the way he called out my name in the hall. I could feel the stifled pain behind it.

Mr. Brightside: I'm really sorry, Hutch.

SoccerStar: It's all good.

SoccerStar: After I got cut from the team, I tried finding a job, but when the only professional experience you have is kicking a soccer ball, it doesn't make for an enticing resume. I got a cashier job at a big box store, but then some Troubadour fans posted pictures of me online, and I became a cautionary tale. People thought it was drugs.

Mr. Brightside: Why didn't you tell them the truth?

SoccerStar: I don't know.

SoccerStar: I was embarrassed. I really thought I'd made it. And I held out hope that my knee would get better. I went to physical therapy religiously, wracked up some nice medical debt.

Mr. Brightside: Is it any better?

SoccerStar: For the most part, but I'll never be able to play like I used to.

SoccerStar: My dad had an injury at work a few months ago. I came home to take care of him and decided that there was nothing keeping me in Nashville. That city was just a constant reminder of failure. And for the life of me, I could not get into country music. Cowboy hats don't fit my head well.

Mr. Brightside: You didn't fail. You were a professional soccer player. How many people can say that?

Mr. Brightside: What is failure anyway? I've been teaching for four years. I've taught lots of students. The only kids who fail my class are the ones who never try. You tried. You gave soccer your all for years. You made it. You lived your dreams. How many people can say that? 10% less knee mobility doesn't take away from that.

SoccerStar: :)

Mr. Brightside: What does that mean?

SoccerStar: It means I'm smiling.

And I was, too, the kind of smile that sent tingles down my spine. Hutch was dangerously easy to talk to, and I let myself get pulled in. Giving him the silent treatment at school was excruciating.

SoccerStar: What about you? How'd you wind up back at South Rock?

Mr. Brightside: It wasn't planned. At my old school, there was a teacher who got handsy at the Christmas party. He was beloved and won awards. Oh and married to a woman and father to two kids. When I'd told the principal what happened, she didn't believe me, said I must've drank too much and hit on him. I'd never felt so small in my whole life. I tried to forget about it, but every time I saw him in the hall or getting a hearty applause at an assembly, I felt sick.

Mr. Brightside: When I got the job offer at South Rock, I could breathe again. I felt saved.

SoccerStar: Who is this guy? Where does he live?

Mr. Brightside: Why do you want to know where he lives?

SoccerStar: I may have a bum knee, but my fists work just fine. [angry face emoji.]

Mr. Brightside: It's not worth it. It all worked out. I love teaching at South Rock. I've met some of my closest friends.

SoccerStar: I love being at South Rock, too. I really love coaching. I love it more than playing.

SoccerStar: Things worked out for the best.

Mr. Brightside: They did.

SoccerStar: Sorry for spilling my whole sob story earlier. You're really easy to talk to.

Mr. Brightside: I spilled mine, so we're even. And you are, too.

The phone was hot in my hand. My screen wasn't the only thing glowing. Our conversation came to a pause, and I didn't want it to end. That was the thing about Hutch. He was like a bag of chips: you promise yourself one chip but blink and wind up eating the whole thing.

It was getting late, and we had to be up bright and early for another day of school.

SoccerStar: I'm hungry.

Mr. Brightside: Me, too.

On the other hand, my stomach rumbled at the mention of hunger. Popcorn and wine were not filling, and all this typing was giving me a workout.

SoccerStar: I think I'm going to order pizza. You in?

Mr. Brightside: Share it?

SoccerStar: Virtually. You get your own. Do you still like mushrooms on your pizza like a madman?

Mr. Brightside: Says the guy who only eats yellow and green Skittles. And I thought we had a deal not to bring up the past.

SoccerStar: Right, right. So, Mr. Brightside, what do you like on your pizza?

Mr. Brightside: Mushrooms.

SoccerStar: Madman!

I burst out laughing, then navigated to a new window and put in an order for pizza. I didn't feel tired at all.

8

HUTCH

"What are you doing ordering pizza? It's eleven o'clock at night!"

"Pop. I'm a grown man. I can eat a late night pizza." I thanked the delivery man with a generous tip, then shut the door with my foot. The salty aroma of the pizza seeped through the box. The greasier the pizza, the better.

Pop stared at me from the couch bug-eyed, his stare toggling between me and the box.

"I was hungry."

"Don't you have school tomorrow?"

"I have work, Pop. I work at school."

"Shouldn't you get to sleep?" He crossed his arms, and the old Pop of my younger days scolding me for being up past my bedtime came back. He still managed to send a chill up my spine at twenty-eight-years-old.

"I have to work on the playbook." That was true. The team was in the thick of practicing; our first game was coming up. But I didn't know if I'd be working on the playbook tonight.

Tonight entered a new realm of possibility. Amos and I were

talking again. I missed his jokes. I missed the way our conversations unraveled.

"Don't worry, Pop. I won't be up late. That's why they invented coffee." I kissed him on the cheek. "And shouldn't you be in bed? You need your rest."

"Once the news is over."

I tilted my head to see the TV. "They're doing a story about a man who collects used stamps."

Pop waved me off, then pushed himself off the couch. I grabbed him with my free hand, and together, we made our way upstairs, two fucks with bum legs.

"What'd you get on your pizza?"

I opened the box and offered him a piece.

"Since when do you like mushrooms?"

"I'm trying something new."

He gave me a screwy look as if to say *what've you done with my son?* He took a piece without taking his eyes off me before retiring to his room for the night.

And I raced to my bedroom. I leapt onto my bed and grabbed my phone, displacing all the pillows but miraculously holding onto the pizza box.

Mr. Brightside: Yummm.

Mr. Brightside: I'm already two slices in.

SoccerStar: I have some catching up to do.

I slapped two slices together like a pizza sandwich and crammed them in my mouth. The mushrooms added a unique texture, and because they were vegetables, they made this healthy.

I leaned back, pulled my pillow from the floor, and got comfortable. Well, as comfortable as one could be on a twin bed.

SoccerStar: Confession. I got mushrooms on my pizza.

Mr. Brightside: Oh? And?

SoccerStar: Officially, not bad. I'm thinking of them like vegetarian pepperoni.

Mr. Brightside: Whatever you need to do to get through.

SoccerStar: I have a theory: the day someone orders mushrooms on pizza is the day they officially become an adult. Discuss.

Mr. Brightside: False.

SoccerStar: No kid in the history of the world has ever willingly eaten mushrooms. It's a food adults force us to eat for alleged vitamins. Once you ask that mushrooms be sprinkled on pizza, it's over. You're an adult. Lower back pain and electric bills and all.

Mr. Brightside: There are kids that like mushrooms on pizza.

SoccerStar: Name one.

Mr. Brightside: I'm Googling this.

SoccerStar: Me, too.

———

Mr. Brightside: It's 2 am

SoccerStar: 2:01

Mr. Brightside: Should we go to sleep?

SoccerStar: Probably.

SoccerStar: You first.

I stared at my phone, eyes wild. A half-eaten pizza sat in a box on the floor. My body was tired, but my mind was wired. I was talking with Amos again. My whole body buzzed, but that could've just been the mushrooms.

SoccerStar: Still there?

Mr. Brightside: Yeah :)

———

SoccerStar: A milestone. I just got my first dickpic message.

Mr. Brightside: Was there any message or just the pic?

SoccerStar: Just the tip.

SoccerStar: *pic

Mr. Brightside: And?

SoccerStar: Someone needs to trim.

Mr. Brightside: Yeah, that's just rude. If you're going to send a picture, clean up down there.

SoccerStar: Pop was right. Guys love showing their ding-a-lings on here.

Mr. Brightside: So was your dad cool with you coming out?

SoccerStar: Yeah. He wants me to be loud and proud. Rainbow flags everywhere.

Mr. Brightside: I like the way he thinks.

SoccerStar: How did your family take it when you came out?

Mr. Brightside: They didn't really care.

SoccerStar: As in, super supportive?

Mr. Brightside: As in...they didn't really care.

My heart sank at the honesty of the answer. From what I remembered, Amos didn't talk much about his family when we dated. We kept our families out of our business to stay private. Yet even when I mentioned Pop showing up at games, Amos never mentioned his parents doing anything similar for him.

Mr. Brightside: My family and I have never been that close. There wasn't any falling out, but we're just different people. I'm nerdy and wanted to discuss cool facts I learned in school. They preferred to eat dinner in front of the TV in silence. I wanted to go to the indie theater to see a foreign film I'd read about. They wanted to take family excursions to wrestling matches. I'm the perpetual odd man out, even before I came out. Coming out was just another aspect of me they couldn't connect with.

Mr. Brightside: Was it because I was gay? Because I was a bookish nerd? Because my sense of style and sense of humor were so fabulous that they felt constantly upstaged? Who's to say.

I cracked a smile, but my heart broke for him. I appreciated how supportive Pop was, but now I was fucking grateful to have a dad like him.

SoccerStar: They can't handle your fabulousness.

Mr. Brightside: My sister dropped out of college and moved to New Orleans, where her boyfriend-now-husband was from. My parents joined them a few years ago to be closer to their grand-kids. I'm holding out hope that one of my sister's kids will be nerdy like me. It'll give me proof that I genetically belong in this family and I'm not a total fluke.

SoccerStar: You're not a fluke. You're exactly who you need to be. I love watching wrestling, but I also loved listening to all the weird facts you'd spout.

Mr. Brightside: I preferred the found kind of family. My friends are like extra siblings. What could beat that?

Damn. I wish we were having this conversation in person so I could wrap him in a hug and remind him how awesome he was. He was really living up to his username.

SoccerStar: Listen, if you ever feel the need for a father figure, I can loan Pop to you. He's a little slow and a little stubborn, but he gets the job done.

Mr. Brightside: What does Pop do, pray tell?

SoccerStar: He'll provide an unlimited supply of dad jokes which he'll laugh at before he gets to the punchline. He'll provide unsolicited commentary on pop culture and political figures, rele-gating most of them to the dingus or doofus bucket. And he can give you a call whenever you need and ask exactly two questions: "are you feeling okay?" and "how's your car running?"

Mr. Brightside: Does he come with an old wallet, stuffed to the breaking point with receipts and loyalty cards?

SoccerStar: You know it.

Mr. Brightside: Sold!

———

MR. BRIGHTSIDE: It's 4 am.

SoccerStar: We have to get up in 90 minutes.

Mr. Brightside: We should stay up. If we go to sleep now, we'll wake up in the middle of a REM cycle and be even more tired.

SoccerStar: Is tonight even real? It feels like a dream.

SoccerStar: I've really liked this. I feel like I haven't talked to anyone in years.

Mr. Brightside: You didn't keep in touch with all your friends from high school?

SoccerStar: We drifted, like your family. Just different people.

Mr. Brightside: Did you see one of your teammates is a conservative blogger?

Mr. Brightside: Barf.

SoccerStar: I did, and I second your barf.

SoccerStar: After I was cut from the Troubadours, I went to work, worked out, and went home. I got into a routine. You never realize how lonely you are in the moment. It's something I look back on like oh wow, I was a step above a hermit.

Mr. Brightside: Loneliness just becomes another layer of clothing you wear. You don't even realize it's on.

SoccerStar: Until someone helps you take it off.

My face turned red. I was really grateful he couldn't see me.

SoccerStar: Seems like you have a good group of friends and a great life here in Sourwood. You've really come into your own.

Mr. Brightside: It wasn't always like that. When we broke up, I felt so alone, Hutch.

Pangs of pain hit me in the gut. The past never truly went away. No matter how close we were, no matter how great tonight felt, what I did would always be in the middle.

SoccerStar: I'm sorry about what I did, Amos. I really am. I hate how things ended.

Mr. Brightside: So you didn't realize you were straight after all?

SoccerStar: Fuck. Thinking about that text still makes me cringe.

Mr. Brightside: Why did you do it?

One simple question. One answer that I wished was more complicated.

SoccerStar: Because I was scared. I was scared of losing my friends, my family, my future.

Mr. Brightside: But you weren't scared about losing me.

Mr. Brightside: I was scared, too. I was scared to lose all those things. But we would've been scared together.

Beep beep.

My alarm clock blared its heart out. Its rhythmic screeching jolted me back to stark reality. Life didn't exist inside of an app. The world had real consequences. All the apologies in the world couldn't change the past. I had my chance with Amos, and I blew it.

I slammed my hand on the alarm clock, shutting it up.

It was time to wake up.

9

AMOS

I arrived at school exhausted and buzzing, my mind and body in a weird battle of trying to stay alert. I hadn't pulled an all-nighter since college, and back then, I could nap in the middle of the day.

A nap sounded good. Were morning naps a thing?

I'd picked up the largest coffee Starbucks sold, which was helping me survive so far. I got to my classroom early and caught up on grading the papers that I'd let lapse when Hutch and I began our epic conversation.

Did last night slash this morning even happen? It all unfolded like a dream. My heart swelled with thoughts of Hutch, and that anything was possible. But in the cold light of day and caffeine, I reminded myself that we could be friendly, but that was it.

I'd been devastated by Hutch before. I had to protect myself from false hope. He had one foot still in the closet, and the other foot was on an online dating app looking for new love.

My morning crawled by. I was very tempted to put on a video, but I pulled myself together and led engaging, fun Thursday classes where we discussed the lingering artifacts of medieval times in our society. Teaching always cleared my head and energized me. And to my pleasant surprise, most of my students brought their A-game to class today.

In fourth period, I was fading. I did my best to turn away from my students whenever I needed to yawn.

"Are you okay?" Reynash asked. "Do we need to call you a doctor?"

His question was half-concerned and half-hoping this tangent could take us to the end of class.

"I'm fiiiiine." I yawned into my fist.

"Late night?" Dale raised his eyebrows.

I wish I could blatantly sleep in class like Tommy was doing in the back row. I didn't have the energy to go there.

"Yes," I said, making more of my students raise their eyebrows. "Not that kind of late night." Not technically. Last night had the intimate glow in my memory as if we'd had sex, but with words.

"Did you go out?" Rosalee asked.

"No. I was–I had trouble sleeping. It happens." That was the boring cover, and I could sense their deflation at the lack of drama and gossip in my answer. If they only knew the truth, they'd be buzzing like bees.

"If you need to nap under your desk for the rest of class, we won't tell anyone," Dale said.

"That won't be needed, Dale."

"Did you know that lack of sleep impairs your brain in the same way as being drunk. So in a way, you're teaching us while intoxicated." I could hear Reyansh building his case.

If he wanted to play games, we could play games. I resorted to my desk drawer of tricks and pulled out a stack of papers.

"Now that I thought about it, Reyansh, it's been a while since we had a pop quiz." I held up the papers, like I was waving a flag of defiance.

The kids groaned.

———

WHEN I GOT to cafeteria duty, there was a coffee sitting on my table, waiting to be drunk. The warm smell of roasted beans made me salivate.

"Sugar and half-and-half, right?" Hutch returned to the table, hands full of snacks and his own cup of joe. "I figured you needed the caffeine boost."

"Thank you." I tried not to ravage the cup and drink like a normal person.

"It's from the faculty coffee machine."

"It'll do." I took a big gulp.

He slid a sharing size bag of Skittles across the table. "A little wake up snack. Have you been yawning like a maniac today?"

"My students accused me of teaching drunk, so I gave them a pop quiz." I broke open the bag and scooped up a handful of colorful orbs. I parsed out the yellows and greens and dropped them into his palm like it was the most natural thing in the world.

"You are stone cold, Mr. Bright." Hutch handed over the reds, purples, and oranges from his handful.

"You know, this isn't really going to wake us up. It's just going to give us a temporary sugar high which we'll crash from."

That felt like an apt metaphor for last night. I was in the middle of crashing from its highs. Still, I shoved a glut of Skittles in my mouth.

We looked at each other and awkwardly smiled, not knowing where to go. Was last night something to be talked about in the light of day?

"Hey, hey now." Hutch put his hand over mine as he slid the Skittles bag to the center, eliciting a rush of sparks through my tired self. "Don't bogart the Skittles. We're splitting those."

Hutch arched an eyebrow at me, sending my stomach on a roller coaster ride. We ate and drank in silence while students flooded in and filled the caf with noise. Eventually, Hutch got up to do his first round.

We didn't bring up our conversation on Milkman. It belonged in its own special corner of the ether, and the less I swooned over the memory, the better.

————

THE AFTERNOON WAS A STRUGGLE. It was a beautiful afternoon, so getting the attention of my students was near impossible. And my sugar high from lunch was quickly plummeting, sending me on a crash course. I kept mixing up facts. Maybe Reyansh was right about me being technically intoxicated.

I had seventh period off. Usually, I'd spend it in the faculty lounge working on lesson plans for the future. But today, my mind could not focus. I needed a nap. Hard.

Outside, the air was breezy and filled with that perfect spring warmth. I unlocked my car, but before I got into the backseat, I spotted that the person parked next to me had a similar idea.

Hutch slept in his car's backseat. I gazed at him a moment, taking in his peacefulness, but trying not to be a creepy stalker who watched someone sleep. His eyes fluttered open, and he greeted me with a sleepy half-smile.

"I had the same idea," I told him when he rolled down the window.

"I need my rest for coaching."

Yikes. He still had practice after school. I did not envy him. "I'm sorry for waking you."

"My eyes were closed, but I couldn't fall asleep."

"I hate when that happens." I hoped the same fate didn't befall me.

"Do you remember when we used to fool around in my car during free periods?"

I blushed with the memories of hot back seats, seat belt buckles jammed into my spine, and looking up from his dick every few seconds to ask *did you hear that?*

"Good times," I said.

"I can't believe how ballsy we were back then."

"Me neither." I got into my car's back seat. For a second, I wondered if he'd asked me to join him.

"Have a good nap," he said from his car.

"You, too." I shut my eyes, but of course, my brain was far from sleepy. Not when Hutch was a life-sized dopamine hit.

I tried blocking out the outside world and listening to my breath so I could lull myself to rest. It didn't work.

I peeked over at Hutch's car. His eyes were closed, but he wore a perfectly pleased smile.

"You're staring at me, Famous Amos."

How could he know that? Was I just finding out Hutch Hawkins was psychic?

"Am not," I said in lame response.

He laughed with his tongue poking out from his teeth.

"Have you been able to fall asleep?" I asked.

"Nope." His eyes sprang open, two twinkling blue orbs that matched the cloudless sky. "You?"

"Nope. I'm tired, but not tired enough."

"Let's try it again," he said. "Once more with feeling."

He closed his eyes, and I did the same.

I scrunched down and got as comfortable as was possible in the back seat of an old car. I took in the peaceful silence outside. The cawing of birds. The rustling of a spring breeze. The sounds of cars driving in the distance.

And...nothing.

Truth be told, my best rest happened when I was wrapped in Hutch's arms. The man could lull me into the most tranquil sleep, whether we were on his twin bed, on mine, or looking up at the stars from the hood of his car.

Maybe we could share one more snuggle today to ensure that we optimize our midday nap. My willpower was shot from my lack of sleep; I'd give anything to be wrapped in those arms again.

"Hutch, you awake?" I asked. "Psst. Hutch."

I looked over, and he was fast asleep, his lips puckered in a peaceful slumber.

Oh, well. It was probably for the best.

10

AMOS

After sleeping for eleven hours Thursday night, I was so ready for Friday. I was refreshed. I had energy. And more importantly, I had growing feelings toward my ex that I needed to dance off.

Amos: Did you hear that?

Everett: The bell rang.

Amos: School's out. Time to party!

Chase: Who are you?

Amos: I'm a guy in desperate need of bangers to dance to.

Everett: I just caught a student rubbing up against one of the velvet stage curtains...BRB

Julian: TGIF

Julian: Where should we go?

Amos: REMIX!

Julian: Again?

Julian: Should we take a group vote?

Chase: Like Amos, I, too, would prefer to dance to bangers.

Julian: We could go to the ballet. They're putting on Swan Lake.

Amos: Bitch, are you joking? How about we compromise and watch Black Swan tomorrow?

Julian: Ha. Deal.

Amos: Want to meet at my place for some pre-gaming? 8ish?

Chase: Cool.

Chase: I still have a bottle of Fireball that a parent gave me for Christmas. Why they thought that was a suitable gift for a teacher is beyond me, but nevertheless, I'll bring that.

Amos: Now it's a party!

Amos: So 8ish. My place. Then we can Uber to Remix.

Julian: See you then.

Chase: Party!

Everett: What'd I miss?

Amos: Literally scroll up the text chain...

Everett: That's a lot of work.

Amos: My place. 8ish. Then Remix.

Everett: Remix!!! Dicks for everyone!

Chase: Dick firesale.

Amos: Dick smorgasboard.

Julian: Dick Van Dyke.

Amos: minus 5 points, J.

Julian: Rude.

Julian: How's your stage curtain, Ev?

Everett: Traumatized.

REMIX WAS the saving grace of Sourwood. I couldn't imagine living in a small town without a rowdy gay bar. In high school, I was mystified by, and terrified of, Remix. I didn't have the courage to try sneaking in with a fake ID. When I finally turned twenty-one, Remix was like Xanadu to me.

It was located at the end of a strip mall on the outskirts of town. Its rainbow flag and pulsing music were a stark contrast to the quiet stores surrounding it. Men hung out smoking outside. My friends and I made a beeline for the door.

I could smell the alcohol, and the sweat of bodies on the dance floor. I was ready to cut loose.

Inside, there were two bars and a dance floor in the middle. Colored lights flickered around the darkness, making this feel like a magical land, at least for me. Everett raced to claim our usual table by the dance floor. It gave us the best view of the joint, and all the guys therein. At my condo, we took a shot of Fireball. One was enough for me. That shit burned. I came to Remix with a slight buzz and room for more debauchery.

"I'll get the first round," Everett said.

"Actually, it's Julian's turn." Chase adjusted his glasses as he looked over at Julian.His brain was literally amazing. I wondered if he could've been an actual NASA scientist instead of using his brain to teach high school chemistry and remember bar tabs.

Julian whipped out a credit card and handed it over to Everett. Everett was the best at pushing through the crowds and getting the bartender's attention.

I stared out across the club. It wasn't even ten. The night was embryonic. The Friday night rush wouldn't happen for another half hour. Guys were filtering in, groups setting up camp. We were all eyeing each other like animals on the savannah, determining who was predator and who was prey.

Once I had a drink in hand, I did a casual loop through Remix. Having a drink in hand somehow made it not creepy to walk around checking out guys. There was a mix of regulars and local college students, rowdy thirtysomethings and debonair older gentlemen. Some cute, some hot, some I wouldn't touch with a ten foot pole.

None were as boyishly handsome as a certain substitute gym teacher slash soccer coach, though.

I returned to our homebase and drank with my friends. See, the thing was, I wanted to be a predator, but in my heart, I was prey. Or worse, someone destined to sit on the sidelines. Charlie had helped us with flirting techniques a while back. He said it was all about confidence, which wasn't my strong suit.

"Any luck?" Chase asked.

"Just surveying the scene. I need more liquid courage." I took a healthy sip of whatever fruity cocktail Everett ordered us. The sweetness masked its strength, encouraging me to drink more.

"Remember to start with the eyes, then the lips, then go," Chase said.

"Right, right. Make eye contact. Then look at their lips. And if they respond..."

"Fucktown, USA." Everett brought round two back to the table with perfect timing.

"You know what, I just want to dance." I didn't want to think about trying to hook up with some random paramour. I needed to forget about guys for a night. I was here with my friends. We were healthy, we were young.

I took Julian's hand, then Chase's. "As David Bowie commanded, let's dance!"

And dance we did.

The DJ played bop after bop, the music flowing through me, moving my limbs like a marionette. There we were, four single guys living it up in a strip mall gay bar, having the time of our lives, dancing the world away. I let my head go blank, filling with the sound of pulsating jams flowing through my ears, cleaning out my overthinking mind. We were electric. Friends ready to conquer the dance floor, then the world. Other guys joined us in the fun, and the dance floor was quickly the place to be.

Everett brought another round back to the table. "Ugh, so did you hear that the football team is getting brand-new training equipment for the fall? Meanwhile, the sets for the spring play are a step above crayons on cardboard. Raleigh must be thrilled."

Everett rolled his eyes as he drank. At South Rock High, sports ruled and the drama department drooled, except they couldn't afford a towel to wipe their mouths with. It wouldn't be a Friday night without an anti-sports tirade from Everett, whose wrath always centered on Raleigh.

I took him with a grain of salt. Raleigh was cocky and kind of a buffoon, but in an endearing way.

"We really should ban sports. I don't see what good it does." Everett took a swig of his drink, which got him off his regular soapbox. He pulled out his phone and opened the Milkman app. "Let me see if there are any available and interested guys here tonight."

My phone felt heavy in my pocket with the message chain from Wednesday. Admittedly, I found myself reading through it when I was bored, reliving that night.

"Gross." Everett scoffed at something on his phone.

"Nobody good here?" I asked, wondering if the search was fruitless, ironically.

Everett snapped out of his phone haze. "What? No. Raleigh posted some idiotic pictures of him and his girlfriend-of-the-week at some sports bar. Why does he think people care about him going to a bar?"

Everett cared, apparently.

"Why do you follow him on Instagram?" Chase asked.

"He friended me, and I couldn't not friend him because he'd know I hate him."

Julian cocked his head. "That makes no sense."

Everett ignored him and returned his eyes to his phone. "Oh shit."

"What?" I asked.

"Hutch is on Milkman."

"Oh," I said innocently. I hadn't shared updates with the guys. I wanted to protect the intimacy of that night.

"And he's on his way here," Everett said.

"What?" I darted my head up. "How do you know that?"

"You can see how close people are on Milkman. Hutch is getting closer. He was three miles when I first opened his profile. Now he's two point five."

Of course Everett knew every feature of Milkman.

"Mine says two point four," Chase said. "And he has some cute pictures."

I pulled out my phone to confirm the news. "You don't know that he's coming here. He could be driving past."

"There isn't much to do past this strip mall. The most likely scenario is that he's headed here," Chase said.

Unease boiled inside me. Who was he coming here with? Was this a first date? A quick drink before fucking like jackrabbits?

"One point nine miles," Julian shouted out like we were playing gay Marco Polo.

"Stop!" I put my hands over as many phone screens as I could. "This is–this is an invasion of privacy. What does it say about our society that we can track people's movements? That means the government is watching everything we do. That's not right. What about freedom? I've studied this in past societies, and with this kind of overreach, at some point in the near future, people will start to rebel. And, you know, we could have another revolution on our hands."

I gasped in breath. I stared at my friends in silence, waiting for someone to say something.

"How far away is he now?" I asked.

"One point one." Everett shot me a snarky grin. "But I loved the monologue. Shakespeare is shooketh."

"Okay. That's cool. Remix is a big place. He'll hang out with whoever, and that's fine." I shook around the ice to get the last traces of liquid courage from my drink. I could use every drop.

Hutch strolled in looking like a million of the sexiest bucks ever produced by the United States mint. He wore a baseball T-shirt that stretched across his jacked chest with green sleeves pushed up his thick forearms. His hair was mussed to perfection, a few sneaky strands falling in his sparkling eyes.

This was easily the hottest he'd looked since he returned to Sourwood. But who was keeping track?

"Is he alone?" Julian wondered.

When I finally pulled my eyes away from his body, I noticed that Julian was right. There were no other people at his side.

"He's probably meeting people here," I said. Some hot date. A registered nurse who never shops Amazon.

"Or hoping to meet someone here," Everett offered, a comment that made my stomach turn.

"He seems to be walking fine, Julian. No sign of a limp," Everett said. I kept the story of Hutch's knee to myself. It was still a painful subject for him, and I didn't want to reduce it to a bit. Hutch walked with a shy swagger. He had underlying confidence, as evidenced by the puffed-out chest, but his face screamed *out of my element*.

"Well, if he was fresh from rehab, he wouldn't be coming to a bar by himself." Julian raised his eyebrows in gotcha fashion.

"Will you both stop?" I hissed at my friends.

Hutch took his drink to a hi-top table in the corner. He scrolled on his phone, the universal sign that meant *Please don't think I'm actually here alone.*

But he was.

"I can't believe he's here alone," Julian said with sympathy.

Despite myself, I felt bad. I didn't get any satisfaction seeing him alone. I didn't have a karmic chuckle. Hutch kept checking his phone, his brave face only holding for so long. The crowd on the dance floor helped block his view of our table.

As the minutes wore on, his aloneness became more stated. Nobody met up with him. A few sketchy guys walked over to flirt with him, which made my stomach violently twist and thrash. Yet after a few minutes, they'd leave defeated, and he went back to nursing his beer. Hutch rudely put a serious wrench in my enjoyment of this evening. How could I try and find a guy to forget him when he was being all sad boy in the corner?

"Do you think we should invite him over?" I asked.

The guys all traded looks as if I suggested we jump off the roof.

"Sure," said Julian.

"That's cool with us." Everett leaned over the table. "Is that cool with you?"

"Of course that's cool with me! Why wouldn't it be?" I flitted away before I could hear their answer and before my internal objections could kick in.

11

HUTCH

Like a vision in the desert, Amos appeared through the
sweaty bodies on the dance floor and approached my small
table.

Shit. As if being caught alone and awkward at my first gay bar
wasn't embarrassing enough. I stood up straight and put on my
best nonchalant smirk as I scrolled on my phone.

I waited a second before acknowledging him coming over.

"Oh, hey," I uttered with a detached coolness that instantly
made me sound like a tool.

"You're here."

"I am."

"You do know this is a gay bar, right?"

"I do." I nodded and looked down at my drink, nervous as shit.
I was at a gay bar for everyone to see. It was another step forward,
and my heart was taking a giant leap out of my chest. "I realized
that my text all those years ago was wrong, and I'm not straight."

"Huh. You don't say?" His face lit up with understanding. He
clapped a hand heavy with support on my shoulder, which sent a
current directly to my dick. "Welcome."

"I'd been curious about coming here for a while. Maybe ever since high school."

"What finally did it?"

"Pop. We were watching TV and eating Chinese take out. He told me that a good-looking kid like me shouldn't be wasting the prime of his youth watching TV with his dad on a Friday night. He dared me to go to a gay bar for one hour, and I don't back down from a dare."

Pop could be a stubborn asshole, but he was pushing for me to be the best version of myself.

"I hope it lives up to your expectations." Amos smiled at the surroundings. Men dancing, carousing, music playing. Yep, expectations met. Amos looked great tonight, light and breezy in a fun button-down shirt.

"Did you ever come here in high school?"

"I wasn't cool enough to have a fake ID."

"Same," I said. I forgot about the struggles of being underage now that I could go anywhere and not get carded. I could even rent a car, a fact which was less fun than it seemed.

Amos licked his top lip, one of his nervous tells. I liked that he was nervous. That made two of us. "Are you having fun by yourself in the corner?"

"It's all right. Just scouting out the joint."

"Are you planning to rob it later?"

"You've found me out."

"Why don't you come hang out with me and my friends?" Amos pointed his thumb behind him, and I followed it across the dance floor to a large hi-top with three familiar-looking fellow teachers.

"Your faux brothers," I recalled from our message chain.

"Correct." Good on him for having a tight-knit group. A twinge of jealousy hit me because I didn't have something similar.

"Join us," he said again.

"I don't want to barge in on your night out."

"You're not barging. I'm inviting you."

"Are you sure?" I asked.

"Yes!" He rolled his head back and exhaled a heaving, frustrated sigh from deep within his lungs. He returned to normal and flashed me a fun little smile. "Must you make everything difficult?"

"Trying to live up to my bad ex-boyfriend image in your mind."

"Mission a-fucking-ccomplished." He grabbed my elbow, his fingers slipping onto my bare forearm, sending another current down south.

———

IF I'D KNOWN teachers could be this ribald, I would've hung out with more teachers earlier.

Amos's friends were hilarious. They played off each other so well, it was incredible they'd only been friends for a few years. The hell of teaching hordes of puberty-crazed teenagers must have expedited their bonding.

"So, Hutch..." Julian bobbed his straw around his drink and had that look that made me steel myself for an awkward question. "What brings you back to Sourwood?"

"Pop—my dad, he collapsed a few weeks ago at work. His health hasn't been great, so I wanted to take care of him." I didn't want to bring down the energy talking about Pop, but I felt an instant comfort around these guys. They were genuine.

"Is he okay?" Amos asked with grave concern.

"Yeah. He's doing better. He's being a baby about taking his medication and taking it easy, but what can you do?"

"If you need any help..." Amos started, then stopped himself. His eyes brimmed with concern.

"Thanks." I went to pat his hand. Was that too much? An overstep when I was lucky to have a literal seat at the table? I went for it anyway. His thumb gave the side of my hand a stroke, a subtle caress that rivaled my drink for biggest buzz provider.

"Are you going to stay here once he's better?" Chase asked, breaking that little moment between Amos and me.

"I'd like to. We'll see how coaching goes. Hopefully I'm asked back for next year." I caught myself. I actually...did like Sourwood. I couldn't wait to get out of here when I was a kid, but now that I was back, the familiarity and friendliness was like a warm blanket. "I love it here."

Amos met my eyes, and before I let myself get lost in their beauty and made things even more awkward, I rubbed my hands together.

"All right. I've been at South Rock for a few weeks. Give me the dirt on all the other teachers. We can't be a group of gay men at a gay bar drinking fruity drinks without gossiping."

"Way to stereotype," Amos said whilst slurping his cocktail.

"Be careful engaging with Mr. Zepowitz in the faculty lounge. No matter what you talk about, he'll always bring it back to a thirty-minute rant on the latest conspiracy theory he's obsessed with," Everett said.

"Back in January, I asked him how his Christmas break was, and it somehow wound back to him trying to convince me 9/11 was an inside job." Julian made the emoji cringe face. He was a sweet guy. I could totally see him being too nice to extricate himself from that situation.

"Mrs. Lucci will try to set you up with her daughter. She tries with everyone," Chase warned me. "Even after you tell her you're gay."

"I've become a pro at getting out of those awkward setups. It happens a lot," I told them.

"Humblebrag," Amos muttered.

"What was that?" I shuffled closer to him. My arm nudged his, another bolt of heat hitting me. I didn't plan for us to stand next to each other around the table...but neither of us were moving away. In fact, we had shifted closer.

"Humblebrag," he repeated.

"What's that?"

"You've never heard of the humblebrag?" Amos's eyebrows twitched on his smooth forehead, bringing attention to his blazing eyes.

"I have not. Did you just make it up?"

"No. It's like a thing, been a thing forever."

"If it was a thing, I would've heard about it." I flashed him a cocky smirk. Was I flirting? Perhaps.

It was Amos's fault for being such a good sparring partner.

"A humblebrag is...I can't believe I have to define it. It's like..." He waved his hand at his friends searching for an answer. He reminded me of game show contestants looking to the audience for help. "Ugh, this is hard. This is why I don't teach while drunk."

"*This* is why." I snorted.

Chase pushed his glasses up his nose. "A humblebrag is when somebody says a statement about themselves that's meant to be self-deprecating but actually makes them look even cooler."

"What he said." Amos pointed at Chase. "It's like if you complained that you couldn't fit into your shirts anymore because they were too tight against your chest."

A wave of self-consciousness hit me. I looked down at my shirt on my chest. Was Amos saying that my shirts were too tight? Was he noticing my chest too much?

"I'm not saying you—or that your shirts—it was just an example." Amos bit into his straw.

"Are my shirts too tight? Because this is the largest size this shirt goes to." I moved an arm to shield my chest.

"That's a humblebrag," Everett said.

We all burst into laughter. None of us knew exactly what was funny, but the good vibes around the table were so strong that we had to let it out. I hadn't enjoyed myself with a group of friends like this in a long ass time. I was buzzed and happy and alive with the excitement of a Friday night.

And a little adventurous.

I leaned into Amos's ear. "So does that mean a humblebrag is just a long-winded term for saying I have a hot body?"

I liked to push against my limits. That was how I became a good athlete, and it might be how I get myself kicked out of this inner circle.

Amos kept a neutral expression, but I could feel his body tense up with heat.

"Way to be modest," he said back, through the strains of a held-back smile.

I kept pushing. I wanted to see more of his sparkling eyes, more of his blush sprinkled on his cheeks. We had such good chemistry. We were baking soda and vinegar: put us together in a confined space, and we'd inevitably overflow with flirtation.

This was like old times. Better than old times

"I think you're humblebrag, too," I said, my hand drifting down his side, sitting at his waist. I unleashed every flirt and charm tactic in my arsenal. "Very humblebrag."

Red flushed his face. He licked his top lip again. Damn, was it sexy. Nervous energy bounced around in my chest, the pull of Amos as intoxicating as my drink.

"I'm going to get some air." He excused himself from the festivities.

———

OUTSIDE, the night air had a haze of smoke from the vapers getting their nicotine fix. Amos walked around the corner where it was quiet. He leaned against the brick facade. A streetlight illuminated his face in silhouette. I took a mental snapshot and committed it to memory.

"Fun night," I said.

"Yeah." He didn't tell me to scram, which was a good sign. "I'm sorry about my friends. I think they were all born without filters."

"They're awesome."

I walked up to him. The closer I got, the more electricity crackled between us. I pictured a Geiger Counter making rapid lines back and forth.

His red lips pouted in thought. I loved watching Amos think, wondering about what new meanings and insights churned through his mind.

"You okay?" I put a hand on his shoulder. More electricity shot through me. He didn't shrug it off. Another good sign.

"Uh huh." His eyes were a sea of wonder pulling me into their waves.

"If our high school selves could see us now, huh?"

"What would they say?" he asked pointedly.

"My high school self would be pumped that I was here with you. He wouldn't be able to get over how cute you are."

Amos's head dipped, a flash of red on his cheeks. I took my chance and moved my hand from his shoulder up his neck, massaging the muscles. His skin was as smooth as I remembered, the little hairs at the base of his head prickling the pads of my fingers.

He rolled his head back in bliss. Amos was always a slut for massages. You'd think he worked in construction or something by the way he seemed perpetually sore and in constant need of rubs. He let out a tiny groan that went straight to my dick.

The world around us shut off. Time stopped. We were high school lovers. We were adults. We were everywhere in between, infinite dots connected on the same timeline.

He dipped his head back, leaning deeper into my massage. His eyes fluttered shut, lips puckered as his cheeks flushed with perfect calm. Another soft groan that went straight to my dick.

All the years that we'd been apart weighed on me. I missed him. I missed talking and laughing and cuddling with someone. I could feel it crackling in the air, pounding in my chest.

His eyes slid open, a peaceful buzz turning his gaze glassy.

This was it. One of those moments where you either had to shoot your shot or get off the pot.

And...I got off the pot.

I let my hand drop away, then tucked it into my pocket.

"I'll see you inside." I shuffled back into Remix.

12

HUTCH

I drove home replaying the night over and over in my head. I completely chickened out. I was the guy who made daring line drives down the soccer field to score. Now I couldn't even work up the nerve to kiss a guy?

Sourwood was quiet. I wound through the streets of downtown, all the shops and restaurants that I'd frequented as a kid. I tried to seek out places where I didn't have any memories with Amos.

There was Caroline's, where I shared plates of fries with my soccer teammates. But it was also the place where Amos and I cut class to have a decadent breakfast of pancakes and waffles. He tried to convince me why waffles were superior to a soggy, syrup-drenched stack of pancakes.

There was Throw a Wrench In It, the hardware store where I stocked up on tools for DIY projects with Pop. Also where I made out with Amos in the back corner amid paint supplies.

Fuck, I was gonna have to find a new town.

I pulled into the driveway, and a light glowed from the living room.

"It's past your bedtime," I announced once I came inside. Pop lay across the couch channel-surfing, the TV giving him a washed-out look.

I had cleaned up the kitchen from dinner, but it looked like Pop had gotten hungry again. Clumps of plastic wrap which formerly held leftover mushroom pizza and beer caps sat on the kitchen table.

"You're home early," he said from the living room.

I cleaned off the kitchen table and counters. I joined him and handed over his night time pills.

"You thought I'd forget? When you don't take all your pills, the Bat signal turns on."

He reluctantly took the tablets from my hand, then the glass of water I offered. He rolled his eyes just like a teenager as he swallowed them. He showed me his tongue as a slight FU.

"Excuse me for trying to keep you healthy."

"I'm already healthy."

"Let's stay that way." Ever since I got the call from the hospital, there would always be a piece of me constantly on edge, waiting for the next phone call.

I sat at the opposite end of the couch, lowering his feet on me as if they were the safety bar on a roller coaster.

A sitcom laugh track echoed from the TV.

"What are you watching?"

"*The Golden Girls*. Did you know that some people call the MacArthur Center the Bea Arthur Center?"

"They do? Who's that?"

He pointed at the tall woman with a football player-like build on screen.

"Huh. Interesting."

"It's catchy. I may start calling it that." He smiled to himself, pleased with learning something new. "I watched this show when I was your age. Now I'm the same age as these broads."

"They seem to be having a ball." His wrinkled skin crinkled with a smile. When had Pop gotten this old? I knew plenty of people his age who were spry and active. This was a temporary setback. He'd be back to his old, strong self in no time.

"Did you really come home early because of my pills?" His eyes found me from the far end of the couch.

"I wanted to. I didn't like thinking of you here all alone."

"Bullshit." He cocked an eyebrow. "You struck out."

"I didn't strike out." What happened with Amos defied all sports metaphors. I was still wrapping my head around the fallout.

"Then how come you're home early? It's just midnight."

"Do you want me to go out all night and come home with random men? Remember when you used to give me a curfew?"

"Yeah, and you beat it tonight."

Even when he was recovering, Pop loved to bust my balls.

"I'm going to respect my elders and let that one slide." I drew circles with my finger on his ankle, like I'd done as a boy. "I went to a bar, and Amos and his friends were there."

Sad but true, Pop was my closest friend in Sourwood. I wouldn't be able to sleep unless I talked about tonight.

"Oh?" He sat up as best he could. His wiry eyebrows raised slowly. "Did you have a good time?" He was being cautious, something I should've been.

"I did, until the part where Amos and I were outside, and I completely blew it."

"Uh oh. What did you do?"

"I really stepped in it, Pop." A weight began to lift off my chest. I thanked whatever lucky stars there were that we had this kind of relationship. It might've been cringey to have him sign me up for apps, but when I needed him, we could talk without limits.

I told him about the flirting inside the bar, and the massage outside the bar, and how the earth opened up and presented this perfect moment for me to go in for a kiss...which I didn't take.

"What's the soccer equivalent of fumbling on the one yard line?" he asked.

"Pop." I smacked a hand over my face, forever replaying the moment in my head.

"Maybe you didn't want to?"

"I wanted to. I really wanted to. But we're finally at a place where we're talking again and on friendly terms. I don't want to blow that up because I still like him." I tapped my finger on Pop's leg. It was time to be honest with myself. "I still love him. I don't think I ever stopped."

Was it possible to be in love with someone I hadn't seen in ten years? Maybe love was like one of those diseases that stays dormant until an outside stimulus triggers it again. Amos was definitely my stimulus. His smiles, and the way we could joke and care about each other... I'd never had something like that with another person.

"Maybe he feels the same way."

I shook my head no. "He's moved on, Pop."

"Is he with someone else?"

"No, but he has a whole life. He has a career and friends and a part of him will always hate me for what happened."

"You don't know that for sure. Hate is a strong word."

"Well, I did a really shitty thing back in the day. I bailed on him when he needed me most. I was so scared." *We would've been scared together.* I always thought dumping him like I did was cruel, but it was much worse. The past replayed in my head on a constant loop. "What if Seth Collins was right? What if this followed me around forever? What if it cost me my soccer career? What if you cut me out of your life? What if people tried to chase you out of town when I left?"

"You really thought that would happen?" Pop asked. "We have a gay mayor."

"He was still married to a woman at that point."

"You actually thought I'd cut you out of my life? Seriously? And you really thought people would chase me out of town?"

"When you're closeted, you're pretty much wired to prepare for the worst. You want to believe that people are good at heart, but when you see enough articles and viral videos showing how bigoted and cruel people can be, it leaves a mark. It makes you not able to fully trust people."

Pop listened and cared, but he'd never truly get it. He sat up and wrapped me in a tight hug. I smelled his familiar Old Spice scent, and remembered how safe his hugs used to make me feel. But being an adult meant knowing that parents couldn't protect you from everything.

"I choked tonight, Pop."

"What were you afraid of?"

"That he wouldn't want to kiss me back." I wasn't ready for that answer. I'd rather live in this what-if state, because if Amos rejected me, then any hope for us would be done forever.

13

AMOS

Julian: Someone's birthday is in a week...

Everett: Birthday boyyyyyy.

Chase: All this means is that I have traveled around the sun once again.

Everett: And lived to tell about it. Time to celebrate!

Everett: What do you want to do?

Chase: Something lowkey.

Julian: Awesome! That sounds perfectly Chase.

Everett: Boooooo. Blackout drunk or bust.

Amos: Easy there. Have you been watching fraternity house porn again?

Everett: No comment.

Julian: Speaking of, one of my AP students handed in their paper, and in between the pages was a condom wrapper.

Amos: The smart kids are having more sex than us?

Chase: We're still the smart kids.

Everett: This is bleak. Maybe we can live vicariously through the sex you and Hutch are having.

Amos: We are not having sex! We're friends. I told you.

Nothing happened outside Remix. Just got some fresh air, and he helped me with a neck cramp.

Everett: So that's what they're calling it nowadays?

Amos: *mutes Everett*

Amos: Let's have Chase's party at my condo. We'll have drinks, cake, music. It'll be lowkey but fun. Good times will be had by all or else your money back.

Chase: Thanks, Amos! I'll put together a guest list.

———

THE WEEK BREEZED BY UNEVENTFULLY. I kept busy with lots of tutoring gigs and mulching gigs after school, adding to my travel fund. Each job activated a different side of my brain. Whatever awkward moment happened at Remix with Hutch and me was a distant memory; we had a good time at caf duty chatting about random school things. It was better than forced silence. I cleaned my apartment thoroughly throughout the week to prepare for the party; Everett and Julian and I went party supply shopping.

My classes stayed fun as we dug into the world of knights and how awful it was trying to fight in armor. I waited until a minute before the bell rang to hand back papers I'd graded. As students gathered up their books and backpacks, with Rosalee and Dale effusing about what a great class it was, I summoned Tommy.

After asking him again, he finally got out of his seat and shuffled up to my desk like he was being dragged by a chain.

"Tommy, I noticed that I didn't see an assignment from you. I was grading them this week, and there was one missing."

"Uh...yeah..." He looked at the other students leaving, as if any of them had a lifeline. "I handed it in. Maybe you lost it?"

My frustration dialed up, but I held it in. "I don't think I lost it. Did you hand anything in last week?"

"Uh, yeah..."

His eyes darted open with relief when the bell rang.

"Tommy," I said firmly when he tried to leave. "We're not finished with our conversation."

"Maybe it's still in your bag?"

I folded my arms, ready to go to defcon 2. "What was your paper about?"

"Huh?"

"Your paper. What was it about?"

"Uh...feudalism?"

Well, that was correct on a technicality. I knew he was lying, but I had to be careful about how I caught him in this lie. "Can you email it to me tonight?"

"I have practice."

"When you get home from practice."

"It's pretty late. And that was my only copy."

"You're telling me you typed up your paper and didn't save a copy?"

"Yeah."

I heaved out an over-it breath through my nostrils. This kid was going to make me go in circles, and I didn't have the time.

"Tommy. I find it hard to believe that you didn't save a copy of your paper."

"My computer crashed, and I lost all my files."

"Mrs. Healy in the computer lab has worked wonders with computers and extracting files. If you bring in your computer, she can probably extract it from your hard drive."

Mrs. Healy was the most tech-savvy person I knew, but I had no idea if this was possible. But I wanted to see if I could call his bluff.

"Uh, that's okay. I already threw my computer out and got a new one."

Damn rich kids. I quickly grew tired of this conversation. It had all the logic of an improv sketch.

"The assignment was due on Friday. There was no paper from you. I'll have to mark that down as a zero."

"Ugh, whatever." He didn't even have the energy to continue the fight. His face twisted into that straight bro *over it* glare that made me want to scream.

"You're already at a D-plus average for the marking period. If you get one more zero, you're going to be failing."

He shrugged with as much interest in his GPA as he had in learning history. "I'm gonna be late for class."

"Tommy, as I've said all year, if you need extra help, we can discuss ways to help you. But you need to meet me halfway."

"Yeah, cool."

I wasn't sure what that meant, and he was gone before I could follow-up.

———

I SWUNG by Chase's classroom on Friday to verify the snacks and beverage menu before Julian and I went to the store after school.

The day hadn't started yet, and he was already busy scribbling away some chemical equations on the chalkboard. I had learned all of this once upon a time, but my knowledge of high school chemistry had fallen out of my brain, pushed out by my encyclopedic knowledge of finalists on *Rupaul's Drag Race*.

Chase squatted down to write to the very margins of his blackboard.

"Hey, Chase. Got a second?"

He was in the zone with his equations. His eyes were wild and big behind his glasses. White powder got onto his shirt.

"Chase." I tapped his shoulder forcefully.

He needed a second to snap out of his trance. He looked around amazed that myself and other students were already in class.

"You were really going at it," I said. "With the..." I waved my hand at the board. "Science. All the science."

"Today I'm going over how to combine chemical equations and getting into the transitive properties of metallic alloys."

"That's...awesome." I wished I remembered more about my science classes. I took the maxim that we wouldn't need it in real life to heart.

"There are so many chemicals in real life that people don't even know about. Chemistry is the bonds that hold us together, quite literally."

"That's poetic." I took a step back to admire what Chase had written on the board. I didn't understand it, but I admired the way his brain worked and the passion and artistry involved in science. I had really interesting friends.

"What's up?" he asked, brushing chalk dust off his shirt, which only smeared it around.

I handed over my phone, open to the Notes app with the snack list. "I wanted to make sure we had your favorites there. I'm going to attempt to make spinach artichoke dip, your favorite."

"You can just get the store brand."

"Nah. You love that Ina Garten recipe."

"Thanks, Amos," he said, touched. Only the best for my friends. He handed back my phone. "I'm already hungry reading this list." He bit his lip slightly. "Is it cool if I add to the party list?"

"Yeah." I wasn't a hosting dominatrix who needed to tightly control a party. Social gatherings were fluid, which made them fun. "The more, the merrier."

"I invited Raleigh."

We shared a laugh. "Does Everett know?"

"Maybe you could break the news?"

I nodded yes. I would take that hit.

"He's cool. We've gotten to know each other during our free

period this year. I'm helping him infuse some mathematics into his defensive and offensive plays."

Before he taught chemistry, Chase was a math teacher. He was easily the smartest person I knew. If he was more versed in pop culture, he would kill on *Jeopardy!*.

"Cool. Anyone else?"

"Yeah. Hutch."

"Oh. You invited Hutch?" I asked, wanting to make sure I wasn't mishearing.

"Yeah. I liked hanging out with him at Remix. I went ahead and invited him today."

I felt a little guilty for not being the one to invite Hutch. It'd been on my mind all week, but I hesitated over saying anything. Were we friends that hung out outside school? Were we even friends?

Hutch would be in my apartment. In close proximity to my bedroom. Why my mind instantly went there was something I would not be unpacking anytime soon.

"So it's cool that I invited him?" Chase asked.

"Sure!"

14

HUTCH

W as it sad that this was my first party in...I tried doing the math in my head but it got too depressing.

Pop was at a poker night with his buddies, the first one he'd been up to attending post-hospital. I ordered him to stay away from the booze and cigars. He was relieved that I wasn't sitting home alone tonight. That made two of us.

The doorbell rang. I hustled downstairs and yanked open my front door.

"You're not ready?" Raleigh asked, eyeing my white undershirt and unbuttoned jeans.

"Can you come upstairs?"

Raleigh groaned, but still followed up to my room, where a tornado of outfit choices waited. Piles of clothes were strewn across the bed. Other outfits that hadn't made the cut flopped on the floor. Never in my life had I had this much trouble figuring out what to wear. Guys were supposed to have it easy in this department, I thought.

It was a piece of cake for Raleigh, who wore a fitted, sleek gray T-shirt and jeans.

"Jesus." He took in the surroundings, stepping slowly like he entered a crime scene. "Is that a twin-size bed? We gotta level you up, bro."

"It's on the to-do list."

"I just stepped back in time, man." He laughed as he found his way to the Fall Out Boy poster hanging above my desk. "I totally had that poster in my room, too."

I bet he didn't have a crush on Pete Wentz, though.

"Can I get your opinion on outfit choices?" Raleigh wasn't my first choice for fashion advice, but he was the only one I had. Beggars couldn't be choosers. No offense to Pop whose fashion evolution stopped in 1988.

"Are we really doing this? It's a small party at someone's condo. I doubt anyone will even be doing a kegstand." He plopped into my desk chair and wheeled himself in circles.

"Hey, this is my first social function in a while. I want to look nice."

"We're guys. It's not rocket science."

I ignored his logic, my mind scrambling with other thoughts. "Well, it'll be a quick decision then."

I threw on option number one, a black polo and dark jeans. I checked the collar and my hair in the mirror on the door.

"What do you think?"

Raleigh bounced a pencil between his thumb and forefinger. "It looks fine."

"Fine how?"

"I don't know. Fine fine. Those are clothes one would conceivably wear to a party."

"That's all you got? In your designer gray T-shirt?"

"This was a gift from an ex-girlfriend. I can FaceTime her if you want her opinion. You look fine. Here, watch this."

I turned back to the mirror before Raleigh could wow me with his pencil-bouncing prowess. "Okay. I look fine. Cool."

I sat on the bed to put on my most unscuffed sneakers.

"However."

I whipped my head up.

"What do you mean however?"

He teetered his head, much like the pencil had been moving.

"What's with that look?" I asked. He turned up his nose as if he'd smelled garbage.

"It's very basic."

Oh, *now* he was going to start being a Project Runway judge? I stopped in mid-knot with my left shoe. Why was I even listening to Raleigh? Ninety percent of his wardrobe were South Rock Football-branded shirts.

"Basic isn't good," I said. "I can't wear something basic."

"What message are you trying to send with your outfit? Because that says nothing."

I re-checked myself in the mirror. He was right. It was...blah. I didn't know what kind of impression I wanted to make tonight, but I didn't want to fade into the background.

"What about this outfit?" I whipped off the polo, threw on a navy-and-green checkered shirt. "This says something, right? I mean, there's colors!"

"Meh."

"Meh?" I had no faith in any of my clothes anymore. Maybe I should stay home.

"That's a shirt you could wear to school. You don't want to wear a school outfit. You want a party outfit. You want something that's going to be fun and make noise." He hopped out of the chair, the take charge side of him coming out. "You want to stand out. You want these teachers to be like 'Holy shit. Raleigh and Hutch are here.' One teacher in particular."

A lump lodged in my throat. I tried laughing it off. "What do you mean?"

"Dude, you have a thing for Amos."

That lump metastasized across my entire body. He said it so easily. Every light seemed to be on and shining right on me, interrogation style.

"What are you talking about?"

"You take a roundabout way down the history corridor to get to the gym. Hell, I've even watched your face light up whenever you passed his mailbox cubby in the main office. And look at you right now. You're freaking out about what to wear to a party at his place."

The evidence was stacked against me. Was I that transparent? Were my puppy dog actions common knowledge among teachers? Among the whole school?

Raleigh's usual sarcastic smirk softened as he put a hand on my shoulder. "I'm ridiculously handsome, charming as fuck, and above all, modest. What I'm not is oblivious."

I found my bed under my hand and slowly sat down, multiple realizations hitting me. It was now or never. I was tired of the nerves, of being careful. Raleigh's gaze seemed to convey that this was a safe space.

"I'm gay, Raleigh."

"Yeah. I know. That's what I was saying...about you and Amos. What part was unclear?" He grabbed the pencil from behind his ear. "Do you think I could balance this on my nose?"

I swiped it back. "So you're cool?"

"Yeah." He looked at me like I was crazy. "Wait, did you just like come out?"

"Kinda?" I hated that my out status was in this forever gray area. Who knew, who didn't. I realized how freaking tired I was of all of it. "You're the first friend I've come out to."

Perhaps technically, I'd come out to Everett, Chase, and Julian first, and I could consider them friends. But Raleigh would appreciate believing he was my first.

"Shit. I didn't know." Raleigh's cool demeanor dropped for a moment. "That's awesome."

"So you're cool with it?"

"Yeah, why wouldn't I be? I'm bi. What do you think about tying a sweater on your shoulders like a preppy tennis player? That could be a look." He sifted through the pile of clothes on the bed.

"Wait. What?"

"You're right. That's too much of a costume."

"You're bi?"

"Yeah. I've been with mostly women, but I've hooked up with guys before." He shrugged. The biggest NBD there was. "I consider myself a hole-sexual."

I did the Mona Lisa of double takes. That was graphic, yet I supposed accurate?

"Hole-sexual?"

"Yeah. I'm all about the hole, dude. Doesn't matter the gender. The hole is what matters most."

"I, uh, that's quite a take. Do you have a preference for one over the other?" No wonder he was with women mostly. They had guys beat with two holes to our one.

"Nah, man. A hole is a hole."

"I guess that's true. Did you always know you were a...hole-sexual?" I would never get used to saying that word aloud.

He sifted through the clothes on my bed, pursing his lips like he was damn Anna Wintour, someone I only knew from my Nashville teammates who got to go to the Met Gala one year. My confidence plummeted in the face of his withering expressions.

"I figured it out in college, like most people." He tossed rejected outfits on the floor, until my bedspread was coming into view. "I was torn between this guy and this chick, first time that had ever happened. I didn't know if I was gay because I really liked the chick. And then I realized that the whole package of a person was what I was looking for. The male or female or non-binary part of it was only part of what attracted me to them. It was the whole that I cared about more than the sum of their equipment."

Then, it clicked for me. "You're a *whole*sexual. W-h-o-l-e."

"Yeah. Wholesexual. What'd you think I meant?"

I could feel my face turn red. "Nothing. I'm out of clothes."

I pointed to my bed, completely devoid of clothes.

"This all you got?"

"There was nothing good on that," *deep breath, Hutch* "whole pile?"

"It's like if wet farts got into designing clothes." Raleigh strode past me and fished through my closet. Hangers swished across the pole with lightning speed. "My friend, if you want Amos to notice you, then you need to peacock tonight."

"What's that?" I steeled myself for another TMI explanation.

"Peacocking is when you wear something flashy to get people's attention. You don't want to dress as your normally preppy self. You want to get to that crowded party and immediately stand out to Amos."

"Or other people," I said sheepishly.

His cocked eyebrow called bullshit. "That is your goal, right?"

It shouldn't have been. I told myself that flirting with Amos was a no-go, but Raleigh got me all excited about the possibility of pulling his attention. And so I nodded yes.

"Found it!"

I wasn't sure what I expected Raleigh to find in my closet, but my loud, garish '90s shirt was at the bottom of my list. Loud wasn't the right word.

It *screamed* at me.

The short-sleeve button down shirt was covered in circles and triangles and squares and waves in various offensively bright colors. It was a relic straight out of the '90s, something that would fit in at a Blockbuster or a Radio Shack.

"That's not a real shirt. I found that online for South Rock's '90s Day when I was in high school. It's a novelty shirt. It's not meant to be worn in public except for explicitly ironic reasons."

The more Raleigh stared at it, the more he nodded at his genius idea.

"No way, dude."

"Aw, c'mon. Try it on." He tossed it over.

I made sure he didn't have his phone out before I slipped it on. My mirror nearly exploded from the retro vibes and vivid colors. I turned as pink as some of the shapes floating across my chest.

"I don't know about this, man."

"Dude, trust me. You look awesome." Raleigh looked at me with wide eyes like he was Dr. Frankenstein watching his monster walk. "It rocks. This is going to make a statement. And you and Amos went to high school together, so he might remember you wearing it."

I hated and loved Raleigh's logic. Either Amos would get a kick out of this shirt, or I'd be laughed out of the party.

Only one way to find out.

15

HUTCH

Chase's face lit up when he opened the door. He had a similar idea, wearing a shirt with dancing flamingos on it.

"Love the shirt!" He threw his hand up for a hi-five, which I had no choice but to proudly reciprocate. "I thought I was going to be the only person wearing a fun shirt, which I suppose makes sense since it's my birthday."

"Your shirt is awesome. Makes me want to go to Florida." I clapped him on the shoulder, happy to have at least one person here who likes my shirt. It gave me a swell of confidence.

"Thanks for coming, guys." He stepped aside. "We've got drinks and snacks and cupcakes."

"Happy birthday, bud. Sorry my guys almost set your lab on fire last year." Raleigh gave Chase a pat on the back.

"That's why they invented fire extinguishers."

Raleigh turned to me. "Some of my players are really into fire."

"Noted," I said and waded into the party.

I had to take a second to soak in how nice Amos's condo was. The kitchen had a breakfast counter that looked out on an open living room with woodsy views. It was sweet digs that I wish I had.

Hats off to Amos for having his shit together enough to afford a place like this. That was one area where he had me beat.

Speaking of Amos, I wasn't looking for him, but I was curious. I mean, he had to be here. It was his place.

Meanwhile, my shirt was peacocking exactly as Raleigh intended. Heads turned my way and guffawed and nodded at the retro-ness. Overall, the response was positive. People were taken aback, but they dug it. I walked around with confidence. I owned it, and was ready to party.

By the TV, the head I cared about most turned my way. I couldn't take in Amos's reaction because I was too busy having a reaction of my own. He looked fucking hot. Damn. He wore slim black jeans and a v-neck black T-shirt that reminded me of how delicious his chest was. This was atypical Amos wardrobe, a one-eighty from nerdy chic that I fully endorsed.

When I snapped back to reality, I was presented with his intrigued eyes, crinkling with laughter.

"If you hate it, blame Raleigh."

"No. No, I like it...you do know this wasn't a theme party. You could've worn normal clothes."

"Eh, I wear normal clothes all the time. I decided to shake things up." I puffed out my chest to fully embrace the corniness of my shirt. Amos liked it, and that was all that mattered.

Amos smiled to himself, something brightening his eyes. "I remember that shirt. Spirit Week senior year. You wore it for '90s day."

"Guilty. I decided to peacock tonight."

"Success." Amos leaned in slightly, giving me an extra glimpse down his shirt of his smooth chest. I wanted to lick it like an ice cream cone in hundred degree heat. "Did you want a drink?"

I needed to quench my thirst because my throat just got uncomfortably dry.

"Sure!"

He led me to the breakfast nook counter which had a bar set up and stools that were likely used for quick meals during the week. A short guy with a big smile poured tropical drinks into plastic cups.

"We have a special drink menu for Chase's birthday." Amos handed over a laminated menu with fun drinks. Fanciest party trick I'd ever seen.

"And if you don't like those, I can make you something else," said the bartender. "At least for another hour. Then I have to get to my actual job."

"Charlie's my friend and the assistant manager at Stone's Throw Tavern," Amos said. "Hutch is a teacher at South Rock, and we went to high school together."

Amos's ears got a touch red at what I can imagine was the information that he left out.

If Charlie had any inkling who I was, he didn't show it. He mixed me up a Sodium Chloride Dog, which was a fancy (or nerdy) way of saying a Salty Dog, which had grapefruit juice and vodka. The pinkish color reminded me of burning summer sunsets.

"Cheers." I held up my glass to Amos's. The clink sparked in my chest. "This is much nicer than the parties we used to go to in high school."

Memories of bad beer, kegs, crowded basements all flooded back. Our quest for alcohol and party space as underage kids meant that we had no standards and were fine with it.

"*You* used to go to," Amos said, correcting me. "I didn't go to parties. Not ones with alcohol. Mine involved board games, pizza, and watching Netflix DVD's we got in the mail."

"Some G-rated Netflix and Chill." Honestly, that sounded like a good time.

"How's your drink?" Amos asked, his lips pert and wet from his sip. I used every piece of willpower not to rake my eyes over his body.

"It's good. Wanna try?" I handed the glass over.

My dick twitched in my pants as our fingers touched. *Down boy.*

"It's good." He took a sip and handed it back. "Has a kick to it."

I didn't take my eyes off him as I drank my Sodium Chloride Dog, putting my lips right where his had been.

I had to enjoy this sip because this would be as close as our lips got tonight.

———

THE PARTY FLEW by in a blur of merriment and cheer. Good people, good conversation, good drinks. I got to chat with teachers from school that I'd only seen in passing. They pressed me on how the soccer season was going. We sang "Happy Birthday" to Chase as he blew out the candles on his pyramid of cupcakes, then somehow, in the oddly sound logic of party flow, that led to Amos putting on the OG *High School Musical* and turning it into a drinking and karaoke game. Nostalgia was a helluva drug. The condo shook with the good vibes of singing and laughing, and I wanted to bottle this night and come back to it over and over again. I hadn't had this much fun in a long time.

I did all this while looking over at Amos repeatedly. I tried to exercise willpower. It was difficult because he looked so damn good. It was like we were back in the halls of high school sneaking peeks.

Maybe it was because it'd been so long, but my body craved all this social time. Raleigh had to leave early, and I said I'd get a ride home. Eventually, things began to wound down, and I found myself wandering into Amos's room for a breather.

There was a queen sized bed and packed-but-organized bookcase plus a desk in the corner. For a room of this size, he made use of every available square foot. Above the desk was a cork board filled with postcards from cities all around the world. Rome, Paris, Tokyo, Santiago. The world was humongous, and I'd barely scratched the surface.

"Hey."

I whipped my head around, broken out of my daze. Amos hung by the door, still sexy in his black outfit but small circles ringing his eyes.

"Tired?" I asked.

"Hosting a party is not for the weak of heart." He leaned against the threshold. I wanted to trace the side of his torso and hip with my hand. And other body parts. "Is Raleigh still here?"

"He went home a little while ago. I think Everett finally got to be too much for him."

Raleigh admitted that he'd dozed off trying to watch *Hamilton* and said it wasn't his jam, which set Everett off on a quest to prove to him why it was the definitive piece of modern theater.

"Strong theater opinions aside, your friends are really good guys."

"They're your friends, too, now."

The quiet between us let me hear the low buzz of music coming from the hall.

"Am I the last one here?" I asked.

"Yeah. Everett and Julian just left to drive a drunk Chase home."

How the hell did I wind up the last one here? I got sucked into a void of combing through Amos's room. "I'm sorry. I didn't mean to overstay my welcome. I'll help clean up."

He waved it off. "It's fine. I got most of it."

"I can't believe I'm the last one here." I prepared myself for the gentle ask to leave. The tightening in my pants hoped for a different outcome.

"You were busy going through my stuff." He said it with his typical Amos sarcasm, but I still felt a bit embarrassed.

"I wasn't going through anything. I opened no drawers or closets." I put my hands up for added effect.

"But how can I be so sure?" Exhaustion added a sexy rasp to Amos's voice. My throat went dry, old desires roaring back. Amos had moved on, but I was working on it.

"I was just admiring all the places you've been." I nodded at the postcards. "Your passport has been getting lots of action."

"Not quite." Amos swung into the room and admired the postcards next to me. "This is a vision cork board of all the places I want to visit one day. I never got the chance to study abroad in college, and my family only ever wanted to go to amusement parks for vacation. Which, don't get me wrong, amusement parks slap. But there's a big ass world out there beyond roller coasters."

"Well, your parents can enjoy all the roller coasters they want in New Orleans."

"How'd you know they're down there?"

"You told me, Mr. Brightside." It was yet another instance of him and his family being on two different planets. I felt bad that his family kinda sucked, but Amos was too good of a person to write them off.

I gulped back the heat climbing up my neck. I could feel the way his light arm hairs danced on the pads of my fingers, our bodies dangerously close.

"I've been saving up for a big vacation, which you'll soon discover is hard on a teacher's salary."

"Where do you want to go most?"

"Rome." He tapped the postcard of the colosseum without a moment's hesitation. "I want to see where it all began."

"Didn't it all begin in, like, Mesopotamia?" Huh, maybe I did remember some things from class.

"True. But I loved studying the Roman Empire. It's my favorite unit to teach."

"Were all the Roman guys gay for each other? They invented bathhouses."

"They were more *fluid* with their sexuality. And bathhouses were used for bathing."

"And a quick handy." I smirked, happily throwing a wrench in his glowing historical image of ancient Rome. I'd seen the statues of naked boys playing and hot guys with chiseled six-packs. The Romans invented Instagays. "You should teach your students about how our ancestors were super horny."

"I'm sure the school board would love that."

"We know that the Magna Carta was signed in 1215, but how did those guys celebrate hmm? A little slap and tickle."

"Slap and tickle." He snorted, his laugh the most beautiful sound in the world. Maybe next to his moans. "How did you remember when the Magna Carta was signed?"

"No idea. I don't know what it is, but I know it was signed in 1215." It was one of those random facts that stuck in my brain and would probably be there until I died.

"I want to see the ruins." A wistful smile flitted on his lips. I was grateful for the left turn away from sex talk. All the talk of horny ancestors wasn't helping me keep things under control. "People think that the Roman Empire was this long-standing civilization, but it was only in existence for about 1,000 years. And of those thousand years, it was only in power for about four hundred."

"That sounds like a long time to me."

"In the grand scheme of world history, it isn't. But isn't it crazy that there are still remnants of ancient markets and coliseums? That we can imagine what random Romans were doing thousands of years ago. They went to the market, they lived in apartments, they watched a gladiatorial battle, which is similar to watching a football game. Not much has changed." He smiled at the postcard, his eyes wild in thought, the academic side of him unleashed. "Sorry."

"What for?"

"Historical tangent over."

"I like it." I could listen to him talk about history all day. It was intoxicating to watch someone be passionate.

I pushed back a stray curl of his hair, tempting fate.

"I hope you get to go to Rome."

"That's the plan for my thirtieth birthday."

Amos sure knew how to plan for things. He was the more organized of us two. He had a plan for everything.

I took a seat on the edge of his bed, my hands stretched out over the soft, navy blue comforter.

"Do you ever wonder what the last ten years would've been like if..." The truth got caught in my throat, but I pushed through. "If we had gone to prom together?"

The light in his eyes went out, thanks to me and my terrible choices in the past.

The wheels turned in Amos's head. He sat in his desk chair, hunched over like that thinking sculpture guy.

"Yeah," he said softly.

"What would've happened?" It was dangerous to go down this path of what if, but I needed to hear it.

"We would've walked in holding hands. I'd be squeezing your hand so tight, but you would give me this look that calmed my nerves. People would talk, but we would ignore them. We'd slow dance together to 'You & I' by One Direction. People would be looking at us, and some guys would probably mutter slurs, but it wouldn't matter. They wouldn't be able to bring us down." A glow took over his face, so bright I felt it in my heart. "Because we had each other. Whenever we got scared, we could look at each other."

"And then what? What about the next ten years?"

"We'd go to different schools as planned. We each had scholarships, so I wouldn't want to jeopardize those."

I let out a soft laugh. Leave it to Amos to be practical in his wildest dreams.

"But we would visit each other on weekends. I'd cheer you on at all of your games. You'd introduce me as your boyfriend to all of your teammates."

"And I would cheer you on at all of your quiz bowl tournaments. I'd bring handmade signs and brag to everyone in the audience that I was your boyfriend. When your team won, I'd jump up and scream FUCK YEAH."

"And then you'd get banned from attending all future quiz bowl tournaments."

"It'd be worth it." I would be the biggest quiz bowl groupie in history.

Amos pushed his chair closer, narrowing the gap between us, and adding kindling to this fire. I desperately wanted to grab him, pull him into me, and taste his salty skin.

"And then what?" he asked.

I closed my eyes and let myself dream. "I would get drafted into Major League Soccer, but I'd be a top pick. All your support at college games would make me more focused. I'd play for New York or LA, and you would come with me. You would teach at some ritzy prep school and dish about your spoiled, overprotected students over dinner. You would come to most of my games, schedule permitting. You would be my lucky charm, keep me from busting my knee."

"I'd watch cooking shows and prepare a new meal for you when you got back from away games."

"I'd be traveling a lot. We'd be apart for days or weeks at a time." I sighed. Things wouldn't be all sunshine and roses.

"It'd be hard, but we'd make it work," he said, his emerald eyes sparking with pure warmth.

"Would it? I knew quite a few guys in the league who'd gotten divorced because the strain traveling had put on their marriages."

"Let's try this then." Amos scooted closer, a whisper of space between our knees. "We'd be living in some tiny apartment, only seeing each other a few days a month. You would play a few years, but then decide coaching was where you excelled. So you'd take a job coaching at your old high school, shepherding the same team to victory that you led all those years ago. And I would take a job teaching history there, too, and in between classes, we'd sneak off to the janitor's closet to make out."

He pushed me back on the bed. Before I could question what was happening and if this was part of the game, he crawled on top of me, our lips meeting in a ferocious blend of lust and want.

Those lips. Those blessed lips that I'd dreamed about, that had wrapped me in ecstasy all throughout high school were on me again. They were better than anything I remembered. Salty and hot and all mine.

I fucking melted. An ice cube plopped on the equator.

Amos heaved heavy breaths against my lips, moaning into my mouth like a geyser of need. He rutted against my aching crotch, my cock fully hard and fully wanting to be free. My hands swooped down the curve of his back and slipped under his shirt, letting his sizzling skin pulse under my fingertips.

He moaned harder into me, his teeth grabbing my bottom lip.

I ripped off his black T-shirt and flicked my thumbs over his nipples. He writhed atop me, a fish out of water, pushing me down and taking the life out of me.

I clamped both hands on his ass, just as firm as it'd been. I gave it a hard slap.

"Need you." He panted out. His eyes were heavy-lidded and ablaze with lust.

He shoved his hands under my shirt and groaned as he hit the ridges of my abs and pecs.

I couldn't unbutton this stupid '90s shirt fast enough; my fingers tumbled over buttons.

"Amos." I cupped a hand around the back of his head and pulled him to me. I needed to kiss him more.

I needed him with such a primal urge that wrecked my body. I thrust into his crotch, letting our denim-covered cocks make contact.

"Need to taste you." And with that, Amos slinked down my body and whipped open my belt, then my fly, then pulled down my boxers.

I was fucking engorged. Leaking like crazy. The head of my cock disappeared into his mouth. A guttural groan ripped out of me as Amos sunk further down, taking me to the base. We'd started our relationship two closeted teens fumbling in the dark. But by the end, and with lots of practice, we had turned into each other's sex gods, knowing exactly how to turn each other on.

Amos bobbed on my dick, his tongue doing things that should be illegal.

"Feels so good." Heat and passion choked my throat.

Amos moaned with a mouthful of me. He licked down my shaft and took my balls in his mouth. I grabbed the comforter in my hands and squeezed back the orgasm. No way was I going to blow less than a minute into this thing. I needed to savor this because I didn't know if it'd ever happen again.

"Fuck, Amos. So good."

His hands and tongue were in perfect coordination, hitting every button of mine. I looked down, watching him in action. He shot me a playful smile (as best he could with a dick in his mouth) that let me know that he had me in the palm of his hand.

I had never been so destroyed by a shit-eating grin.

I could only hold on for so long. I was only human.

"Gonna come," I muttered out, but it was barely warning. I was already there.

I bucked my hips up and exploded in his mouth. Amos didn't let go until he sucked me dry.

He fell back onto the floor, catching his breath.

I needed a damn respirator. I think I lost contact with the outside world during that orgasm. How the fuck had I existed on this planet as a functioning human being, working jobs and paying taxes for the past ten years, without that?

"Shit." I didn't have anything eloquent to say. *Blow job good. Come lots. Want another one.*

Amos wiped off his mouth, which I found all kinds of sexy. "Well, that was...we..."

I sat up and stared him dead in the eye. "We're not doing that yet."

We could be adults in a few minutes. But first, I was a gentleman and was dead set on returning the favor.

"Stand up," I growled. My torn ACL limited how agile I could be during sex, so I had to get creative.

A new wave of lust burned in his eyes. His cock was rock hard in his pants, pressing against the fly like it was being suffocated. I rubbed a firm hand over his erection and grunted as I peered up at him.

Proving I could be just as fast as him, I unbuckled, unzipped, and yanked down his boxers. His cock was hitting the back of my throat in seconds. Sense memory came back with a vengeance. All the little things that Amos loved, I remembered and I did. I cupped his balls as I sucked on his fat head. I twisted my fist around his shaft.

"Yes," he groaned out in one long note, like he'd been holding it for a decade. He interlocked his hands behind my head, steering me back and forth.

He fucked into my mouth, which was such a turn on I felt myself stiffening up for round two. Amos might play the nerdy guy, but he knew what he wanted.

"Hutch." His voice broke in that way that alerted me his orgasm was imminent.

"Come for me, baby."

He jolted and flopped like he'd been struck by lightning before filling my mouth with his hot seed.

He collapsed onto the bed next to me, catching his breath and laughing at the same time.

We stared up at the ceiling. It was safer than looking in his eyes and wondering what he was thinking.

"Just like old times?" I asked with a smirk.

His chest rose and fell with ragged breath. "Better."

16

AMOS

For the rest of the weekend, I ran errands, graded papers, changed three light bulbs that had gone out, and cooked myself a delicious bowl of rice pilaf. I had to congratulate myself for getting anything done after the showstopping blow job I received (and gave, thank you very much) on Friday night.

Holiest of holy shits.

All weekend long, I kept replaying everything in my head, pinching myself that it wasn't a fantasy. It was very much reality. Hutch and me alone in my bedroom. Hutch sitting on my bed. Hutch looking up at me with those unnaturally gorgeous blue eyes.

Was it any wonder that I had no choice but to climb him like the dreaded rope in gym class?

I earned some extra cash putting down mulch for one of my neighbors on Sunday. They were amazed that I enjoyed doing it since I couldn't stop smiling.

Hutch and I exchanged a few messages on Milkman over the weekend. Hutch was busy coaching South Rock High men's soccer to their first two back-to-back victories of the season.

After our bedroom blow jobs, there wasn't much to say. We'd see each other at school. I wasn't going to be the needy boyfriend who wanted to talk about things.

I refused to be needy, and we weren't boyfriends.

I got to school early Monday morning and put together a quiz for later that week. My heart beat wildly when someone knocked at my door.

It was palpitations over nothing. Principal Aguilar strolled in.

"Good morning! How was the party?"

Heat absolutely strangled my neck. "It was a good time."

My friends and I sometimes hung out with Aguilar. It was a complicated situation since he was our boss, and a little quirky, but he was also a fellow gay guy in town. It wasn't as weird as we imagined when we did get together with him. Outside of his shirt and tie, he was a warm, friendly man.

"I'm sorry that Clint and I couldn't attend. We were out of town at a green thumb conference. I have three words for you: water wise gardening."

He emphasized each word with his hand, like they were inscribed on a billboard.

"Wow," I uttered with mild enthusiasm. "Maybe next time?"

"Definitely. I'll bring my karaoke machine. Clint and I are practicing a duet of 'One Sweet Day.' We're sounding really good. Not Mariah and Boyz II Men good, but getting there."

Did this middle-aged man *really* just say he was nearly as good of a singer as Ms. Mariah Carey?

"Can't wait." I worried about the future of my ears.

"I stopped by to let you know that we'll be having a pep rally during eighth period. It's for men's and women's soccer, which both had victories over the weekend. Fun fact." He raised an excited finger. "Soccer is called football in England."

"Yes. And yet ironically, the word soccer comes from British slang." I beamed with the victory of finally being able to share that tidbit with someone.

"Whoa." Aguilar's eyes blew open with the new information. "Your fun fact blows my fun fact out of the water."

"Isn't learning fun?"

"I prefer my fun fact, though. Anyway, I'll see you later." Aguilar held out his hand, and it took me a few seconds to realize he was asking for a hi-five.

"Don't leave me hanging, Amos."

———

MY STOMACH WAS in knots when I walked into the cafeteria. This was like our version of the morning after. Did the glow of Friday night only exist in my bubble?

Hutch was hanging by the athlete's table, his natural habitat, flanked by students who were probably shooting the shit over the soccer victories. After a lackluster football season in the fall, South Rock needed this boost. He held court as he gave them a play by play. Hutch had this inborn ability to be popular. It astounded me that he was a loner in Nashville.

He'd probably be too busy to eat today, and that was fine. He deserved this moment. He and his team worked hard.

When I got to our table, on my chair was an opened bag of Skittles consisting of only reds, purples, and oranges. I glanced over at the star of the hour, and he shot me a subtle wink that was like its own version of a quickie.

The rest of the day flew by as a raucous energy took over the school the closer we got to the pep rally. After sixth period, where half of my class was fully checked out, I got a message notification on Milkman.

SoccerStar: Meet at my car for a quick nap?

Mr. Brightside: You're tired? You have a pep rally in 40 minutes.

SoccerStar: Hence the nap.

Mr. Brightside: You want a nap. Sure.

SoccerStar: Just a nap. No Shitheads Allowed.

I met up with Hutch in the teacher parking lot. He leaned against his car like he was auditioning to play Jake Ryan in *Sixteen Candles*. The sight of him drove me wild.

"Funny running into you here," I said.

He flashed me a sexy smirk that made my stomach do a somersault. "Want to take a quick ride?"

"What happened to the nap?"

"Do you trust me?"

Who was I to say no to a cute guy?

Hutch drove us to a familiar spot: the parking lot of an abandoned ice cream stand. Scoop's Ice Cream had been a big deal up until the mid-2000s, when code violations forced it to shut down. It was too far from downtown to attract new tenants, which was a shame because it was on a hill that overlooked the Hudson River. That view was one of the things that attracted us to this spot in high school. That, and it was secluded.

"And what are we doing here?" I asked.

Hutch launched at me, pulling me into a kiss. "No time for banter. I have a pep rally in half an hour, and I'm way too hard to nap." He pulled my hand to his crotch for proof.

Without saying a word, we climbed into his backseat. We kissed and groped in a maelstrom of heat and hunger.

"Today's been crazy. Everyone's been coming up to me, congratulating the team. We were expected to lose the second game. It's been amazing, but exhausting recounting the games. I love it, though. After years of feeling out of the loop, I'm back on the field, just in a different capacity."

"I'll have to come to the games." I leaned into him, letting his hardness dig into my thigh. I remembered his back seat as being more spacious. Maybe I was more flexible back then.

"So I came out to Raleigh this weekend," he said. He massaged his fingers softly through my hair, then down my neck. He knew all my spots. I tipped my head forward, giving him full access.

"You did? How'd it go?"

"Cool. Shockingly cool. He was whatever about it."

"Nice. This also feels nice," I said, rubbing against him in between kisses.

"Did you finish the Skittles?"

"You know it. But there's something I still don't understand, something that will keep me up at night. Why do you only like green and yellow skittles? They are the worst ones."

His chest rumbled underneath me. Our heads were turned to the sunroof where soft white clouds floated past our vision.

"I only eat them because I know you love the reds, purples, and oranges."

I sat up, looked at him to make sure he was serious. I'd never felt so touched in my life. I kissed him softly at first, but with more heat when he cupped my head in his hand.

We were breathing heavily and laughing and our hearts were thumping in our chests. I wanted to bottle this moment and open it when I'm ninety.

"Wait." I activated a thirty-minute timer on my phone and placed it in the backseat cupholder, where it still fit.

"Genius."

The second I grabbed his hardness through his pants, I knew this wouldn't stop at kissing. To be fair, I couldn't let the man walk into a pep rally with blue balls. And by the ferocious hue of his heavy-lidded eyes, he wasn't going to let that happen either.

Hutch pushed me back onto the seat, his towering frame heavy over me. He grunted as he thrust against me, our dicks rubbing against each other through thick layers of pants. I did some impressive acrobatics and lifted my legs so he could dry hump right against my ass. I was on fire, melting into his heat.

"We're supposed to be napping, Amos."

"Don't blame me. Blame friction."

His heavy breathing against my lips cast a spell on me. We were going to make the most of these remaining minutes. I moaned at the delight of his tongue, of his body on mine, of the sound of his crotch hitting my hole, wearing down the fabric of our pants.

"Need you," he heaved out, barely able to form words, his pink lips slick.

In lusty, desperate seconds, we both unbuttoned and unzipped each other's pants. He freed my cock from its tight quarters, and I let out a guttural groan as my hands made contact with the hot flesh of his rod.

Hutch took control, taking both our dicks in his hand, pumping us together while rutting against me, heat and need building and building. I stared into his eyes, blazing with hot lust.

"Feels so good," he uttered.

"Hutch." I pushed my head back against the seat, letting this feeling roll through my body. I didn't even have the breath for a witty retort. The jokey part of the sexytimes was officially over. This was a race to the finish.

"Gonna come," he strained out, his voice husky and desperate. He tried to point at something. "My gym bag. On the floor."

My hand felt around desperate for gym bag contact. I was so turned on and so close to coming, I could barely function. The orgasm was tearing through me, ready to unleash all over our nice school clothes. Hutch couldn't stand in front of the school with come stains on his clothes.

Inside the bag, I pulled a fresh towel, likely for the gym showers. I handed it over, and he wrapped it around our dicks. The new sensation sent me over the edge.

Hutch grunted and his voice cracked as the towel and my dick were soaked with his release, and then mine. He kept our cocks covered as he wiped up, then threw the towel back into the bag.

I glanced down.

"All clear," he said. "No stains."

"Fantastic." My head smacked back against the seat. "Ten out of ten. Would definitely recommend we do that again."

Above me, Hutch hovered. He leaned down and pressed the softest, tenderest kiss on my lips.

"And we still have twenty-five minutes. Enough time for a nap," he said. "Get over here."

We returned to our natural positions of spooner and spoonee. Like clockwork, Hutch's arms sent me off into a blissful cat nap.

———

PEP RALLIES WERE HELD on South Rock's indoor basketball court, with students and teachers filling both sides of the bleachers. I led my eighth period history class to the gym. All of the classes that walked down to the gymnasium mashed together in the hallways. Friends found friends, everyone mixed. Teachers were only responsible for getting their students into the gym.

Julian had arrived first and saved us our usual spot at the far end of the bleachers. Two of us sat in front of the other two. We found it was easier than us all sitting in a row and trying to talk.

But could I talk? I still felt flushed and wired from the backseat adventure I took with Hutch. My body continued to tingle with afterglow.

"Just so we're all aware, this is a waste of time and school resources." Everett sat down behind me and Julian. "There are posters?"

He scoffed at the freshly printed posters celebrating different soccer players adorning the walls. They must've been made within the last forty-eight hours.

"I begged and pleaded for a new prop budget last year for our production of *The Glass Menagerie*, but was told there wasn't any funds available. We almost had to cancel the show because Laura had no menagerie to show off." Everett rolled his eyes and took a calming breath. It wasn't worth anyone's energy to rebel against the sports-industrial complex, as he called it. "Anyway, what's up with you? You look winded."

"Me?" I could feel my cheeks turn red. Everett had eerily good powers of deduction. "I had to run here from my car. Because I was getting something there. At my car."

"The teacher parking lot is actually very close to the gym, though," Chase said. "I can't see why you would've needed to race here."

"I was cutting it close running back."

"Did you leave something in there?" Julian asked. "You're usually pretty anal about having everything on you so you can avoid running back to the parking lot."

Damn my friends for knowing me so well.

"I'm not perfect, Julian. I'm a human being and sometimes I forget chapstick in my car."

He put up his hands in defense. Everett smacked them down.

"Who cares about Amos running away from cars. We want to hear what happened on Friday night. When we left your apartment, Hutch was still there, if I'm not mistaken."

My three friends faced me, three spotlights blinding me. Since the band was playing at full blast and the nearby students were ensconced in their own conversations, I had some cover that this story wouldn't be overheard. Still, I kept my voice low.

"You are correct. Hutch was the last to leave my party."

"You two seemed to be getting along well," Julian said.

"I think the slutty outfit Everett picked out for you helped." Chase shrugged, not one to mince words.

"It wasn't slutty. It was different. Black is inherently sexy." Everett had convinced me to take a wild swing with my outfit. We danced around the why, saying it was to make an impact as a party host when really, I didn't want Hutch to see me in my normal, nerdy outfits.

"But you did look great," Chase added. He could be blunt but he always cared.

And he was helping me stall for time. I had to get it out before Aguilar started. He was known to call out people for talking while he was speaking.

"Anyway," I said.

"Anyway..." Everett gestured for me to keep talking.

"He and I were talking in my bedroom, and one thing led to another, and we wound up exchanging birthday cards."

The guys and I had come up with a code language to talk about certain topics in school without getting in trouble. The last thing I needed was a student hearing about me going down on his gym teacher.

Three slack jaws and unblinking eyes faced me.

"Happy birthday to you," Everett said.

"Wow." Julian blushed a little, as he usually did with sex stuff.

"Yeah." I nodded along, still processing that wild Friday night. And the backseat adventures of forty minutes ago.

"Was it a nice card? Did he write something personal in there?" Chase asked.

"It was. One of the best cards I'd ever received."

I'd said before that I'd been ruined by Hutch Hawkins, and I stood by my statement. His mouth and entire body were gifts from the gods above to us mere mortals. My entire body was on fire from that blow job.

"Do you think you're gonna–" Everett stopped himself, hissing

Ancient History   137

with frustration. He had a hard time sticking to the code. "Is this going to be a regular exchange?"

"I don't know. I'm just taking it one birthday card at a time."

"But you like him," Julian said. "You two were cute together at Chase's party."

"Like him? It was combustion. An outburst of magenta tension."

Magenta = sexual.

Was that true? I wish it was. I wish the feelings that I'd sworn off from Hutch didn't come charging back. Hutch had wandered in a sexual desert for years and wanted to get his rocks off. I refused to make things awkward with feelings.

"And actually, I wasn't winded from running from my car. I was winded because we also exchanged business cards during seventh period."

Their mouths dropped. I smiled triumphantly. Although our code language clearly had zero consistency.

"Birthday cards and business cards? You fugly slut," Everett whispered to me.

"We're just having fun. The last time I tried to make things serious, he bolted." I didn't want to open myself up to being hurt again. So I looked at this for what it was: sexy times with an old boyfriend.

"Maybe it's for the best. Trying to date a guy in the closet is a struggle you don't want."

"Very true," I said.

Aguilar got on the mic and thankfully kept his speech short, ceding the time to the cheerleaders, who introduced both soccer teams. I let myself get into the pep rally, losing myself in school spirit.

The men's soccer team ran out through a crafty tunnel that I was sure pissed Everett off for being so extravagant. I scowled when Tommy darted out and hi-fived his teammates. I knew he had to be some kind of jock.

"And last but not least, let's hear it for the coach who helped them bring in their victory. Coach Hawkins!" Aguilar yelled his name into the mic as the school went wild and Hutch trotted out with a self-conscious grin and wave, thankful but also uncomfortable with the attention. He shot me a stealth wink. It was all one major deja vu that hit me square in the gut.

I'd been here before. Sitting in the bleachers, pining for Hutch during pep rallies, receiving the subtle wink. This story was getting eerily familiar, but would it be ending the same way?

17

HUTCH

P op just laughed and laughed as he watched me from the hallway. His deep chortle, which I'd always found a comforting presence, was really pissing me off this morning.

I peeled my eyes away from the mirror, where I was getting my hair into place. "I'll be done in a second."

"Sure you will." He was having such a good time, like he was watching a movie or something.

"Do you gotta use the can? Is yours clogged?"

"Nope."

"Then why are you staring at me like that? It's creepy." Maybe there was something really wrong with my hair. I checked it again. "Go back to bed. You don't have anywhere you need to be this morning. I have to get to work."

"You're gonna be late with all the time you're spending prettying yourself in front of that mirror."

"I'm not prettying myself. That's not even a word. I'm getting ready for work. I have to look presentable and shit."

That elicited another chuckle of deep laughter from him. While I should've been happy that Pop was in such good spirits, I didn't want it to be at my expense. He was just jealous because he was bald.

I dropped my comb into the sink. "What is so funny, Old Man?"

"Just thinking back to all the arguing we used to do about getting your ass to school on time," he said. I didn't have time for one of those reminiscing moments, though there were mornings where we got into shouting fights about using the bathroom. Good thing we could laugh about them now.

He was the only one laughing currently.

"I'll be done in a second. I'm shutting the door now."

But even from behind the door, I could feel him smiling with glee.

"What's so funny?"

"It seems to me you want to get yourself all pretty to impress a guy."

"That's..." I bit down on my lip to hold back the wave of embarrassment quickly coloring my face. Even though I had privacy now, I couldn't face myself in the mirror. "Nice try, Pop."

"You've been spending an awful lot of time in there in the mornings. Just making an observation."

"That means you have too much time on your hands." I had to get Pop a hobby. Monitoring my bathroom activity and speculating on my love life didn't count.

I checked my hair in the mirror, making sure the strands laid just right. My chin and cheeks were clear of any razor nicks. Teeth were pearly white. I was good to go.

"It's all yours," I said when I opened the door, ignoring the shit-eating grin stamped on his wrinkled, still lovable face. I stepped aside like a gentleman.

"Looking sharp." He clapped me on the shoulder.

"Why do you talk like you're in the Rat Pack? You're not that old."

Downstairs, I heated up two bowls of instant oatmeal in the microwave and cut up a pair of oranges into quarters. I laid out the breakfast on the table, two mirror images. Except one had pills and a glass of water on the corner of the plate.

Pop joined me in silence, still highly amused. Only the sounds of our spoons clanging against bowls filled the kitchen.

"It's my job to look professional." I shouldn't have brought it up, but I didn't want to give him the victory.

"You look very professional." He bit into his orange. "Amos will be impressed."

I dropped my spoon.

"Pop."

"You never told me how the birthday party last week was."

"We all wore those paper party hats, played duck duck goose, and ate birthday cake."

"You came home late." He raised his eyes, having the time of his freaking life this morning. He spooned oatmeal into his trap. "This tastes like paper."

"I made it with water and no salt or butter. Oatmeal is high in fiber and helps to lower cholesterol."

"I'd rather drink toilet water." He reached for the salt shaker, but I moved it to my side with two meddlesome fingers.

At least we could both torture each other this morning.

"And take your pills."

He stared me down as he gulped them back.

"I can stay out late if I want. I'm not on curfew anymore."

"Fair enough." His face softened, breaking this game of chicken we were playing. "Did you have a good time?"

A genuine question deserved a genuine answer. But the answer was, of course, complicated. Two guys knocking boots could never be simple. Fuck, I'd been thinking about that night nonstop. The hungry look in Amos's eyes as he pushed me back. His exquisite moans of pleasure. Tasting him again.

I had a fucking time, that was for sure.

And we'd been having repeats in the Scoop's parking lot this week. Three seventh period car naps that turned into hand jobs, that then turned into actual car naps. My gym towel desperately needed to be washed. I could crack it in half at this point.

I wasn't sure what was going on between us, but my heart was fully involved. This was one of the best weeks I'd had in a long time, but I kept this sentiment to myself. Even though things were better between us, a part of Amos was still raw from how things ended last time. If I tried moving into more serious, romantic territory with him, I could trigger that hurt again and scare him off. It was better to stay in hookup limbo. For now, I'd just blow my load, not my chances.

"Yeah. It was fun times. It was good hanging out with people my own age. No offense." I stood up, my chair squeaking on the chair. "Gotta get to school."

I kissed him on the head before he could ask me more questions. "Love you, Pop. See you tonight."

———

Amos and I had caf duty again. I stayed busy cooling down a table that was getting rowdy and on the verge of breaking into a fight over accusations of boyfriend stealing. In a way, I was grateful for the distance. My willpower against not petting him and kissing him was not strong. Especially when he wore adorkable sweater vests like he had on today.

"Good job," Amos said, eyeing the table that almost broke out in World War III. "What was that about?"

"Just some petty high school drama. Someone's boyfriend was DMing this girl and I'm already exhausted."

I hunkered down into my chair.

"Do you want one of my Ding Dongs?"

Chocolate sounded good right now.

"You'd share one of your beloved Ding Dongs with me?"

"Act fast before I change my mind." He held out the chocolate disk which looked like a hockey puck. My stomach moved at the sweet smell.

I didn't realize until I'd already leaned forward and bit into the Ding Dong that Amos wasn't trying to feed it to me. He was giving it to me, like a normal non-boyfriend person would do. Friends and colleagues do not feed each other food.

I slowly moved back to my seat, Ding Dong sticking out of my mouth like I was a damn dog with a frisbee. Amos's eyes were wide and awkward, but there was a smile in there somewhere.

"Um, thank you," I said with half a Ding Dong in my mouth. I swallowed, the snack and my pride, in one big lump.

"Yeah. No problem." He laughed to himself. I joined in, too. Laughter was the fastest way to wash away this weirdness. And the swoon I felt by the gesture.

"Do you want some of my chips?" I offered the bag of potato chips to him.

"Okay."

I thought about trying to feed him chips before just handing over the bag.

I ate his Ding Dong, and he ate my chips in comfortable silence.

"This is good," I said of the snack cake. "Really freaking good."

"I know, right? That burst of cream in the middle is..." he made a chef's kiss gesture with his fingers. "I doubt it's real cream. Probably ninety-nine percent chemicals."

"Still edible."

I reached for a napkin in the center of the table. Scooting in, our knees touched. Heat rushed up my leg. I thought about the heat of his body on top of mine.

And because I was a rebel, I didn't pull away.

Neither did Amos.

I reached under the table and gave his knee the slightest caress. Would we have to make another pit stop in my backseat this afternoon?

He snacked on more of my chips. We talked about classes and soccer games, all the while our knees kept touching.

Life was good. It was like I was drunk and loosened up.

"Do you want to go to a movie this weekend?" I asked, continuing to feel bold.

"Like a date?"

Before I could fumble for an answer, a foursome of guys marched into the cafeteria wearing matching sunglasses and fedoras. A loud song blasted from one of their phones.

They strode up to a table filled with girls who were either screaming or about to be.

The guy in front whipped off his fedora and held it over his heart. "Ereka Fraser."

He pointed her out, and heads inevitably turned. The three non-speaking gentlemen carried her in her chair to the open space in the center of the caf. Her face was the brightest red I'd ever seen on a human being. Other kids had their phones out to record.

The lead guy kissed his lips and pointed at her. He changed the song on his phone to something current, a love song I'd been hearing on the radio.

The fedora foursome was actually a quartet. They exploded into a choreographed dance that had been thoroughly practiced. It was a mix between boy bands and breakdancing. The cafe went absolutely bananas. I looked to Amos to see if we had to stop it, but he was equally transfixed.

At the end of their dance, the lead guy pulled a rose from his inside pocket. "Ereka Fraser, will you go to prom with me?"

Fucking promposals. Some things never changed. It was the official kickoff of prom season.

Ereka's face was streaked with tears as she jumped into his arms nodding like a maniac.

The caf cheered them on, and I appreciated that everyone in here was a sap for this stuff.

I had to be the adult. I strolled up to them, gave them a nice golf clap. "Okay, guys. Very nice. You gotta get back to class."

"Cool cool. Got it, Coach Hawkins." The lead guy gazed at Ereka, right through me like I was invisible.

"She said yes. Congratulations." I guided him and his fedora'd friends to the exit. I wasn't sure the protocol for promposals, but this seemed like the responsibility of caf duty.

The lead guy gave his prom date a wink. She clutched her rose tight, her cheeks as red as the petals. Ah, young love. So wide-eyed. I smiled to myself, happy to have witnessed such a sight. Deep down, I was a sucker for this stuff.

"It's promposal season," I said with an eye roll when I returned to the table.

Amos didn't have any reaction. He stared off into the blank space where the foursome had performed, his usually expressive face muted.

"I can't believe kids do that," I said.

"It's nice," he said, his voice hollow.

I returned to my seat, but Amos had pushed back so our knees could no longer touch.

18

AMOS

Watching promposals happen on a nearly daily basis hit me harder than I expected. Usually, I laughed them off. Except for the promposals done by queer students. Those rocked! I cheered them on like crazy when they occurred.

But this year, I got a tiny ache whenever I watched a student profess their heartfelt desire via song, dance, or poster to take their fellow classmate to prom. It made me think of the promposal I never got and the prom I never got to attend. Was I setting myself up for another round of disappointment by letting myself fall for Hutch again?

This wasn't love, I reminded myself. This was car sex.

Even if I wanted it to be more.

Even if the feeling of being cocooned in Hutch's arms as we (actually) napped brought me a sense of peace I'd never before experienced.

Hutch could get scared again and end this with another text message. That thought refused to leave my mind, despite telling myself that Hutch would never be that cruel again. He had grown. Things were different this time.

But were they?

History repeated itself. That's what it did with laser focus, like a shark hunting prey.

I became a bit of a grump, admittedly. I told my students that class couldn't be interrupted with promposals, so warn their dates accordingly. I hated being that teacher, but it was for my own mental health.

A week after that first promposal in the cafeteria, I was grading papers at home. With no roommate, the condo felt extra quiet. Good for concentration, but bad for letting thoughts flit through my mind. I focused on the papers. It was quite incredible the spread of writing capabilities among my students. Some students had truly interesting ideas, and I was impressed by how thoughtful they could be. Others I could tell were doing everything they could just to score an A, no real passion.

I pulled up Tommy's paper and steeled myself for tossed off garbage. But to my complete surprise, his paper was...incredible? Well thought out. Thought-provoking. Beautifully written with sentences that exploded with passion. He challenged the very notion of what I was teaching.

I was blown away. Had Tommy turned over a new leaf?

And then I came back to stark reality.

————

"YOU PLAGIARIZED THIS PAPER."

I slapped Tommy's paper down on my desk after class.

"What? No I didn't."

I expected this answer. Denial was the first stage of grieving, and pretty soon, Tommy was going to have a lot to grieve. I removed a printed-out article from my drawer and slapped it on top of his paper.

"Yes you did. This is an article on fiefdom from a website

called *History on the Regular*." I picked it up and cleared my throat. "The fiefdoms of the Middle Ages stifled intellectual growth among its citizens, slowing the development of culture and thereby keeping European society in the dark ages. Famine and disease, while negative aspects, proved..."

I put down the article and read from Tommy's paper: "...to be agents of change as much as chaos. They pushed people to leave their farms and travel to cities for help, for new starts. The co-mingling of people energized new ideas."

I let his paper slip from my hands and flutter onto my desk, like a paper teardrop. Everett would be proud of the dramatics.

"That's a coincidence," Tommy said. His eyes bugged out, and he couldn't look at me for more than two seconds at a time.

"I don't think it is. You lifted your entire paper from this essay. Word for word."

Panic snaked across his face. "How did you find that essay?"

"I used this specialized academic technology called Google." For a digital native, he hadn't grasped the basic tenets of the internet. Everything was searchable.

"Why were you searching my paper on Google?"

"I run plagiarism checks for all student papers. I told the class back in September."

"This is like an invasion of privacy," he said.

"How?" I folded my arms, perversely excited for an answer.

He couldn't answer the question. His mouth was a series of opening and closing, eyes never once looking at me.

"Fine, so I copied a few lines."

"A few lines?"

"So I didn't have anything to write about fiefdoms. Nobody cares about stuff. How is learning about fiefdoms going to help me in the real world?"

Complaints like this were the quickest way to get under my skin. Nobody took history seriously. They thought math, English, and science were the only valuable subjects. A lack of taking history seriously was why we had Holocaust deniers and anti-vaxxers.

"It's *fief*doms," I said with a tight expression. "And it may not help you in the real world, but neither will copying someone else's work. You know, I would've helped you. If you had shown any willingness to learn, I would've met you halfway. But because of your actions, I have no choice but to give you a zero on this assignment. That means you are now officially failing this class." I jammed both his and the copied essay in my briefcase.

"Dude…"

"Mr. Bright." The only person allowed to call me Dude was Charlie, and that was only because he made me free cocktails from time to time.

"Mr. Bright, you're failing me?"

"I'm not failing you. You failed yourself. You've missed assignments, plagiarized papers. This is on you, Tommy."

"But I've been really busy with practice."

"There are kids in your class who are involved in sports, too. And clubs. And part-time jobs. And they still manage to get the work done. I gave you chances." I zipped up my briefcase.

The cold look Tommy had began to slip away, showing me the scared little boy inside. I softened my stance. Kids thought teachers liked to be vindictive and fail students. We didn't. We hated it. I hated this! I hated giving zeros and F's as much as a doctor hated watching their patients get sicker.

"Look, you still have a chance to turn things around. There's two more months left in the school year. If you really work hard and put in the effort—I mean it—then you can pass this class. I'm happy to meet for extra help after school."

"I can't meet after school. I have practice." His voice was soaked in annoyance, as if I were the one not paying attention.

"We can arrange to meet during lunch."

Now, I'd seen kids roll their eyes and scoff. It was a hallmark of teaching teenagers. I was immune at this point, but hearing Tommy let out a very audible ughhh and deliver a very visible eye roll to me challenged all of my anger management skills.

"This isn't fair."

I swallowed back an incredulous laugh. The balls on this kid. "Please explain to me how it's not fair."

I blinked at him, waiting for a cogent answer. As predicted, he stammered and shrugged and stared at the floor.

Because I was the adult, I couldn't march out of there, even though I had things to do.

"This is so not cool." Another eye roll, this one filled with even more attitude. "Enjoy your power trip."

Fortunately, he shuffled out of class right before I lost it.

———

I HUSTLED to meet my SAT prep student in the school library. Being around a student who was eager and attentive helped me cool off from my conversation with Tommy.

The South Rock library had large windows that overlooked the football and soccer fields in the back of school. It was a reader's paradise, which was a shame since nobody used it for pleasure reading. Students looked up texts for term papers or fumbled around on the computers until their parents picked them up. What I wouldn't give to spend a Saturday afternoon sinking into an armchair with a good book and enjoying the view.

Perhaps this was a reason why I'd had trouble getting laid.

The soccer team practiced on the field, Tommy included. Our conversation seemed to have rolled off him as he laughed with his teammates.

My attention to tutoring kept getting pulled away by Hutch coaching on the sidelines. He'd blow his whistle and jog out to the field, go over drills and moves. He was electric out there, and even from here, I could see how coaching lit up his entire body.

And watching his ass jiggle in his gym shorts was a huge benefit, too.

But I couldn't let myself get excited, both literally since I was with a student, and emotionally. Watching those promposals happening reminded me how quickly things could change. Hutch and I were having fun. So even though my heart was getting in on the action, I couldn't get attached.

"Mr. B?"

My student awaited instructions. We went over the practice test and jotted down words to add to her SAT prep list. I didn't quite understand how we measured a student's aptitude by having them memorize tons of words, but regardless, I was here to help.

We worked through analogy questions. *If X is to Y, then A is to what?*

I assigned her practice questions and let my attention get pulled back to the soccer field. Even from here, I could make out with Hutch's wide smile.

Er, I could make out his smile.

It beamed in the sunlight.

Hutch lifted his head up, and we locked eyes. Shit, had he caught me staring? I forgot that this was a giant window and not a one-way mirror. I shuffled around in my seat and pretended to act busy.

"Good. Good job," I said to my student.

"We haven't gone over it yet."

"Right. Well, I could see that you were focusing very intently on the questions, and that's always a good sign. Mindset and focus is incredibly important. You don't want to be one of those students who chokes on test day."

Her face dropped as panic set in. "Does that happen? Do students choke?"

"Oh yeah. Occasionally you have a student who cracks on test day. When I proctored the test one time, a student broke down sobbing in the first section then ran out. But that won't be you. You have great focus." I tapped my fingers on her practice test. "So keep focusing."

She returned to her work, and I breathed a sigh of relief. These kids weren't paying me to stare at the soccer coach. I moved my chair so my back was to the window. But before I sat back down, I let myself have one more glimpse outside.

Hutch was looking my way. He flashed me a smirk that I felt in my bones.

If Hutch is to sexy, then I am to trouble.

———

HAZY ORANGE LIGHT illuminated the teacher parking lot when I finally got to my car. The sun had begun its descent into night. This long day was almost over. Almost time to do it all over again.

I unlocked my car and threw my messenger bag into the passenger seat. I was about to get into the car when I heard an unhealthy noise.

The muffled sounds of a failing engine resonated in the lot. I followed the noise to Hutch's car. He turned the key in the ignition, eliciting another round of struggling machinery.

I knocked on his window. "Are you having trouble?"

"I almost got it."

"Are you sure about that?"

Hutch turned his key with all of his force. His arm and neck muscles tensed up as if he were trying to turn the wheels himself. More ugly sounds came from the hood.

I knocked again, and this time he rolled it down. "You okay?"

"Yeah. She's just being stubborn." He strummed his fingers impatiently on the steering wheel.

"Can you pop the hood?" I asked him.

He was skeptical of my automobile prowess, but I dared him to call my bluff. As a lifelong owner of cheap used cars, I had to become my own de facto mechanic.

"I didn't know you were an automobile expert," he called from the driver's seat.

"I'm not. I'm an experienced novice," I said, lifting the hood.

"Don't try to fix it if you're not sure."

I thumbed through the weeds of the engine. I didn't know much, but I had cursory knowledge of what to check in a car. Oil, dipstick, things like that. YouTube was my saving grace. I went through all the tricks in my bag, but when Hutch turned the key, the same ugly noises emanated from the engine.

I jumped back from the noise.

"I'll call a tow truck." His phone was already to his ear.

"Why didn't you buy a new car when you went pro? Isn't that what professional athletes do?"

"I got this beautiful truck. I used to go into the mountains with it. Then one day, I was on a hike, and I forgot to put the emergency break on. I reached the peak of this trail, with a beautiful view of watching my car roll down the mountain into a ravine."

I smacked a hand over my mouth to keep from laughing.

"Whoops." He smiled to himself, his lips curling up in a perfect half moon. Did this man know how watchable he was?

The tow truck eventually came, and we watched Hutch's car get pulled away like a child dragging a toy. His face curdled when he glimpsed the bill before folding it into a tight square and shoving it in his pocket.

"I can give you a ride home."

"Are you sure?"

I nodded yes.

His blue eyes beamed megawatts of gratitude my way, which gave me an excuse to gaze into them. "Are you hungry?"

I had leftovers waiting for me in the fridge, but I'd been eating them all week. It was a law of diminishing returns. "It's dinner time, so yeah."

"Let's grab something to eat. My treat."

"We can go Dutch." The tow truck bill had to be considerable.

"I left my wooden clogs in my car. No, my treat. My house is in the opposite direction of your place. And besides, going Dutch implies this is a date."

Had I implied this was a date? Hutch laughed it off before I could get fully embarrassed.

"Excellent." Hutch made a triumphant fist. "I know just the place."

19

HUTCH

I willed my stomach not to growl in excitement as Amos parked. CJ's was located at the corner of two residential streets. Since it wasn't in downtown Sourwood, it was sometimes overlooked. That made it the town's best-kept secret, and also the perfect place for two closeted teenagers to secretly meet.

The guy and girl at the register tossed pizza slices into the giant ovens behind them. If I worked here, would I ever get tired of pizza? That seemed biologically impossible, but stranger things had happened.

Behind the glass partition were several pizzas with different toppings ready to be ogled by hungry customers. They were most known for their mac 'n cheese pizza, but it was too decadent for me. I liked mac 'n cheese, and I liked pizza, but not together.

"We'll take four slices of mushroom pizza," I said. The kid behind the counter made a face, proving my point. He was a kid, not yet an adult.

After we ordered, we slid into a red booth by the window. Maps of Italy decorated the paper placemats and the walls.

We looked around, admiring all the details of a place that was preserved in amber. Aside from the Facebook and Instagram decals on the window and the sign advertising free Wi-Fi, the place hadn't changed.

"I haven't been here in forever," Amos said. "I've gotten so used to getting it delivered."

"Remember when I got you to try red pepper flakes?" I fiddled with the shaker, ringing it like a bell.

"I do. That was a cruel joke."

"A cruel joke?"

"You said they tasted like red bell peppers. You said nothing about them being hot."

"I dared you to try one flake, and you tossed a handful into your mouth."

"I was hungry!" Amos's eyes bulged out of his head, the same reaction he had to trying the flakes.

I couldn't stop laughing. He was so animated, so full of life. I'd been living the past ten years in a world of gray.

The girl serving us, who I recognized from gym class, dropped off our order, each slice on a different paper plate.

I slid the napkin dispenser Amos's way.

"You're taking off the best part."

Amos ignored me as he dabbed at the layer of oil atop his slices.

"The oil is what makes the pizza so good."

"The pizza still tastes great." He laid out a fresh napkin to hold the oily, wadded up ones. The man had a gift for taking simple foods and turning them into a process.

"Cheers." We held up our slices and let the tips touch, which sounded much dirtier than it was. I bit into a literal slice of heaven. "There truly is no substitute for New York pizza."

"What's pizza like in Nashville?"

"Boring. I went to a place that billed itself as New York pizza. It was not. You couldn't do this with the pizza." The crust cracked as

I folded my slice in half, music to my ears. "Pizza was meant to be folded."

True pizza was a fat, greasy triangle. Not squares or rectangles. I dug into my pizza, and it tasted even better than I remembered. Everything here was better than I remembered, including the guy across from me.

"I once saw a guy eating his pizza with a fork and knife. I wanted to call the police." Amos smiled with a mouth full of pizza, his cheeks bunched up and fucking adorable.

I wanted to reach across this table and pull him into a kiss. My phone buzzed, snapping me away from my hornier impulses. This wasn't a date. This was pizza.

"What?" Amos asked, probably because he saw me rolling my eyes at the text.

I showed him the pic Pop sent of his empty pill slot for the day.

"He doesn't like taking his pills. Thinks he can use willpower and grit to recover."

"How is he doing?" His voice filled with concern, which warmed my heart. I'd wished they'd gotten to know each other. Pop and Amos would've gotten along great, had I not kept him this big secret.

"Healthwise, he's improving. His leg is healing. He hasn't had any more dizzy spells. The last checkup went well. But he's bull-headed. He thinks he's healthy and just had a slip."

"It sounded like a pretty bad fall."

"It might've been a blood clot or a heart thing. The doctors weren't totally sure, so they gave him medication to handle all of it. He's recovering but..."

"He almost didn't."

"He wants to act like it didn't happen, but it did, and it was fucking scary." The terror of getting that phone call came rushing back me. Whenever I got a call from an unknown number, my blood went cold. Would it be the hospital again?

"Y'know, Pop could fix anything. If he was in the parking lot, he probably could've fixed my car. He could do anything. He was the strongest guy I knew." I cleared my throat. "He is the strongest I know."

Memories of Pop flitted through my mind. Roughhousing and sitting on his shoulders and being his assistant when he was fixing things around the house. These montages in my head made it seem like he was on death's door. Every adult reached a point when they realized their parents were going to die. Maybe not right away, but someday. They were no longer invincible. They were mortal.

He was still here. I wouldn't let him go yet.

The next thing I knew, Amos's hand was on top of mine, stroking me with his thumb. His soothing touch calmed down my heart. I gazed into his warm, entrancing eyes, full of all the comfort in the world.

"He's going to get better," Amos said with full conviction. "Thanks to you."

I beamed at him, letting myself believe it.

"Stay on him with the pills. Maybe mash them into a banana."

His thumb continued to stroke mine. We continued to stare at each other. I got that gut feeling again that if I didn't break away, I would try and kiss him.

"Hey, do you wanna play?" I got up and strolled to the arcade game in the corner. Pop said it'd once been a pay phone booth. "I bet I can still kick your ass."

Amos coughed up quarters.

We each took a steering wheel. I gave him an *it's on* nod, which he reciprocated. And then we were off to the races. I focused on my screen, racing down the track, bending around curves. Amos was on my tail.

As I left him in the dust, he bumped me in real life, his hip hitting mine.

"Technical foul," I said.

"There's no technical foul in this game." He bumped his hip against me again.

I bit back the surge of lust when our bodies connected. Two could play at this game. I gave him a shove.

"That's cheating!" he said through laughter, his eyes never leaving the screen.

"It's payback."

"I gave you a hip bump. You shoved me."

I shoved him again.

"Fucker." He shoved me back, but I tensed all my muscles so I wouldn't budge.

When he felt my flexed pec, a look of hot fire scorched his eyes, which made my throat get dry.

"What else you got?" I savored my impending victory. The black-and-white checkered flag was in the virtual distance.

He said nothing back. I powered ahead, the W oh so close.

Or it was, until Amos dragged a finger over the crack of my ass. And squeezed.

I sputtered out, my car spinning out off the course and over a cliff. My mind was in similar shape.

Amos's car rolled to an easy victory. His screen lit up with computer-generated confetti.

I hadn't recovered yet. Not only had Amos stolen victory from me, he'd made me ragingly hard. Every synapse in my brain went into meltdown mode.

That was devious. But man, was that hot. Amos seemed taken aback by what he'd done, too.

"If that wasn't a technical foul..." I started, but I couldn't finish my sarcastic comment. The slap and squeeze had awakened all of my horny feelings, and I needed absolute focus to come back to earth. I didn't realize how sensitive I was to Amos's touch, how thin the ice I skated on was.

"I had to think of something." He shrugged his shoulders and returned to the table to finish his pizza.

After I was one thousand percent sure the boner in my pants had subsided, I joined him.

————

AFTER THE ARCADE GAME, we finished our pizza and kept shooting the shit. We talked about old memories, college stuff, Sourwood, on and on it went. When I was having a good conversation, the subject matter wasn't important. Time flew regardless.

It was dark out by the time we rolled up to my house. The glow of the TV shined through the curtains. I stared at my house, tired but not ready to call it a night.

"Thanks for the pizza," Amos said, his lips practically in silhouette.

My heart was racing all over again. This was a moment when two people would kiss. This wasn't a date, but it sure felt like one.

"Thanks for driving me home and helping with that." I could barely string together a coherent thought. My pulse raged in my ears.

If I didn't get out of the car, I would kiss him. Not a backseat-foreplay kiss. A real capital-K, I-wanna-be-with-you kiss. And that would be a mistake.

A glorious mistake.

"Let me know if you need a ride in the morning."

I checked out Amos's crotch to see if he was hard like I was getting. I'd played packed soccer games, and still I never felt more nervous than I did now.

"I'll be fine. Raleigh lives close by, so I can have him pick me up."

"I don't mind."

"I know, but it's out of the way for you. So, yeah, it's fine. He owes me one."

Raleigh didn't owe me anything. I hoped he didn't give me shit about asking for a ride to school.

"Cool." Amos gripped the steering wheel. "Well…"

The next move was on me. Time to get my ass out of there so he could drive away.

I didn't want this night to end, but I had to leave. We couldn't stay in this car forever.

"Yeah. Thanks. I, uh…it was good pizza." Lord, I sounded like an idiot. The pizza was like the eighth best thing about tonight.

I drifted my gaze away from his eyes. He had some crust crumbs on his collar.

"Looks like you took the pizza home with you." I leaned forward to brush the crumbs off his shirt. Amos blocked me with his lips.

We were kissing. Or rather, our lips chilled out against each other. It was a moment of hot awkwardness.

He moved back slowly like his body was a stiff corpse.

"Sorry," he said, crushing his eyes shut. "I thought you were—"

"I was brushing off some of the—what did you think I was doing?"

His bright red, mortified face said it all.

"You thought I was leaning in for a kiss?"

He nodded yes.

My jeans suddenly became incredibly tight. Every part of me tingled with pins and needles.

"And you were kissing me back?"

His eyes were pinched closed in tight slits as he continued nodding. He collapsed onto his steering wheel.

"I'm sorry," he said, his voice muffled against his sleeve.

His nerdy awkwardness turned me on like never before.

"Why?"

"I don't know what's wrong with me. I attacked you in my bedroom. I'm attacking you in my car. You need to carry pepper spray when you're around me."

"Amos," I said firmly. I'd found a new calm, a sense in the universe that we were doing exactly what we should be doing.

He tilted his head to look at me, those green eyes gleaming in the moonlight.

Before he could launch into another apology, I did what I should've done hours ago and capital-K kissed him. Our lips met in a perfect symphony of heat that made me melt into the center console between us. I could taste the hint of pizza from before, entwined in a clean scent that was one hundred percent pure Amos.

No kiss could last forever, though I wanted to try. He pulled back slightly and smiled against my face. I was ready to build a forever home in this moment.

"We shouldn't do this," he said.

"Why not?" I stroked his clean-shaven cheek.

"We tried this once before, and it didn't end well."

"It ended because I was a scared idiot, not because I ever stopped loving you."

His eyes widened, wanting those words to be true.

"I still love you, Amos. I've thought about you every day since we broke up. That was the worst day of my life. I wish I could've done things differently."

"I doubt you thought of me everyday. Even on Flag Day?"

"Yes, Amos. Even on Flag Day."

"Hutch, I don't want to get hurt again. What if we get in this cycle where we get together, then break up again?"

"You say that history repeats itself *unless we learn from our mistakes*. Well, I've learned. I'm not running anymore. I'm not letting myself be intimidated out of love. And you're not this shy, awkward kid anymore." I see-sawed my head. "You're still a little awkward, but in a really cute way."

"Thanks?" He raised an eyebrow, all his adorable awkwardness spilling out.

"Oh, yeah. It's a compliment. Look, I don't have any historical examples to whip out, but I know soccer, and the game isn't over until the final seconds. There's always time for a team to shrug off their losses, get their shit together, and stage a come from behind victory." I kissed him softly, then gazed into his eyes, trying to parse out what he was feeling. "Amos, I know I broke your heart before, but if you give me one more chance, I'll never break it again."

Amos lunged forward and kissed me with ten years worth of pent-up things he couldn't say. This was an all-timer of a kiss, shooting down to my toes.

"One more chance," he said, smiling against my lips. "Don't fuck it up."

"I won't. I promise." I meant every word. There would always be a part of myself upset for what I did, for the fear that led me to cut the most important person out of my life. Just like a part of me would always rewind the day I tore my ACL to see what I could've done differently.

But living in the past was pointless. And maybe I needed to go through rough times to enjoy these current highs.

We made out in his car, our heavy breathing and moaning fogging up the windows. The center console made it tough for things to progress. That, and we were parked on the street where anybody could drive by.

"I don't know about you, but I'm ready to sex," Amos said. "For sex. Shit. Sorry."

"Agreed." I nibbled on his ear lobe. "Let's go up to my room."

He pulled back. "But your dad's home."

"So?" I did not want to be thinking about Pop at this moment.

"So, you just want me to come in with you and go up to your room? Are you even allowed to have boys up in your room?"

Pop would probably throw a ticker tape parade, which would make things weirder.

"I don't want your dad's first impression of me to be some guy you bring up to your room. If we're really going to give this another shot, then I want my first meeting with your dad to be more traditional. Maybe brunch?"

I wasn't sure what signals Amos was giving me with his etiquette conundrum. I imagined guys had the same challenges hooking up with Emily Post.

"So should we hold off?"

"Probably." Amos took a deep breath and put his hands back on the steering wheel.

For approximately two seconds.

Then we were making out again, and he grabbed my dick through my jeans like it was the gear shift.

"We can go to your condo."

"I can't drive with this boner."

"We could find a secluded spot," I suggested, catching my breath. "Scoops?"

"Kids use the Scoops lot at night to skate and get high. Besides that, there are no more secluded spots in Sourwood. They've either turned into a park, a housing development, or they're being used by other horny teenagers."

"I have an idea." I didn't know if it'd work. I was thinking with my other head. "But you have to trust me."

20

AMOS

Was I willing to die to have great sex?

The answer was yes, apparently.

Less than ten minutes after Hutch told me he loved me (He LOVED me! No layover in Likeville.), I was on the precipice of plummeting to my death. Because the only way to sneak into his bedroom was by climbing a freaking tree like we were in some deranged buttsex-flavored Romeo and Juliet redux.

I was not a climber. I kept my svelte figure not through exercise but via genetics. I came from a long line of proud people with zero upper body strength.

Hutch swore the tree could support me, as he'd climbed it tons of times in high school to sneak in after curfew. The last thing I'd climbed was...well, Hutch.

We stood under the mighty oak, the window of his bedroom high above us. Hutch pointed out which branches and stubs to step on.

"It's a piece of cake."

"You know what's a piece of cake? A piece of cake," I whisper-screamed back.

"I climbed this tree drunk all the time. It's so thick with branches, it'll be like climbing up a ladder. Once I give you a push, I'm gonna go inside, say hi to Pop, and I'll be upstairs to help you in no time."

"I'll be climbing this alone?" I gulped back a lump of fear. Another one plopped in its place.

"I can't follow you because of my knee. But I promise, you can do it. If I didn't think you'd make it up there, I wouldn't have suggested it." Hutch slid a finger across my deepest forehead stress wrinkle, then kissed it calm.

"Did you ever play on the monkey bars?"

"All the time."

"I never did. I tried, but I couldn't pull myself across a single bar. Because these guns are two pieces of wet spaghetti." I flailed my rubbery arms for emphasis.

"You make me laugh, Famous Amos." He cracked a cheshire cat-esque smile, which made my pants tighten. It was good to know that despite all my raging anxiety about climbing a tree, I was still horny for sex. Something to look forward to if I made it out of this alive.

Hutch cupped my face, getting serious for a moment. His electric eyes swallowed me whole. "Do you trust me?"

"Yes." Because he loved me. He never stopped loving me.

"I meant what I said in the car. I love you, Amos. I asked for a second chance, and I'm not going to waste it by making you go splat on the ground."

"Splat? Who said splat?"

"Figure of speech. My bedroom isn't that high off the ground. If you fall, at most, you might break a leg."

That was a pretty big might. If he wanted to calm me down, he was doing a subpar job. "The only time I want to break a leg is in a musical."

"That won't happen. Trust me. Once you make it into that

window, I'll make it worth your while." Hutch leaned in and whispered all the things we'd do once we got to his bedroom. Then he capped it off by sliding a tongue in there, turning me to jelly for a moment.

He clapped my shoulder and gave me a thumbs up as he stepped back. It was showtime.

I looked up at the window. Pure ecstasy waited for me in that window. Time to Romeo and Juliet the fuck out of this.

Hutch hoisted me up, and I grabbed onto the first branch. Then the next. Then the next. His path seemed to be working. The branches were sturdy under my feet, and before I knew it, I was solidly above the ground.

"Good work!" Hutch whisper-yelled up to me. "I'm gonna go inside."

I went to give him a thumbs up and almost lost my balance. That was enough looking down for me.

Soreness shot into my biceps and quads as I gathered strength I didn't know I had to pull myself up. The branches became denser the higher up I got, making it easier to climb them like a ladder. The things people did for sex.

And love.

In my near-death adventure, I realized that I was doing this for love, too. Maybe that was why my heartache never fully went away. Because deep inside me, I never stopped carrying a torch for him.

I made it up to the thick branch that ran perpendicular to his window. Phase two of this operation. I hung tight and hugged the tree until he appeared.

I could see his whole neighborhood. I could also see the grass beneath us. Grass was not mother nature's padding that we all assumed.

Relief washed over me when Hutch's bedroom light turned on. He opened the window.

"This is romantic as fuck."

"That'll look great on my tombstone. What do I do now?"

"You need to lay down on the branch and shuffle your way to the window. Imagine that you're on a stripper pole that's parallel to the ground."

"Did you really just compare me to a stripper?"

"Hell yeah." His eyebrows jumped up, sending a jolt to my re-tightening pants. Mortal panic couldn't even eliminate my sex drive, apparently.

I very slowly squatted down while hugging the tree until I reached the branch in question. I put out one hand, then the other, and hugged my arms around its thick circumference.

"That's it."

I shimmied myself down the branch, one stressful inch at a time.

"You're halfway," he said. "Relax, Famous Amos. I won't let anything happen to you."

"I know you won't, but gravity is another story."

Little by very little, the window got closer. Hutch came more into focus. My fingers maintained their white-knuckle grip around the branch.

"Okay, in the homestretch." He held out his hand and motioned me to come forward.

I reached out to take it and lost my balance. I felt myself sliding down the side of the branch. I was in such shock I couldn't react. No screams, no sassy remark. Only the realization that this was actually happening.

"Shit." Hutch grabbed my shirt and pulled me rightside up just before I lost my fight with gravity. He yanked me forward the final part until my hands made contact with the window sill.

"What'd I say? Piece of cake?" Hutch pulled me upright. I hugged his neck as we maneuvered inside.

Once I sensed that I wasn't going to die, I scowled at Hutch, but his sweet, scared look made all my fear dissipate. He wasn't going to let anything happen to me.

"This had better be the most mindblowing, incredible sex of my life. No two pumps and done. I demand stamina."

"Amos, I got you covered," he growled in my ear. He pulled me flush against him. "Are you hard?"

"Yes. I don't know why. Just shut the window."

"I take it as a compliment."

That cocky shit. Ugh, he should, too.

He whisked us into his bedroom, and I was hurtled back in time. His bedroom had not changed since high school. It was eerily intact. Memories of sneaking up here filled my head. (I snuck in through the front door, back when his dad worked full time.)

"Time warp," I said. Hutch gestured for me to keep the noise down.

Right, the whole reason we snuck across a tree.

I ambled around the room, running my hand over old trophies and feeling the leather of his letterman jacket in my hands. We had good times up here.

Hutch came up behind me and kissed along my neck. "You can walk down memory lane later."

He spun me around and continued the kiss from the car. I was more revved up, sparks flying through me. Maybe narrowly escaping death added to my lust.

Hutch pulled me close. His kiss was tentative, a bit nervous, which I found endearing. Our bodies mashed together, and his hardness dug into my leg. I reached a hand between us and stroked him.

A crash of glass downstairs broke the magic.

"Did you hear that?" I asked.

"Pop is like a bull in a china shop." Concern washed over his face. "Wait right here. I'll be right back."

"Just so you know, if we ever do this again, we're doing it at my place," I said.

"Baby, we are so doing this again." He kissed me goodbye and off he went.

Alone in his bedroom, I returned to my walk down memory lane. But there was one thing I needed to make sure he still had. Taking quiet steps, which was difficult with creaky floors, I went to his closet and found the shoebox for his Vans.

He hadn't worn Vans in years. It didn't matter. The lube and condoms he kept were still there. I thanked the angels that his dad never cleared out his room and turned it into a study or greenhouse or whatever empty nesters did with their kids' bedrooms. But my heart sank when I checked the expiration dates. Both the condoms and lubes expired six years ago.

Did condoms and lube really expire? Or was this a marketing gimmick that forced consumers to buy more?

I Googled *Can you use expired condoms and lube?*

Expired condoms were drier and could break more easily. While there were no known dangers of using expired lube, there was a chance that bottoms could experience burning.

It was just a chance!

I'd climbed a damn tree. I was invincible! I could handle a little potential burning. Maybe...

Was this a cruel metaphor? Had our relationship passed its expiration date?

Hutch returned and clicked his bedroom door shut. "Pop dropped his beer bottle in the kitchen. It's the third time he's done that this month. I need to wrap this house in rubber. Speaking of rubber..." He pointed at the open shoebox at my feet.

"I think our sex life expired." I showed him the expiration dates.

"I forgot I had those." He squatted down and sifted through the box. "Good times."

"No more good times since it's all expired."

"You can't use this stuff after it's expired?"

"According to the internet."

"Oh, well." He shrugged and got up. "I guess you can go home since we can't have sex."

He opened up the window. The rattling of the branches outside were their own evil cackling laughter.

"Okay?" Why even bother climbing onto the tree again? I should just jump out the window and plummet directly to my death. We were cockblocked by time.

He went to his nightstand, where he produced fresh lube and condoms.

It was a Christmas miracle!

He tossed the boxes my way. They were in their pretty, fresh packaging.

Hello, friends.

"I got these recently," he said.

"How recent?"

"On my way home the night we blew each other."

"You got lube and condoms after we said we weren't going to have sex with each other?"

"What can I say? I'm an optimist."

"You're a genius." I grabbed his collar and threw Hutch backward on the bed to sex the life out of him.

The mattress let out a petrifyingly loud squeak.

"Was that your bed?"

"It's creaky," he said.

"Ya think?"

"We wore it out back in the day." His cheeks blushed, but his smile was full of confidence.

"We're supposed to be quiet."

"We can be quiet." Hutch pulled me down to him, a lusty rasp in his voice. "Pop's hearing has gotten worse over the years, so he keeps the volume way up."

He pointed up for me to hear. The dialogue and music of a television drama floated up from the living room. I tried making out what show it was – was it an NCIS or a Law & Order – until I remembered I should be making out with Hutch.

"Get over here." He kissed away my worry. We had a locked door, fresh sex supplies, and a loud TV.

I sank into the warm, special feeling of his arms wrapping around me, holding me close. His muscles flexed against my chest as he moved me on top of him. I straddled him, his dick willingly poking into my ass.

"It's tight quarters," I said of the twin bed. "How did we have sex on this thing?"

"Sheer force of will. Enough talking. Take your shirt off."

My dick twitched at his command. I looked over my shoulder once more to ensure the door was closed and locked and that the loud, soothing sounds of procedural television were audible. Then I was off to the races.

Hutch's rough, calloused hands ran up my flesh, flicking over my nipples, sending a pulse of desire shuddering up my spine. I ground against his crotch, willing the denim of our jeans to tear so he could be inside me already. I was hungry, so incredibly, tortuously hungry, for his touch, for him to take control of my body.

He sat up, eliciting another squeak from the mattress, and whipped off his shirt. I happily raked my eyes over his muscular frame.

He looked down at his chest, unimpressed. "I've let myself go. I'm not as ripped as I was in high school."

Hutch had an awfully peculiar understanding of the phrase "let myself go." His muscular chest and arms were slightly rounder instead of cut glass, and a little layer of thickness lay over where there once were rock solid abs. I freaking loved it. He was like a weighted blanket I wanted to wrap myself in. Make no mistake, the guy was still sex on wheels.

"I prefer the Hutch dad bod." I gave his shoulder, then his nipple, a quick bite. It was my seal of approval.

Our chests rubbed together as he pulled me into another kiss. He was so close I could feel his heart beating into my chest. I didn't know where mine ended and his began.

Hutch dragged his teeth down my neck and kissed along my collar, making me shiver and pulsate with want. His eyes shined in the darkness, electric currents sparking me to life.

With one fluid motion, and accompanying bed creaks, he took us off the bed and carried us to his dresser, pushing aside random papers and his old soccer jersey.

"I want to taste you," he uttered in a low tone.

There was no need to answer. He could see it in my eyes. I was his, completely his.

Another fluid motion, and I was bent over his dresser, pants and underwear at my knees. I groaned into my arm as his tongue swept over my opening. He pushed me open, swirling his tongue deeper inside me, past the tight ring of muscle

"You're so damn hot. Want you so bad," he said between deep gulps of air to catch his breath.

"Need it," I croaked out.

He spat on my hole, smeared it around with his thick tongue, hitting every erogenous zone inside me like a pinball machine. His thumb slid in and out of my hole, then drifted down to brush against my balls, sending a shiver of heat through me.

"Need you inside me."

"I'm not done yet." He clapped his hand on my cheek. He could've come down on me hard, slapped my ass so hard I'd be branded, were it not for his dad downstairs. "Remember when you touched my ass at CJ's?"

He did it to me, my pale flesh putty in his strong hands.

"Remember that?"

"Yeah," I said, breath choked. "I don't know what came over me."

This was true. I got so into playing the game, and Hutch was so sexy with his focused stare, that I forgot I wasn't supposed to flirt with him.

"You got me really hard." He reached down and grabbed my erection, leaking between my legs.

Every nerve in my body cried out in pleasure as I heard him unzip his fly and snap the waistband of his boxer-briefs. He slid his dick in between my cheeks, slick with his spit, teasing me so bad I was going to disintegrate. I jutted my ass out, hoping for a miracle of him slipping inside me.

"Not yet. We need our unexpired lube and condoms."

Damn him and his thoughtful approach to safe sex.

Hutch swooped me up in his arms and carried me to his bed, placing me down like a delicate flower. He let out a brief wince but powered through.

"How's your leg?"

"Good. I can't do sudden movements, so that means I'm gonna try and fuck you nice and slow. But we'll see how that goes."

I once told Charlie that I couldn't really be with another man because Hutch Hawkins had ruined me. No man could measure up. I stood by that statement. Hutch was commanding yet tender. He was protective of me, making me feel safer in his arms than anywhere else.

My legs were over my head in a heartbeat. Hutch drizzled lube on my hole and rolled the condom on his engorged cock. I leaked a puddle on my stomach. I was never good with being patient, doubly so when I knew I was about to get railed.

He hovered over me, his arms balancing him on either side of my head. Our eyes connected in the tenderest of moments, cutting through the lust.

"Amos..." He said my name like a prayer into the universe.

"Hutch," I prayed back.

"Oh shit, I think I hear Pop."

"What? Shit." I attempted jolting up, kind of impossible with a large man above me.

"I'm fucking with you."

"Yeah, well drop the 'with' already."

I bit my lip as he breached my opening.

"Are you okay?"

"Yeah."

"I forgot that you need a moment to adjust."

I wasn't one of those guys with a porn-ready ass that could take it at a moment's notice. Each time, it was a shock, and my body needed to get used to the feeling before I could enjoy it. Hutch waited above me until I gave him the green light to fully climb aboard.

He filled me up. And it was everything.

His strong body rested above me as he rocked into my opening, making me feel whole. He went slowly, dragging out the pleasure until it became agony.

"You can go faster if you're able."

"If I go faster, this bed is going to sing loudly like it's drunk karaoke."

He jabbed into me with quick, forceful thrusts to demonstrate just how squeaky his bed was.

I moaned into his chest, my fingernails digging into his broad back.

"Don't worry, Amos." He smoothed back a wayward, sweaty curly lock of hair from my eyes. "We may be quiet, but this won't be boring. We'll get you where you want to go."

I smacked my hand over my mouth and tried to hold back the laughs.

"What's so funny?" he asked.

"That's what I always say to my students when they're trying to pull up their grades." *We'll get you where you want to go* had been said to calm down many a student concerned for their GPA.

Screw GPA. I wanted to get to pound town, and I wanted Hutch to take me there.

He laughed into my shoulder. We were naked, tangled, and Hutch was fully inside me. But we still knew how to have a good time. I'd missed laughing during sex. That was the thing about random hookups. There was no history there. No feelings. We were putting on a facade, pretending we were sex gods. When really, I was kind of a mess.

I could be my messy self in front of Hutch.

Hutch leaned over me and resumed his slow, deliberate thrusts into my channel, heat building in my core. He might've been slow, but he was hitting all the right places.

"Yes," I said in a blissed-out whisper. My hands traveled all over his chest as the sweaty tips of his hair hung in his eyes.

"Just like old times?"

"Better."

We met in a kiss, hungry to block out the slow thrusts. I could feel his heartbeat against my chest. The room was quiet except for the heavy breathing and rhythmic sound of skin hitting skin. I bit my lip to hold back the moan dying to come out. I pulled him down and groaned right into his ear so that he had full confirmation of what he was doing to me.

Hutch's pupils were black saucers. "Baby, need to fuck you hard."

In one fluid motion, he sacrificed a loud bed squeak to lift us up and move us up against the wall. That he did all this while staying inside me, with a deficient ACL, made my cock even harder. Pre-come smeared across his stomach.

His thick hands dug their grip into my thighs while he, for lack of a better term, fucked the life out of me. Sharp, needy thrusts, pummeling inside me, splitting me open like a fresh watermelon. Put me on a medical slab and declare me officially dead.

How had I lived my life without this man? How had I attempted to date like a normal person and pretend that Hutch Hawkins hadn't ruined me for all future men?

I looked over his shoulder at the full-length mirror tacked on his bedroom door. His back muscles flexed with power, and his firm ass thrust into me.

"Hutch." He barreled into my opening, leaving it all on the field as my athlete students would say, pulling my sweat-slicked skin against him, closing the physical and emotional gaps between us. "I love you."

Telling someone you loved them, or that you never stopped loving them, should be reserved for really special moments that were thought out in advance. They shouldn't immediately be followed by coming all over yourself.

I dug my fingers into his back as I shot loads of come onto his stomach and mine. His gleaming teeth grit together, his eyes a swirling blue of a tropical storm, as he let out a final groan and spilled his seed.

"Shit," I gasped out when it was over.

He let me go carefully, but I was like a newborn animal still learning how to use its legs. I slid down his wall to the floor, a sticky, sweaty, absolutely spent mess.

And I wanted to do it again as soon as possible.

Hutch brought me his shirt and offered to wipe me off, but I was an independent adult and could do it myself.

"Amos, that was off the charts." He sat on the floor across from me, his back against his bed. His cock was half-hard, sweat glistening his muscles. "Better than anything I remember from high school, and that was epic."

I felt a surge of relief that he found our sex life epic. "Same."

He tipped his head back, and it was like I could see the wheels turning. "Amos..." He said my name like it was a far-off state. "I missed you."

"I missed you, too."

He quirked an eyebrow. "And did I mishear, or did you say that you loved me as you came?"

I pressed my eyes shut, kicking myself for the most unromantic moment to say it.

"Was that something just said in the heat of sex?"

I shook my head no. "I love you, Hutch. I never stopped either."

Maybe this was a romantic moment. We were naked, in all senses of the word.

I could tell more was on his mind, things were on his mind for years. Instead, I kissed him quiet. In that moment, it all seemed trivial. What ifs and what could've beens and rehashing the past wasn't worth it. With Hutch, I wanted to live in the present.

"I should probably get going."

That would entail getting up and walking. Easier said than done thanks to Hutch.

My eyes traveled to the window and the dreaded tree. If I could barely walk, how the hell was I going to do that?

"Maybe you could distract your dad, so I could sneak out the front door?"

"I could." His eyebrows danced on his forehead. "Or, you could stay here tonight."

"Are you asking me to spend the night?"

He nodded yes, his dimpled lazy smile telling me all I needed to know. "We've made my twin bed work before."

That we did. I treasured those afternoons when I fell asleep in his arms before his dad came home. But our bodies were more flexible back then.

"I've had ten years of beauty sleep in a queen-sized bed."

Hutch stood up and held out his hand. "I'll make it worth your while."

He pulled me up with him, meeting for yet another kiss. He shut his lights, letting moonlight streak across our bodies. Then, without saying another word, he undid his sheets, got into bed, and I lay down beside him. His arms stretched across me and lulled me into a soft, peaceful sleep.

21

AMOS

The best sex of my life was followed by an okay sleep. Sleeping in Hutch's beefy arms was incredible. It was so incredible that I kept waking up throughout the night to pinch myself. So yeah, not much actual sleep, but I'd never been so happy to wake up groggy.

I checked my phone. It was five minutes to five. Hutch was sound asleep, with the same slight snore that hadn't improved since high school. Fortunately, it hadn't gotten any worse either.

While I would've loved to wake up with Hutch and cuddle and kiss and potentially have a second round, reality set in. And by reality, I meant dried come pulling at my skin. I needed to shower, get dressed, and get my ass to school on time. And no way in hell was I climbing down the tree of terror by myself before the sun came up.

It was early enough that I could sneak out unnoticed. I slid out of bed and replaced my body with a pillow for Hutch to spoon. I stood up and remembered that I was buck naked.

And hard.

But that would have to wait.

Hutch looked peaceful and beautiful sound asleep. I wasn't one of those guys who liked to watch people sleep, but I took a quick moment to admire his pouty lips. Even in his dreams, he was primed for making out.

I used my phone light to go on a scavenger hunt for my clothes. My shirt was on a desk chair. My pants spread out on the floor. My boxers were bunched in a ball under the nightstand.

We truly sex tornadoed.

Right shoe poked out from under the bed.

Left shoe behind right shoe.

One sock. And...

And...

Where was my other sock?

I swept the phone light across the floor searching for the last piece of my wardrobe. I had a thing for funky, fun socks. These socks had repeated images of Mount Rushmore with all four presidents wearing sunglasses. They couldn't be hard to find.

Time was ticking. I didn't want Hutch to wake up; he needed his beauty sleep. I definitely didn't want his dad to find me either. That would've been awkward.

After another moment of frantic searching the corners of his room, I gave up. I went barefoot with my left shoe, but I would survive.

I gazed on Hutch for one more slightly creepy moment before I clicked his door shut.

I crept down the stairs, taking each step with utmost care. This was an old house. Everything creaked. If Hutch really got to have his way last night, he would've humped the bed so hard it crashed into the living room.

I tensed my body as one foot, then the other, slinked to the bottom of the stairs. I was doing full on cat burglar moves, like a mime dance. I took one step into the kitchen to use the side door, which I thought would be more secretive.

"Morning." Mr. Hawkins stared at me before shoveling a spoonful of Froot Loops into his mouth.

"Hi," I said, trained by society to be friendly no matter how awkward the circumstances. "I...think I'm lost?"

"Are you looking for the way back to my son's room?" His eyes were direct spears holding me in place.

"Whatever do you mean?"

"I take it you're not a burglar."

"Heavens no. Don't believe such happenstance."

Why did I start talking British when I got nervous?

I thought he was going to rip me in half. With his rugged face and bald head, he gave off Bruce Willis vibes. But then his rigid glare broke into a squinty-eyed smile and a deep chortle. I became a tad relaxed, still on alert.

"Just so I'm clear, you're laughing because you've decided not to kill me, yes?"

That made him laugh more, grizzled cheeks bunching up like he was a child. "The name's Bud."

He held out his hand. Was it normal to shake hands with the father of the man I just slept with? My innate politeness won out.

I took his hand and was surprised by his firm handshake. "Lovely to make your acquaintance. I mean, nice to meet you."

I sat at the table as instructed. "I'm sorry, sir. Hutch snuck me into his room last night. But nothing happened."

I didn't want this nice man to think I was a slut right off the bat.

"Nothing happened? Well, that sounds boring. Do you want something to eat? We've got toast, bagels, cereal."

The colorful Froot Loops caught my eye and made my stomach rumble. CJ's Pizza felt like a million years ago...and we definitely burned it off in his bedroom.

"I'll have what you're having."

"I'll get you a bowl, so long as you keep this a secret. My son would kill me if he caught me eating sugary cereal. He has me on a strict breakfast of flavorless heart-healthy shit."

I smiled despite myself. There was something cute about Hutch being protective over his dad. Bud opened a cabinet next to the fridge and handed me a bowl that matched his.

"Thank you, sir."

"Bud."

"Bud." Even with my friends' parents who insisted I call them by their first name, it was a knee jerk reaction.

Colorful, sugar-filled loops spilled forth from the box into my bowl, followed by milk. I hadn't eaten Froot Loops since I was a kid. I kept my breakfasts quick and boring, usually eaten while driving to school.

"Thanks," I said before digging in.

"I love this stuff. Much better than oatmeal." He smiled as he shoved a spoonful into his mouth, as if he were auditioning for a commercial. I expected him to have his own catchphrase and everything.

"What do you do when you have to eat with Hutch?"

"I eat slowly until he gets up to leave. Then I toss that shit out."

The super sweet goodness washes over my taste buds. "This is so good."

"It hits the spot, right?"

Not unlike your son. I nearly choked on my loops.

"Easy there," Bud said. "I don't want to kill my son's new boyfriend."

"I'm not—we're…"

He nodded as I stumbled through my answer. "I get it. Too soon."

"You're seriously cool with this?" I pointed between us then up to the stairs where his son slept buck naked after mindblowing sex. "You're like those parents who let their kids host parties with alcohol."

Bud got serious for a moment. He stared into his cereal. "It's just the two of us here. His mother passed when he was young, and secrets in a two-person household don't work. If you're the person he's spending time with, then I'm happy to meet you...I'm sorry, I didn't catch your name."

It took me a second to answer because I was caught up in a father being this loving to his gay son. I had to wonder if I was still asleep.

But I wasn't, and he was waiting for my name.

"Amos."

"Amos. Amos," he said again, as it obviously rang some kind of bell for him. "From high school."

How much had Hutch told him about me?

"Yeah, we work together at South Rock."

"Not that. Before."

He didn't need to elaborate. Hutch had apparently taken advantage of an open father-son relationship. I felt my face go as red as the fruitiest of loops.

I nodded yes.

"He really liked you. I remember the summer after you two broke up, he was quiet, despondent. Couldn't get him to say more than three words at a time. I thought it was because high school was over and he was nervous about college. But years later, once he shared your history with me, I got it."

I fished my spoon through the milky, faded colors of cereal mush, memories of my own summer resurfacing.

"Looks like you two made amends."

"We're on our way," I said, my throat thick, "He hurt me back then."

"If it's any consolation, he was hurting, too." Bud's charming demeanor soured into a grizzled glare before he uttered a name I hadn't thought of since high school. "Fucking Seth Collins."

"What about Seth? They were both on the soccer team, right?"

"Yeah, and if Hutch had any sense, he would've kicked a ball right into his face. He was the one who made Hutch break up with you."

My gay Spidey sense tingled. I leaned closer. "Why?"

"He saw text messages between you two. Threatened Hutch with all this bullshit, like that you would get run out of town if people found out. And Hutch..."

"Got scared." The Froot Loops landed heavy in my gut.

"But let's not spoil such a wonderful meal with the sad stuff," he said. "I'm happy to finally meet you, Amos."

"Likewise."

Bud poured us each a cup of coffee. "I don't know how the hell both of you fit on Hutch's bed."

I snorted.

Ten minutes later, thanks to my tight schedule, I had to jet. I cleaned off my bowl in the sink.

"Bud, this has been an unexpected pleasure, but I must run." I craned my neck to the entranceway. No sign of Hutch. The man could sleep.

"Hope to see you again." Bud shook my hand in a total dad move.

I opened the side door. Fresh air hit my face. "Me, too."

———

I RACED home after that delightful and unexpected breakfast. The sugary cereal gave me a big boost of energy that allowed me to shower, shave, get dressed, and pack my lunch in record time.

Not like I timed myself.

Not officially.

The entire time, I had a big, dopey smile on my face. It made shaving all the more difficult.

Part of why I had to dash early was that I promised to carpool with Everett this week while his car was in the shop. Everyone I knew was having car trouble! He literally rode his car until the wheels fell off. His time was focused on school and plays, not automotive upkeep.

I toweled off my hair as best I could before throwing the towel over the shower bar. I was running late. Before I left my apartment, a tingle zipped through my body.

I had sex last night. Really really good sex with Hutch. That happened.

We said I love you. That also happened.

I leaned against the threshold and let myself have one more dopey, wide-eyed, birds- chirping-like-I-was-a-Disney-princess smile.

The sky was a mix of fluffy clouds dancing over a blue sky. I was in such a good mood, I opened the sunroof. Usually, I wasn't a fan because the wind was loud, but today called for such a celebration.

Everett lived on the top floor of an old house owned by an even older couple. They'd converted their attic to an apartment. Everett found the tight quarters romantic. To each their own.

He skipped down the front steps and slid into the passenger seat.

"Mocha Mellie's. My treat." He blew me a kiss.

"We don't have time for coffee." Although now that he mentioned Mocha Mellie's, my mind couldn't think of anything but their iced coffee.

Well, iced coffee and Hutch's face as he came inside me.

"We'll have coffee in the teacher's lounge."

"But it tastes like piss," Everett scoffed.

"How would you know what piss tastes like?" I realized after I made that joke that Everett might have an answer. "Kidding."

"Come on. It's on the way."

"It's actually not. It's actually completely in the opposite direction of school."

"We live in a small town. Nothing's ever that far."

I rolled my eyes. I loved Everett dearly, but he could be a small doses kind of guy, especially when he was craving coffee.

"I would. You know I would, but we're going to be late."

"That's not my fault. I was ready. You were the one who was tardy for the party," he said.

Damn me and my punctuality. A smile crested on my lips as I thought about why I was late. But I wasn't ready to share it with my friends. I was still processing the past twenty-four hours and didn't need Everett to condense it down into a pithy, sassy comment.

"I got a late start. Had trouble sleeping."

Everett studied me for a moment, and I got very still, waiting for him to call bullshit.

"You feeling okay?" His brow creased with unexpected concern.

"Yeah. Just one of those nights." I shrugged, willing him to drop it.

He relaxed back in his seat and checked his phone. Crisis averted.

My sugar rush dropped precipitously. I needed a coffee pick-me-up soon, even if it was gross teachers lounge coffee.

"So what'd you do last night?" he asked.

"Nothing. It was a weeknight. I graded papers." I breathed slowly and kept my eyes on the road. I was not a fan of lying, but I didn't want Everett to turn last night into a whole thing.

"Yeah. You're right. My night was also–"

"Incoming text message." The monotone, vaguely feminine, Alexa-esque voice of my car's text-to-voice system came on the speakers. "From Hutch."

My eyes darted directly out of my skull. I reached for my

phone, but it was in my pocket, and I was wearing fitted pants. I wouldn't fish it out without hitting a telephone pole. Maybe that was best.

"Are you just going to hit it and quit it?" the robotic voice read out. "No morning sex?"

Everett was eerily silent. I glanced over and witnessed the most slaphappy, giddy expression lighting up his face. Technology was going to ruin my life.

"That's not what you think..." I started before being overtaken by the voice again.

"Incoming text message from Hutch."

I jammed my fingers at the touch screen hoping to hit something that would make her shut the fuck up. Of course we were hitting all green lights this morning so I had no chance to stop. My fingers smeared over the screen, but I only managed to turn up the volume.

"I can't stop thinking about last night," the voice read aloud—very aloud. "I want to be inside you again. Peach emoji. Eggplant emoji."

Everett's hands were clapped over his face, tears of joyous laughter raining down his face.

I wanted to die...but I was also really turned on by that message, making my tight pants even tighter.

"Don't. Say. A. Word," I growled out to Everett.

He held up his hands silently.

"Because I know you want to say something. You're dying to say something. But because you're my friend, you won't say anything, right?"

He mimed zipping his mouth shut.

"Because you asking questions will turn it into a whole thing, and it is way too new of a thing to be a whole thing. It's still a zygote of a thing. You know, like when the Founding Fathers signed the Declaration of Independence, they weren't all 'I guess we're a world superpower now. Because that's a whole thing, and we're just ex-colonies.' You get me?"

He cocked his head, seeming incredibly lost. I was a bit lost in my metaphors. I didn't even teach US History.

"Just, don't say anything."

And he didn't. The silence quickly became unbearable though, its own judgmental weight that stifled the car. I could feel him looking at me. I could hear the questions rattling off in his head.

"Fine. Because you're so damn nosey, I'll tell you. Hutch and I maybe, possibly, one hundred percent definitely had sex last night. I'm not going to rehash every detail because it's personal and private, but I will just say that it was amazing. I'm not going to spill every detail about how we did it on his bed and then he shoved me against the wall and thank god you dragged me to those sunset yoga classes."

"Incoming text message from Hutch." I found myself grateful to be interrupted by AI. "Yo, can you give me a ride to school? Raleigh is coming in late, and I don't have a car dot dot dot."

Shit.

I strummed my fingers on the steering wheel. The school was a block away. But Hutch didn't have a car. And Everett was in mine having the time of his life.

Everett leaned forward and tapped the reply button on the screen.

"On my way," he dictated.

"On my way," the AI voice repeated back. "Okay to send?"

"Yes," I said. I glanced over at Everett, still smiling, but there was a warmth there that let me know that amidst enjoying my embarrassment, he was happy for me.

"Don't say a word," I said to him.

"Don't say a word," the AI voice repeated back. "Okay to send?"

"Yes!" Everett shouted out before slapping his hand back on his mouth.

22

HUTCH

"You're smiling awfully hard considering it's gym class." Raleigh watched me like a hawk as I handed out golf clubs to the students.

I felt my face and realized that yes, I had on a big, dumb grin.

"Just happy to be here."

"In gym class?" Raleigh laughed to himself and strolled down the line, giving pointers to students on their swing. I handled the other half of the line, helping students align their hands and feet. Even though they pretended not to take it seriously, their faces lit up when they hit a great shot.

No matter how trivial, everyone liked to learn and get better at something.

Raleigh and I stood in back while kids continued taking their shots. My mind kept going to last night, how perfect it was. I wish I was able to wake up with Amos in bed with me, but I understood that he had to make a hasty exit to his condo. Fortunately, he snuck out without waking up Pop. That would've been awkward.

"Have you thought any more about what you're doing next year?" Raleigh asked. "You seem to have a knack for coaching."

"Beginner's luck."

I loved helping my players improve, devising strategies, and watching the team dynamics gel. My confidence with coaching was stronger than it ever was as a player. I'd floated around aimless ever since I was cut from professional soccer, but I'd found my place here. Maybe I did have a knack for it.

"Aguilar and I are meeting this week to discuss. I'd like to come back. Part of it depends on how the team finishes out the season."

"If things keep going as they are, then it should be a done deal." Raleigh turned to face me. Even though we were the same height, he loomed larger somehow, his thick blond hair and burly shoulders making him look like Thor.

"Have you given any more thought to getting your teaching certification?"

"I looked into it. It's a lot of work."

"Not as much as you think."

Reading over the requirements the other day was overwhelming. "It's been a long time since I had to study for a test. I'm rusty."

"I can coach you. I'm a great coach," Raleigh said, sorta cocky and sorta jokey. It could be hard to tell with him. I appreciated the support, though.

I happened to know another great tutor. One with a very cute butt.

I snorted. "I'd officially be a gym teacher."

We used to make fun of gym teachers when I was in school. Life was ironic.

"I know people don't consider us real teachers." Raleigh let out a little smirk at his comment, but I could tell it steamed him. "But there is work involved. And I've seen you these past few weeks. You have a real skill with kids. You like working with them. You're a kick-ass coach. Being a teacher is worth it, man. Not just for the summers off."

I ran a hand over my head. "You really think I'll be a good teacher?"

If someone had told me when I graduated high school that I'd come back willingly to teach for the rest of my days, I'd have called them crazy.

"Definitely. It'd be great to call you an official coworker. You can't leave me to be surrounded by a bunch of eggheads. We need more jocks on staff." Raleigh sounded like he was kidding, but also not. "The certification isn't that arduous. And you'll have it for life. You'll be able to keep teaching and coaching."

"People who are teachers usually do it, like, forever right? Until they retire."

"That's the plan. Then you get a pension."

I was going to be a teacher forever. That was a long-ass time. "I could probably get an office job, make about the same. No cramming for a test."

"You could." Raleigh turned to me, instantly cutting through my bullshit. "But do you really want that?"

The answer crystallized for me as a big, fat nope. I had friends at South Rock. I got to joke around with students. I spent my days coaching my favorite sport. And now I was dating the most adorkable guy in school. I loved it here!

"Well, fuck. Looks like I have a certification test I gotta start studying for."

"There you go." Raleigh gave me a hard slap on the back. "Yikes."

He nodded at one of our students, who was trying to hit his golf ball but only succeeded in bringing up chunks of grass.

I gave him a confident nod. "I got this."

———

DURING SEVENTH PERIOD, I sat in my office working through strategies for the soccer team before our next game. We were facing the top-ranked school in the district. There was a lot riding on this win, for the team and for me. I wanted to preserve Coach Legrand's legacy.

Since this office had no windows, except the small square one in the door, it could sometimes feel like solitary confinement, and it was easy to lose track of time. A knock at the door startled me from my work. Amos waved at me through the window.

"Hey!" I gave him a kiss without thinking of who could see us. There were no gym classes and an empty locker room at the moment. Raleigh was on his cafeteria duty. "It's been too long."

"It's been a few hours."

"A few hours too long." Man, I was gushing. But after last night, I wasn't telling any lies. Waking up without Amos in my bed gave me serious withdrawal.

My hands clamped on his slim hips and ran up his sides.

"Hutch." He tried to squirm out of my grip, but his beaming smile told me loved it.

"What are you doing here? Came to surprise me?"

Amos pulled away from my grasp and checked out my office. There wasn't much to see. I hadn't decorated or put up any personal items on the desk, and the cinder block walls were painted in the ugliest shade of industrial yellow that Home Depot offered.

"I like what you've done with the place."

"I went minimalist."

"You should at least get a nameplate." He sat on my desk, which oozed cutesy sexiness. Yes, Amos was a mad scientist who was able to cross-pollinate cute and sexy into one look.

His ass got dangerously close to my playbook. I bit my lip.

"You just came by to say hello?"

"Maybe." He licked his top lip, sending jolts of hotness raging through me. "So, should we talk?"

I crossed my arms, unsure of where this was going. Amos's trains of thought didn't come with directions. "Talk about what?"

"Last night? You, me, the tree of death."

"Yes, all those things were there." I wasn't sure what he wanted to talk about. Amos liked to analyze things. Past moments were historical events to be pored over, whereas I preferred living in the moment.

"Mr. Bright." I stepped into the space between his knees and put my hands on his cheeks, where they'd wanted to go ever since he entered my office. "Talk to me. What are you thinking?"

"I'm not thinking of–"

"You love to think. A lot. It's one of the many things I love about you."

His cheeks reddened under my sturdy hands.

"Are we really making another go of this?" he asked in that pure tone like a child asking if there's a santa.

"Do you want to?"

"I asked you first." He dipped his forehead onto mine. "Hutch, I've spent most of my adult life trying to forget you, trying to forget the past. And now you're all I can think about again. So if this was just another example of people saying things in the heat of sex, I need to know."

He needed to protect himself. I could tell how awkward and tough it was for him to admit that. I didn't want to hurt Amos. That was the last thing in the world I wanted.

I wanted to be the one to protect him.

"Amos. I'm not going anywhere. Last night wasn't just sex, although sex was a big part of things. We connected." I put my hand on his heart, felt it beating just for me. Unless...was this him trying to get out of saying I love you last night?

"Did you say anything in the heat of sex that you wanted to take back?"

I steeled myself for an answer, and I watched the gears move in his mind in real time before settling into a calm.

"I love you, Hutch."

I'd never get tired of hearing him say that. It sounded just as good as it did last night. I'd been lonely and isolated for my entire adult life; knowing there was someone out there in the endless sea of people who wanted to be tethered to me was the best feeling in the world.

"I love you." I'd never been more certain about anything in my life. "My heart has never stopped beating for you, Famous Amos."

"If your heart stopped beating, you'd be dead."

"It's not as romantic when you turn my metaphor into a literal fact." I laughed into his lips as I kissed him. I pulled him close to me, his erection digging into my stomach. "Is this what you want?"

"Do you know that humans were able to evolve because of fire? Fire allowed humans to stay up late and communicate. My fire for you has continued to burn. That's a long-winded yes for you."

I loved my awkwardly verbose guy. Was he my boyfriend again? Those were details to be parsed out later.

"I tried not thinking about you. Didn't work." He shrugged. "Apologies for giving you a big head."

I cupped his crotch. "Feels like you're the one with the big head."

"Hutch." He pushed my hand away and looked behind us at the open door.

Somehow, looking at that door only made my cock swell up more because I knew what he was thinking.

"Fun fact." I kissed his neck. "That door locks."

"We can't!"

"Fun fact number two." I gripped his erection, making him let out an uncontrollable groan. "I can tape paper over the window."

"People could come into the locker room at any time. Put this idea out of your head."

"Fun fact number three." I grabbed his hair, pulled his head back, and licked a stripe up his neck. His pulse quivered under my tongue. "There are no gym classes scheduled this period."

"Still, you never know," he said between gasps, his whole body shaking with need under my touch. "A teacher could come in. Or Bryce the janitor."

"I'll take my chances." I stroked his length through his jeans. "Feels like you will, too."

"That is from friction and is not indicative of my current mental state."

"Okay, then." I stepped back, letting the air fill the space between us. "You're welcome to go." I picked up my playbook and pretended to study its pages. "We can pick this up later."

"Good. That's the sensible thing to do. Just because you can easily push me back on this sturdy desk and have your way with me, doesn't mean you should." He nodded and nodded, and licked his lips again, and if he bolted, I was going to have to rub one out in my car. That'd be sad.

"We're educators," he said.

"You're right."

Silence hung between us. The clock ticked on the wall.

Amos grabbed me by the whistle around my neck and pulled me against him for a hot-as-fuck kiss. He moaned into my lips. His cock was a rock hard dagger. All that talking had been outstanding foreplay.

He pulled on the whistle string harder, nearly choking me. "I don't know why I find these stupid whistles so sexy. Maybe it's because all the coaches wear them in pornos. They take off all their clothes, but keep the whistle on, which is very impractical but I can see the appeal."

"It obviously works for you." I whipped off my shirt, but kept the whistle string around my neck.

"Holy hotness. Did I say that out loud?" Amos raked over my chest like he was cleaning up fall leaves.

"You did. It was sexy."

Amos flicked a tongue over my left nipple, then my right. I bit back the moan that wanted to unleash itself. Between my bedroom and my office, we were doing a shit job of hooking up in places where we could be loud.

He dragged his fingers over my pecs and abs. I flexed them for show.

A moan escaped my lips when he slunk a hand into my waist-band and brushed over my bulge. His hands were magic.

He bit his lip so hard it turned a bright red. I tipped his chin up to gaze into his eyes. Yea, we were about to go at it like quiet chipmunks, but there was something special between us, something I wasn't going to let slip away again.

He slipped his other hand into my shorts. His sweaty palms massaged my shaft, sliding up and down my length. I yanked his hair and kissed him deep, moaning into his lips. He opened for my tongue, exploring his mouth aggressively.

"Fuck. Need it," I muttered.

"Tell me."

"Need to suck you." I wanted Amos inside me, wanting him writhing around under my touch.

Before he could respond with a witty retort, I pushed him back onto the desk. His tented pants jutted up.

I cupped his crotch, the heat of his dick burning into my palm. He rolled his head back, letting me take command.

Before I got completely lost in a sex haze, I taped the piece of paper over the door window and double-checked the lock. There probably shouldn't be anyone coming in, but I wasn't going to make Amos nervous.

I was on my knees in seconds, releasing his dick from his tight pants. It sprung into the open. I let it flop there for a moment. He'd once told me that he loved this feeling of his dick hitting fresh air right before a blow job, getting turned on by the transgressiveness of not being covered up by clothes. I appreciated how Amos thought about little details like that.

But it was time to dig in. I filled my mouth with his hot shaft, the salty pre-come hitting my tongue.

"Hutch," he whispered out my name like he was talking in tongues.

I cupped his balls and licked up and down his rod, taking in the heat and lust seeping off him in waves. I pressed my nose into his crotch, taking in his damp, musky scent. I massaged myself with my free hand. Tasting him and listening to him squirm under me proved to be a powerful aphrodisiac.

"This is so fucking amazing," he huffed out, need strangling his voice.

My playbook fell to the floor. He was on my desk. My desk where I did my job. He was all mine.

"I have an idea." He sat up.

"Now?" I asked. Leave it to Amos to get inspiration mid-blow job. "Is it sex related, because I have a one-track mind right now."

"It is. What if we were efficient and covered two dicks in half the time. Come over here. Let me suck you while you suck me."

"Sixty-nine."

"It'll be more like an eleven since we'll be stretched out, and you'll kind of be standing."

Math aside, I loved his plan.

I went to the side of the desk where his head was and dropped my shorts. My cock flopped in his face. He smiled as it smacked on his upside-down lips. I bent over him and took him back in my mouth. Despite the strange angle, we made it work.

Oh, did we make it work.

It was sex explosions all the way down as my cock slid into his throat.

The angle allowed me to take him to the base. I moaned against his cock as his mouth did wonders with my dick. He tightened under me, his legs flexing and hips jutting upward as he came.

I swallowed him clean.

"Fuck, that was hot," I muttered, catching my breath and standing up.

"We're not done yet." He smiled at me upside down as his hair fell in swirls like he'd been electrocuted. Had someone looked as adorably goofy mid-blow job as Amos?

I glanced down at my dick, hard as ever, in agreement with Amos's statement. There was still work to be done. I stepped forward and slid my dick back in his mouth. At this angle, I was able to cleanly fuck his face, sliding my cock in and out. I watched my thick rod disappear into his pert, little mouth. God, he looked so damn hot taking me.

I pulled out and had him lick my balls. My knees got weak at the sheer brilliance of his mouth. I had to up my game.

My cock disappeared back into his mouth, and soon it was too much to take.

"Yes. Amos," I croaked out as I came. He swallowed every last drop.

Amos pushed himself further onto the desk so he could rest his head. He sprawled and gazed at the yellow light in the ceiling.

"Doing it on a desk was even better than I imagined, although next time I should bring a neck pillow."

I massaged his head and neck on cue, not wanting him to feel any discomfort.

"So you're saying there will be a next time?" I arched an eyebrow.

"Oh, yeah." He reached for my hand, and our fingers slipped together in a sweet moment.

The bell rang, breaking our sweet moment.

"Crap." He shot up and brushed a hand over himself. "How do I look?"

"Sexy. Hot. You need your own calendar," I said with only minimal hyperbole.

"Not that. Wait, really? Thank you." He shook his head bashfully. "I mean, does it look like I've been engaged in sexual activities?"

His face was flushed, but it was also stuffy in this office. South Rock was known for keeping the heat cranked into May.

He gave himself a once over, and I appreciated how he could make me laugh. He picked at his clothes. "No evidence of come stains...same for you. We should be good."

Amos gave me a quick kiss, then ripped off the paper covering the door window.

Principal Aguilar stared back at us.

23

AMOS

Aguilar usually tried to be everyone's friend, the friendly older principal. But he was not smiling. His inscrutable face filled up the glass.

I looked back at Hutch, but he didn't have any grand ideas. My eyes flitted around the office, searching for a vent we could escape into.

I did one more check on both of us for any signs of sex. It was fine. We were in the clear. Why was I freaking out? We were two teachers having a conversation. Just because most of that conversation revolved around putting our dicks in each other didn't mean it didn't happen.

I unlocked the door.

"Principal Aguilar! How are you? Is that a new tie?"

"Good and no."

"Really? You deserve to treat yourself to a new tie." I held onto the door tight. Maybe when he was distracted, Hutch and I could run out. "How's Clint? Is his apple tree blooming yet?"

"Good and yes."

One-word answers were never good. Where was my chatty, aloof principal?

"Hey." Hutch half-waved at Aguilar.

"What was going on in here? The door was locked."

"It was?" I looked back at Hutch like that was crazytalk, but he wasn't following my lead. We had good sexual chemistry, but our improv skills left much to be desired.

"Really?" I twisted the knob to check on it. "Maybe it was accidentally locked. You know how doors can be. Hutch and I were just having a conversation."

"You were?" Aguilar scratched at his chin. "Because it sounded like you two were engaged in sexual acts."

Was it too late to climb into a vent? I could feel my whole body melting into the tiled floor. I did the only thing I could think of. I laughed. A lot.

"What? Are you...what? That's...you're funny." I looked to Hutch to join in my laughter, but he missed my cue. He looked away, his cheeks turning a cute shade of red.

Ugh, now was so not the time to be admiring anything about Hutch.

"That's what it sounded like to me," Aguilar said matter-of-factly.

"It was a heated conversation."

Aguilar cocked his head at me. Sadly, he wasn't as dimwitted as I wanted to believe. "Would you like me to repeat the things I heard?"

Never. I never wanted to hear Aguilar talk about anything relating to sex. Even when I helped him with his romantic drama last year, he kept the conversation G-rated. I was the one who went on a weird tangent about using a cactus as a dildo. Sometimes I wondered why I even bothered saying words.

"How long were you standing there?" I asked, my fake laughter turning into sheer nervousness.

"Long enough to know that the desk should be wiped down. Also, your cheeks are all flush, Amos."

"I'm sick?" I gave the most pathetic fake cough in history.

"Whatever just occurred on school grounds should not be repeated on school grounds. Are we clear?"

Hutch and I nodded, two boys who'd totally been caught.

"You can do that on your own time." A slight smile creased Aguilar's face, as if to say the principal side of him didn't approve, but the hopeless romantic side of him did. "I had a feeling something was going on between you two."

Did everyone know there was something between us? I missed my high school wallflower self because at least back then, nobody noticed me.

"Is this a problem?" Hutch asked.

My heart stopped for a moment. Was he going to call this whole thing off to save his job?

"Are teachers allowed to date?" he continued. He slung his arm around me.

My heart stopped for a totally different reason.

Aguilar let out a hearty chuckle. "Of course! There's no rule against fraternization. In fact, earlier this year, I too had a clandestine relationship with a student's legal guardian."

"Clint," I told Hutch, filling him in. "You guys are really cute together."

"We know. We've started a joint Instagram account for us and our apple tree and cacti. Our handle is JohnnyandCactiGuy. Clint wanted A Couple of Pricks, but I don't think the school board would look kindly on that. I'll send you a friend request."

"Oh, okay." Before I could object, Aguilar pulled out his phone and seconds later my phone buzzed with a notification. I steeled myself for my feed to be flooded with awkwardly adorable pictures.

Aguilar kept watching until Hutch and I took out our phones and accepted his request.

"I'm truly happy for you both. You're both a joy to have on staff."

"Thanks for being cool with this," Hutch said.

"Well, not this." Aguilar gestured at the desk. "While I pride myself on being a sex-positive principal, if I ever catch you having sex on school property during school hours, there will be consequences. Please take your exhibitionism elsewhere."

"Oh, we're not exhibitionists," I said, feeling myself turn yet another shade of red. "We prefer having sex in private. We had sex in his bedroom last night."

Shit. Why didn't my mouth come with a pause button?

"Do kids still say TMI?" Aguilar asked.

"I think so."

"Then TMI, Amos."

"Sorry about all this, Principal Aguilar," Hutch said, sounding like the voice of reason, whereas I was a sputtering fool.

"Hutch, I actually came here to speak with you." Aguilar went to sit in a chair but thought otherwise. "Unfortunately, one of your players is unable to stay on the team and he's restricted from playing in upcoming games."

"What?" Hutch stepped forward from the corner where he'd been hiding. "Who is it?"

Aguilar opened a folder in his hands. "Tommy Alvarez."

"He's one of our best offensive players."

Whatever high was left of this moment washed away.

"He's currently failing one of his classes, and it's school policy that athletes must be passing all classes in order to continue playing."

Hutch went white as I watched him trying to figure out how to salvage his team on such short notice.

"He's not the best student, but he's a hard worker."

"His work on the field isn't translating in the classroom," Aguilar said.

"We've got our big game next week. This could be our chance to be the top-ranked school in the district and make it to the regional playoffs."

"I understand that, Hutch. I want that, too. I want to see South Rock High succeed in all areas. However, I have a firm stance on this. I won't let athletics trump academics. Students need to know that their schoolwork is a priority."

Silently, I made a fist in support of Aguilar. I really respected his position, which was a tough one to hold firm to.

"Well, who's the teacher? Maybe I can talk with them." Hutch asked.

My entire body seized up as Aguilar flipped through his folder. His usually sunny face twisted into an uncomfortable frown.

"It's, uh..."

"It's me."

24

HUTCH

"Amos?"

He stood against the filing cabinet having trouble meeting my eyes.

I had the most important game of the year coming up, the one that could help ensure my place on the coaching staff next year and net our team a well-deserved victory that we'd been working toward all season. We were so close. Victory was in our sights.

"It's me," he said again.

"Well, I just stepped into a lover's quarrel," Aguilar said with a nervous laugh.

Now Amos tried to meet my eyes, and I was the one looking away. I had to figure out what the hell I was going to do with this nuclear bomb that just went off.

"Is there any recourse?" I asked Aguilar. "Can we get an exception?"

"The student can request a hearing, but he'll need a good reason to explain why he's failing. I know this is a surprise, but... it's school policy."

"Yeah, I get it." I gritted my teeth, as my championship season turned to sand in my fist.

Aguilar gave both of us a nod and reminded us to wipe down the desk before he left. It wasn't funny like it would've been a few minutes ago.

"So it's true?" I asked Amos once it was the two of us again.

"Yeah."

The bell rang again. We both had to get to class.

"Can we talk about this later?" I asked.

"He wasn't doing the work, so I had no choice. I didn't know about this rule."

I was too wiped to say something. I needed the escape of gym class to think about what to do. Maybe I could have Tommy work with Amos on extra credit? I'd figure something out.

I kissed Amos. "We'll talk about this later."

———

LATER DIDN'T COME until night, after a hellstorm of an afternoon.

Tommy came to me in tears, ripped up about not being able to play. I spent practice consoling him, giving him pep talks about how this was a speed bump in life.

But it didn't matter. He was devastated. He knew he wasn't the best student, but soccer made him come alive. I understood completely how crushing it was not to be able to play the sport that was in your blood.

Practice was a mess. The boys were sluggish and distracted.

Word had gotten out that Tommy wasn't able to play. Other players' parents called me freaking out about our chances of advancing to regionals and state. The gossip in school quickly turned negative, which dragged down team morale. We were so close, and this threw a wrench into everything we'd been working toward as a team. I couldn't let the bad buzz get in my players' heads or else we were goners.

After practice ended, I thought I could relax, until Chris Bergstrom showed up in my office. He was the director for all athletics programs in the Sourwood school district, technically my boss. A former lacrosse player, he was in his forties with a trim build and close-cropped blond hair that had some stealth gray sprinkled in there.

"Hutch. Good to see you. Have a seat."

It was never a good sign when somebody asked you to have a seat in your own office. I sat behind my desk, but didn't feel like the more powerful one. Bergstrom shut the door.

"What's going on with this Tommy Alvarez situation? Is he really suspended from playing?"

"According to the school's zero tolerance policy."

"I tried getting Aguilar to make an exception, but he wouldn't. We are this close to the championship. Our hopes lie with the hearing on Thursday. I got it moved up so Tommy could still play. I want you to attend."

"Me?"

"You can speak in support of Tommy, talk about what a conscientious player he is, how this teacher is being severe and unfair."

"He's not. Amos–Mr. Bright is a very fair teacher. He says that Tommy cheated."

Bergstrom see-sawed his head.

"Let him defend his actions. What we need from you is to talk about the Tommy you know, the one who made a tiny mistake and deserves to play. You can speak to the unique stress student players are under, which will show how unreasonable this teacher is being."

The whole thing didn't sit right with me. Not one bit. Did Amos know what kind of defense Tommy was preparing?

"I don't think he's being unreasonable. All my other players are passing. And Mr. Bright is a good teacher."

Bergstrom was losing patience. "Hutch, whose side are you on? We have a pathway to the state championship. That will go a long way toward you staying on next year, maybe becoming a staff teacher in the future. Remember, you're here on a trial run."

He stood up, narrowed his eyes at me with a matching bitter smile, letting me know that he wasn't bluffing. "Be a team player, Hutch."

———

BY THE TIME I had a moment to myself, it was early evening. The striking pink sky was one highlight. I beelined to the vending machine in the faculty lounge for the biggest bag of overpriced chips they sold. I gobbled them down in three seconds.

I took an Uber to Amos's condo that night. I had to see how he was doing, and I needed to feel him in my arms to believe that things would be fine.

"Hey," I said after knocking. His eyes lit up with such hope when he saw me, which made me wonder how his afternoon had gone.

Amos got up and grabbed me in a hug. It was the tight hug of someone who needed it. I pulled him to me, giving him the support and warmth he craved.

"Today was a day, huh?" I said, hoping to inject levity.

He groaned into my chest.

I followed him to the couch. He sat on the edge of his seat, still poised and on high alert.

"I'm not a smoker, but if there was any day for me to start..." He brushed a hand through his hair and heaved out a sigh. "Hutch, please know I didn't do this out of spite toward the team or Tommy."

"I know that. Of course I do."

"Tommy stared outright daggers at me during class today. Kids and even some teachers gave me the stink eye. Can you smile at me just so I remember what it feels like to not be hated?"

He laughed to himself about the ridiculousness, but I could tell it got to him. He was wired with stress. He was unfairly framed as the villain in this story. I caressed his cheek and mustered a loving smile.

"Turn," I commanded.

Amos presented his back to me, and my hands went to work on the most epic massage.

"This wasn't part of some evil plan." He dipped his neck. His muscles relaxed under my touch.

"Why did you fail him?" I asked. "If he was struggling, was there a way you could've helped him?"

"You're blaming me for this?" Amos sat up straight, primed like a cat.

"I'm not blaming anyone." I gently pushed his neck back down. "I just wonder if there was a way this could've been avoided. You said it yourself, no teacher wants to fail a student."

"The only person to blame is Tommy. I gave him chances. I was willing to help, but he had to meet me halfway. He didn't do the work, plain and simple."

"Maybe he struggled with the work."

"Then he didn't come to me for help. I offered to work with him after school, before school. He brushed me off. He couldn't care less and put in no effort. He had this 'I don't give a shit' attitude. Didn't study, didn't turn in assignments on time."

That didn't square exactly with the Tommy I knew. He didn't slack on the soccer field. But I believed Amos was telling the truth. People contained multitudes.

"We have a zero tolerance policy for cheating, which includes plagiarism. He barely tried to hide it, too. It was the laziest cheating I'd ever seen. It was almost insulting. He cares so little about my class that he couldn't even put in the effort to mask his plagiarism."

Amos slouched, defeated; Tommy wasn't the only one torn up about this.

"If he brings his grade up, he can go back to playing."

This was our final game of the season. The team's season-long drive to this championship was on the line.

"He works really hard on the soccer field. He knows he's not the greatest student, but he excels in other areas."

"I'm sure he does, but the only area I give out a grade in is Ancient History."

I paced to the window and admired his view. My stomach was a tangle of knots that I couldn't get out of.

"Maybe this is my fault," I said.

"Your fault?" He looked at me like I was crazy.

"I work my guys hard. There's practice, games, the pressure that comes with winning. It's a lot. It's more pressure than just getting an A. Not every athlete can handle the responsibility as well as others. It's hard to understand if you didn't compete."

His face became a white sheet of building anger. I was on thin ice, and any step I took would form another crack. "So because I'm not a jock, I can't fathom what hard work is like? You're defending him."

"I'm not defending him." I heaved out a heavy breath. Today was a never ending shit snowball rolling downhill. "The athletic director wants me to attend his hearing in support."

"You *are* defending him."

"I'm only going to show up to speak to his hard work on the soccer team. I'm not going to defend his plagiarism. I don't have a choice. If I didn't comply, he might not bring me back next season. And if we lose this upcoming game because we don't have Tommy on the field, then he definitely won't bring me back next year."

Amos rubbed his forehead. He let out a pained laugh, as if maybe there was a silver lining somewhere in here. "So we're both screwed, huh?"

I rubbed his shoulders. He let out a groan which I felt, too. I felt it so hard. My brain was exhausted.

"Maybe this isn't worth the trouble. What's the worst that happens if Tommy passes?"

"Who gives a shit about some history paper, right? I do." Amos pressed his lips together tight as tears beaded at his eyes. He was trying to push them back.

"I can't tell you how many times students have told me that my class doesn't matter, how many parents have complained that this class is pointless and shouldn't wreck their precious child's chance at getting into Harvard. History is never as important as math or science or English, right? I refuse to let them belittle what I do. They may not respect it. Tommy may not respect it. But I do."

After some wine and trash reality TV to take our minds off things, Amos and I went to bed. His queen bed was a big step up from mine. Soft covers, firm mattress, and no squeaking. I pulled him close to me and kissed the point where his neck and shoulder met.

"Hey, this is our second night in a row falling asleep together," I whispered.

Amos just patted my hand, no energy to respond. I squeezed him tight, letting him know I wasn't going anywhere.

The next few days were going to be hell, but we'd make it through. We had each other. I just hoped this shitshow didn't get any worse.

25

AMOS

The hearing was two days later, expedited by his parents in the hopes he could still play in the playoff games. Hutch and I got zero sleep the night before, and not in the fun way. After staring at my ceiling, I used my anxiety-driven insomnia to good use: I cleaned the apartment, drafted some lesson plans, and took some online surveys that paid twenty-five bucks. Twenty-five bucks closer to Rome. I put my sleeplessness to use.

Whatever exhaustion lurked within me was tamped down with coffee and a nervous stomach. I'd never been to one of these hearings. I didn't know what to expect.

The hearing happened first thing in the morning. Aguilar had a sub cover my class.

"Are you nervous?" he asked me as we walked down the empty hall to his office. I was literally going to the principal's office. I was never the kid who was sent to the principal's office.

Yes, I was nervous.

"Do you think I did the wrong thing?" I asked him.

"Not at all. But unfortunately, it's been moved above my pay grade."

The school district's three-person discipline panel board would decide Tommy's fate, and luck was on the kid's side.

I was reading online last night (or was it this morning? Time blurred together when one did not sleep.), and one of the school board members used to coach basketball. Another one played football for South Rock in the eighties.

It was the lowly history teacher up against the kings of the jocks.

"The worst that happens is you reverse your grade for Tommy, and he plays out the rest of the season." Aguilar shrugged as he opened the glass door to the main office.

It didn't sound so bad, but it was the principle of the thing. Also, I wasn't a confrontational person. I was ridiculously outside my comfort zone. Tommy didn't deserve to be rewarded for cheating. I didn't deserve to be penalized for upholding a zero tolerance policy.

"Oh, I forgot to ask, but did you and Hutch wipe down his desk from the other day?" Aguilar, with impeccably terrible timing, asked before opening his office door.

"What?"

"This probably isn't the best time. We can table that for later. No pun intended. Get it? Table, desk."

I didn't have the energy to humor him with a laugh. The man had really, really bad timing.

He motioned for me to go in first. Chairs were set up in his office for all the new people here. Aguilar's office was surprisingly spacious.

Three school board members, all men and all in brown suits, sat behind Aguilar's desk. They had gold name plates. Mr. Grenier, Mr. Camp, and Mr. Howard. Three men who looked like the human versions of the curmudgeonly Muppets who heckled Kermit.

On the other side were two groupings of chairs. One was taken up by Tommy, his parents, and a woman in a sharp blazer. The other was for me. His parents had the outfits of well-to-do people, and their stares told me they were having none of my teacher bullshit. The woman in a power blazer had on a poker face. Was she secretly on my side?

"Who's that woman?" I asked Aguilar.

"Their lawyer."

They lawyered up? Did I need one? My legal experience stopped and ended with repeat viewings of *Erin Brockovich*. I suddenly had the feeling I'd brought a rubber chicken to a gunfight.

Tommy played innocent well. He looked like a totally different student in his tie and button-down shirt, as opposed to the grungy clothes he usually wore.

Aguilar motioned for me to take my seat. He sat against the wall by the discipline panel members.

"We are here to discuss the failing grade Mr. Amos Bright gave to his student, Mr. Thomas Alvarez," the lead school board member, Mr. Camp, said in a stern tone. "We'll have Mr. Alvarez and his family give their side first, then Mr. Bright. We may interject with questions, and when it's over, we'll convene and deliver our decision. So it's courtroom-lite," he said with a chuckle, trying to inject levity into a place where it was not welcome.

The tension in the air stifled me.

The lawyer lady stood up and tried to maneuver as best she could in such tight quarters. Her heels clacked on the floor, each one hitting my ear drums. I couldn't even worship her designer shoes.

"Are we all set to begin?" Mr. Grenier asked.

The lawyer looked at the door. "Um, just about. Waiting for one more–"

Hutch walked through the door, looking not at all pleased to be here, with a drill sergeant-looking guy behind him. His boss Bergstrom, I assumed.

He met my eyes and gave me a supportive nod before he sat down on Tommy's side of the room.

"Thank you for meeting with us today," she said, turning on a polite smile for the board members, who were probably all straight and loving this. "Mr. Thomas Alvarez is a hard-working student athlete. He has practice plus a part-time job at his father's company. In between, he carries a full course load."

I tried to keep a neutral face. I didn't know Tommy worked another job on top of practice.

"He's had multiple altercations with Mr. Bright throughout the year, with Mr. Bright holding him to extremely high standards. He doesn't seem to like that my client sits in the back row."

I really tried to keep a neutral face, but she was spinning literary fiction at this point.

"Objection!" I called out.

"This isn't a courtroom, Mr. Bright."

"I'd like to object to what she's saying about me."

"Save your objections," Mr. Camp said with a condescending tone that old straight men seemed born with. "You'll have your turn to speak."

The Alvarez family ate it up. Hutch remained stoic, detached from their side.

"As my client has helped lead South Rock High to a winning season, the pressure has mounted. He's been working in multiple roles—student, athlete, employee. Mr. Bright assigned an extensive paper with a severe deadline. He seems to believe that his is the only class that matters to students." The lawyer let out a little scoff before reeling herself back in.

"Thomas tried his hardest to complete the difficult assignment with a ticking clock. He did voluminous research, but in his haste, he forgot to cite one of his sources."

It took every ounce of willpower not to object again, not to cross my arms like a petulant child at having to listen to this. It'd gone from literary fiction to the lead story of a supermarket tabloid.

"Mr. Bright was unwilling to understand Thomas's side and failed him. Does Thomas own up to what he did? Yes, he does. He's not perfect, just a hard-working young man trying to do what's best. But Mr. Bright was completely inflexible, and because of a vendetta against my client, he's taken away his chance to lead South Rock to victory. He's jeopardized his future, and by extension the fate of the entire South Rock Husky men's soccer team. We have his coach Mr. Hawkins here to say on his behalf what a valuable player he is to the team. We are willing to work with Mr. Bright on compromise. But this punishment feels, frankly, draconian."

She gave a nod to signal she was done.

"Thank you, Ms. Pike," Mr. Camp said.

She swiveled on her heel and walked back to her seat without looking at me. Though she had no problem pointing at me during her speech.

I couldn't see what she was saying to the Alverez family, but they were all smiling victoriously. Tommy shot me the scummiest grin like he owned me, that I was a pawn that got in his way.

I didn't have the heart to look at Hutch.

"Mr. Bright." Mr. Camp gestured at me.

I shot out of my chair, then remembered I had to keep my cool. I couldn't be defensive, but I also couldn't be offensive against a student. I was in a weird spot. I did not do well with weird spots.

"Ladies and well, just gentlemen of the jur—discipline board members." This was already off to a horrendous start. At least I wasn't slipping into a British accent. "When I assigned this paper, I gave the same time to complete it as I did other assignments. There was no unusually tight deadline. Every single student in class managed to hand in the paper on time. Tommy—Mr. Alvarez didn't merely forget to cite a source. He lifted an entire research article from an online magazine, word for word, paragraphs of it. There was no independent thought put into this paper. It was a simple copy-and-paste. I understand that Mr. Alvarez works hard at soccer, and I didn't know he had a part-time job, too. But he acts totally checked out in my class. Coming in late, not doing the homework, not participating, not asking for extra help. Every metric I have for grading, he fails. If you ask my other students, you can see that I care deeply about them and what I teach. I don't want to fail anyone. But students have to do the work. I gave the grade he earned."

I heaved out a breath, staying professional. I didn't look behind me at the Alvarez clan.

"Thank you for your time," I said to the panel, my heart racing.

Ms. Pike stood up as soon as I sat down. "Mr. Bright, I have a question for you."

"Are we allowed to ask each other questions?"

"In this part of the hearing, we are," Mr. Camp said, though he never offered me the chance to ask questions after her speech.

Ms. Pike clacked my way. "Mr. Bright, do you have a vendetta against my client?"

"No."

"Because from your statement, it sounds like you really don't like Thomas."

"I don't like his attitude in class, and I don't like that he cheats. But I have nothing against him as a person." After that sinister grin he gave me, I wasn't sure how true that still was.

"How did you discover that he had allegedly plagiarized?" she asked.

"I did a search online, and the text popped up in Google."

"Do you do that with all of your students?"

A pit sunk in my stomach. I knew where she was headed, and I didn't know how to stop her. It was that queasy feeling of knowing you were about to be outsmarted.

"I use an online anti-plagiarism program to analyze all papers."

"That's different from Googling?"

"I'll Google if something suspicious pops up."

"Something that doesn't 'pop up' on the anti-plagiarism software?" Her air quotes for "pop up" were lethal.

"Correct."

"And how many of your students required a secondary Google scan for this paper?"

"Just Mr. Alvarez." I hung my head.

"Interesting. So you don't think that scouring the internet trying to find out if this one student cheated counts as a personal vendetta?"

"No!" My voice jumped an octave, taking the panel aback. I tried to keep an even tone. "The writing in the paper sounded nothing like his other assignments."

"So you've memorized how all of your students' writing sounds? Or, again, just Thomas?"

I turned to the panel and to Aguilar, who had a sympathetic frown. "You would notice if there was such a big difference! It went from barely English to sounding like a history professor?"

"So now you're calling my client illiterate?"

"No!" I yelled, not caring how it made me sound. I was losing my mind, I didn't care if I sounded crazy because I wasn't crazy. And I knew that didn't make sense, but it also made perfect sense.

I handed over a folder to the panel. "Here are Tommy's previous papers and the paper he submitted. You can spot what a difference it is."

"Those papers are inadmissible." Ms. Pike gathered them from the table.

"So now we *are* using legal terms?"

"How do we know they haven't been doctored by you?"

"Are you serious right now?" I whipped my head to her, to the panel, searching for a lick of common sense.

"If you had enough of a vendetta against my client, who knows what you're capable of."

The school board members listened to her in rapt silence. My grip on sanity was fraying by the second.

I hopped out of my seat, only seeing red. "I am not the villain here. Your client cheated. Anyone could see that. Look at these papers!" I waved them in her face. Ms. Pike lurched back and let out damsel-in-distress gasp that she'd never do in her regular life.

"That's enough, Mr. Bright," Mr. Camp said, his face cold and angry.

Tommy snickered in his seat. His parents had the satisfied grin of believing Ms. Pike was worth every cent.

"Mr. Bright, sit down," Mr. Camp said again.

"Amos..." Aguilar gently took my arm and sat down beside me. I should've had a lawyer, someone from the teacher's union. I felt ambushed. Who was the one on trial?

"While Mr. Bright has been a dedicated teacher at South Rock High School for the past three years, frankly, I am concerned about his judgment and his fairness," Ms. Pike said, smoothing out her blazer, all poise. "Especially with his history."

"What history?" I asked. She spun on her heel, her venomous eyes directed right at me.

"Mr. Bright, you abruptly left your last school, a move that was still mysterious to the people I spoke to over there. Was there another altercation with a student? Another vendetta that you had to run from?"

I tried to answer, but my throat went dry. I tried to match her poise, but the room kept spinning. I looked to Aguilar, but he was as speechless as me.

"I believe Mr. Bright."

My heart stopped in my chest. Suddenly, all of the drama and mania cleared at the sound of Hutch's loud voice booming through the office.

"I believe Mr. Bright," he said again. His chin was up, eyes determined. "Amos is one of the most thoughtful, fair teachers at South Rock. He cares more about his job than every other teacher here combined. He doesn't have vendettas against his students.

"I recently started the process to study for my teaching certIfi-cation. I want to be a staffed teacher, and it's because of seeing what Amos brings to his job day in and day out that I'm inspired to do the same. Tommy is one of my best players, but if Mr. Bright said that Tommy plagiarized, then I believe him."

Hutch gave me a supportive nod that warmed every cockle of my heart. I wanted to run over and wrap him in a hug, but that would not have helped my case.

"Mr. Hawkins, you're here to support Mr. Alvarez, not Mr. Bright," Ms. Pike said with a tense smile.

"I won't sit idly and watch you destroy a good teacher's reputa-tion. And if that means Tommy is out for the season, then so be it." Hutch shrugged his shoulders defiantly. "Every player on my team is passing their classes without an issue. Also, Tommy's part-time job is posting to the Facebook page of his family's business. He's boasted in the locker room about doing next to nothing for it."

"That's not true!" Tommy's dad shouted. "Tommy—Thomas is an integral part of our social media marketing." Not even he could say that with a straight face.

Hutch walked up to the table and grabbed the file before Ms. Pike could stop him. He flipped through the papers.

"Jesus. It's like night and day. A squirrel could tell that this paper was plagiarized." He glared at Tommy. "You really thought Mr. Bright wouldn't notice? You didn't have *any* time to write this paper?"

Tommy hung his head, no victorious grin in sight.

"That's enough." Bergstrom stepped up to grab the paper from Hutch.

"No, it's not enough!" Hutch's yell silenced all of us. Even the school board members were scared quiet. "You were our star player! I came here to defend you because I always have my player's back. I was ready to go to the mat for you, even if it almost ruined..." His gaze landed on me, two electric blue orbs filled with warmth and emotion. He swiped the folder back and then slammed it to the ground. "This is garbage. You didn't even try. You have such little respect for Mr. Bright that you turn in this joke of a paper? Have you read this paper?"

He pointed at Tommy's parents, who had trouble meeting his eyes.

Ms. Pike stood up. "Coach Hawkins wasn't asked to speak. His testimony should be stricken from the record."

"Is this a courtroom? I'm very confused," I said.

Hutch ignored us, kept on Tommy's parents. "If you were in Mr. Bright's position, would you have suspected the same thing?"

Tommy's parents hung their heads. He pointed to Tommy, whose entire face turned red. But not as red as Hutch's.

"And instead of owning up to it, you're trying to what? Get Mr. Bright fired? Smear his name? One of the best teachers in this school you want to put on the street so you can get your way?"

"N-no. I just wanted to play."

"Well, that's not going to happen."

"The school board hasn't ruled yet," said Ms. Pike, the only person here keeping her composure.

"I don't care what they say. You're not playing one single second in a game. You're riding the bench for the rest of the year. Regionals, state, all of it."

"Coach!" Tommy broke into tears, but I couldn't enjoy the sight. I didn't have a vendetta against him. I felt guilty about ruining the season and Tommy not being able to do something he loved doing. I didn't want any of this.

Tommy was learning a lesson today, and the hardest lessons provided the most growth. Or so I hoped.

"Hutch." Bergstrom leveled his eyes at him. "Think about what you're doing." He turned to the school board panel. "Gentleman, Coach Hawkins is a very passionate individual. We want Tommy to play. He's been working so hard to get to this point in the season. Could we start his suspension next week as a one-time exception? Boys make mistakes."

"Just so you know, if you do that, I promise Tommy won't get one second of playtime. If he can work hard on the field, then he can put in that same effort in class." Hutch stared down the panel, daring them to try him.

"Hutch..." Bergstrom growled.

"If you want to replace me and find a new coach, then that's your call. But I'm not going along with this bullshit."

"You're going to give up the chance of a winning season for some history paper?" Ms. Pike scoffed.

"Yeah." He gave me a tight nod. *I got your back.* He turned back to Tommy. "The real shame is that Mr. Bright would've helped you. He would've bent over backwards to help you. You had the best teacher in this school, and you didn't even care."

Hutch marched out, leaving us all to catch our breaths.

26

HUTCH

There was no better balm than pizza. I dug into the delicious slice at CJ's Pizza and sunk into my seat. Gray clouds coalesced over the sky.

The bell rang as a new customer entered the restaurant. His bushy hair and wide smile filled my heart. Amos walked up to my table.

"Hey," he said.

"Hey."

He leaned over the chair opposite mine. "Have you ever seen that Tyra Banks meme from *America's Next Top Model*?"

"I don't know half the words in that sentence." My knowledge of memes and the internet fell off in my twenties as I tried to navigate the adult world.

Amos pointed at the chair, and I nodded for him to sit down. His face was aglow with excitement.

"So there's this meme of Tyra Banks yelling at one of the models, like going off, saying 'I was rooting for you! We were all rooting for you!'"

I was confused where this story was going, but I enjoyed watching Amos be this animated. "I'll have to check it out."

"You were Tyra today."

"Beg your pardon?"

"The way you went off on Tommy. *You were my star player!* I really thought you were going to launch into the Tyra meme, because you really were rooting for him."

I had no choice but to laugh. He was getting so into his impression, tossing fake hair over his shoulder. He cooled down, and quiet came over us. I enjoyed those times when we could live in the silence without it being awkward.

"Thank you for sticking up for me today," he said, his entire body earnest. I got angry all over again for what I witnessed in Aguilar's office. I should've stopped it earlier.

"I got your back, Famous Amos."

"The panel voted to uphold my decision."

"Good. They made the right call."

"They wouldn't have if you hadn't gone full Erin Brockovich for me."

I didn't understand any of his memes. Hopefully, I would learn.

His forehead crinkled with concern. Damn, this guy didn't know how cute he was. "Did I ruin your season?"

"Something I learned from playing and coaching for most of my life is that no team should rely on one player. That's a recipe for disaster." Having a star player meant creating a guy who came with an attitude. It meant off-kilter group dynamics. It meant all other players kowtowing to one person.

That being said, things were going to be more difficult, hence drowning my stress in greasy pizza. Tommy was one of the best on the team. I broke the news to my team this afternoon that Tommy was benched for the rest of the season. There was concern and shock, but to my surprise, a bunch of my players were relieved.

They shared stories of Tommy's huge ego, how he talked about himself as if he were solely responsible for the team's victories.

"The South Rock Huskies are going to be just fine." I gave him a wink. "I'm sorry for defending him at all, for making excuses."

"I get it. You wanted to believe Tommy."

"I just thought he wasn't a great student, but he's worse than that." I reached out for his hand. It was warm to the touch, and he didn't pull away. "I hope you didn't listen to anything that lawyer said about you. You're a badass teacher, Amos. You have more integrity than anyone in the Alvarez family. You're my favorite teacher at South Rock."

"I am?" The way his face lifted at my praise set my heart ablaze.

"Always. I meant what I said at the hearing. I want to be a teacher like you." I gripped his hand tighter, interlocking our fingers into an unbreakable fist. "Amos, I love you. I was terrified about coming back to South Rock. I thought I was a failure. But coming back has been the best decision I ever made because it brought me back to you."

His eyes welled up with tears. He swiped some napkins from the dispenser and pressed at his eyes like he was dabbing oil from a pizza slice.

"I love you, too, Hutch."

"I never want another pissant teenager or school board hearing to come between us again."

"Deal."

I slid my pizza slice over to Amos. He took a bite, and his cheeks bunched up with pizza. I was so overcome that I kissed him right then and there.

"Hutch, I have a mouthful of pizza."

"Don't care." I kissed his lips, tasting the savory pull of pizza and something that was uniquely Amos.

"So, you know what can help take your mind off salvaging your soccer season?"

I took a huge bite of my pizza. "More pizza?"

"Better." A sexy smile slid onto his lips. He reached under the table and grabbed my crotch.

———

FIFTEEN MINUTES LATER, we barged into Amos's condo like a summer flash thunderstorm, hands and lips all over each other.

"Shit." Amos winced as he backed into the table for his keys.

The smart thing would've been to stop kissing for five seconds so that we could find the bedroom and continue to the good stuff. But horny trumped smart every time.

We shuffled backward through his condo, hitting pretty much every piece of furniture. Dings and bangs hit our backs and hips. We laughed through the pain. Sex was a full contact sport.

I couldn't pull my lips away from Amos, couldn't take my hands off his hot skin. I didn't want to let go of this perfect moment.

I yanked at his tucked-in shirt. The thing wouldn't budge. "Jesus, it's like you have on a chastity belt."

We'd deal with clothes later. I picked him up, and he threw his legs around my waist. I led us to the bedroom.

"Ow," he said. We hit a floor lamp. "This isn't the way to the bedroom."

"Trust me. I know where I'm going." My dick was like a compass pointing north.

"You've been here once, and I live here full time. But sure, go off."

I slapped Amos's ass hard. I tugged at his lower lip before shoving my tongue back inside his mouth.

"Less talking." I turned us around and walked backwards. This way, I'd block us from any more furniture fails.

I let out a few expletives as I smacked my ass into each dining chair and dining table. Some kind of wire jammed into my butt.

"What the fuck?" I reached behind me. "You have rabbit ears?"

I held up the antennae. Had we teleported back to the 1950s?

"I need those to watch over the air channels that I can't get from streaming. Also, we're now fully in my living room."

Damn. He was right. We were far from the hallway, farther from the bedroom. Even gay men hated asking for directions. My back was almost up against the sliding door that led to his patio.

"Put me down. Let's go to the bedroom."

My pride, and the boner completely taking over my body, wouldn't comply. I threw Amos onto the couch and towered over him. I stared with heat and fire into his lusty eyes. Here was fine, and we weren't moving.

I kissed his neck as I unbuttoned his shirt, then undid his belt. His lean body quivered under me. I kissed down his chest, flicking my tongue over his nipple. His hips jutted up, wanting the main course.

"Someone's impatient."

Amos couldn't respond, just huffed out nonsense. My tongue dragged down between his pecs, down his stomach and swirled around his belly button. His erection pressed through his pants, the hard outline hitting my chin.

Slowly, for maximum torture, I pulled down Amos's pants, dragging them inch by inch to reveal smooth thighs and firm calves—and a prominent bulge in his underwear. But I'd leave that last.

"Hutch," he breathed out, his chest heaving for air.

I licked up his inner thigh, stopping just before his underwear, smelling the heat and musk coming off him. I did the same on his other thigh, trailing over light hairs.

"I'm taking my time with you," I said in a low voice. "Patience is a virtue."

"Not always!"

"Haste makes waste."

"Mother fucking goose," he exclaimed as I slipped a finger inside his underwear. Pre-come dotted the fabric. I was leaking, too. And fully clothed.

I whipped off my shirt and threw it on the floor. I yanked open my belt and pushed my pants to my ankles. I gripped my engorged cock for some relief.

"Uh uh," he said. "No touching yourself. It's only fair."

"You drive a hard bargain."

Very hard.

I slid a second finger inside his underwear, setting off another groan from his lips. I moved them across his sac and drifted further south.

As if I hit a button to reveal a secret passageway, Amos lifted up his legs to give me a better view. I made out where his underwear dipped for his opening.

Fuck, this was torture for me, too.

"Hutch. I need you so bad. I want you inside me."

My mind scrambled with lust. I was on the edge, ready to combust, as I dragged my two fingers to that glorious dip. He cried out in joy and relief while I circled his hole. He was hot.

I dipped one finger inside him, waves of ecstasy hitting me. Hitting both of us. He dug his head further back into the couch pillow.

I pulled him closer to me and frotted my dick against his opening. I didn't know what I was doing. I wanted him. I wanted to plunge inside him and fully claim him. But I was going to come the second that happened, so I needed to stretch this out. I needed to run out the clock. I never wanted to let Amos go again. No longer would I ever be that stupid.

Okay, patience stopped being virtuous. It was time to feast.

Off went his underwear. Off went mine, both into the pile of clothes somewhere on the floor. I smacked my cock against his hole, drops of pre-come slicking him up.

"I'm gonna make you come so hard."

I jerked our dicks in my hand. Amos writhed under my grip.

"Lube," he squeaked out.

"Where is it?"

"Bedroom."

I stood up and held out my hand. Amos would've let me fuck him wherever I wanted, but I also knew that he liked this couch. Sheets were easier to clean. And the bed gave us more space.

He jumped back into my arms and wrapped his legs around me. His dick smeared pre-come on my abs, while mine was excruciatingly close to his opening. This time, I didn't need directions. I maneuvered us expertly around the furniture, into the hallway, and onto the bed. Amos sprawled out for me, showing me his fucking sexy naked body.

I pulled the condoms from his bedside table and suited up, then got us nice and lubed. We were so turned on I couldn't tell where the lube ended and the pre-come began. I folded his legs over his head and licked his hole.

Amos fisted the sheets as I entered him with my tongue. Feeling him convulse under my touch electrified me, made me curse missing out on ten years with him. But life only moved forward. And I wasn't moving forward without him any longer.

"I'm ready," Amos said. "God, this feels so good."

For me, too. Every nerve ending in my body was alive.

I sheathed myself in the rubber, gave his hole and my dick one more coat of lube, and plunged ahead. Amos gasped as I entered him.

I held steady, waiting for permission to board the vehicle.

He nodded tersely. I sunk into him completely.

It was like home.

His warmth tightened around my dick in a tsunami of pleasure. I fucked him in slow, steady strokes. We weren't worried about being noisy. I wanted to savor this night and this man like fine wine.

"Amos," I cried out, begging myself to not come yet. Feeling completely overwhelmed by emotion and desire.

"Faster," he grunted out.

"You sure?"

"I need you tonight, and I need it hard."

I was not one to disobey my teacher's commands. I pulled him up to me, had him sit on my lap. He bounced on my dick, while I thrust up into him in short, rigorous humps. His ass slapped against my thighs. My arm muscles flexed holding him upright and against my chest. We made out in passionate kisses. I wanted to swallow him whole.

Amos's dick rubbed harder against my abs until he exploded between us, his seed painting my stomach. I locked him into a tight hug as I fucked him fast and hard until I released.

We fell back onto the bed. This time, no funny comments. No awkward silence. Just two men in love.

27

AMOS

"Mr. Bright, why are you smiling so much about the bubonic plague?"

I checked myself in the window reflection. Yep, I was grinning ear to ear like I'd just won the lottery and an Academy Award on the same day.

Sex with Hutch was that good.

Really good.

We were doing it a lot. My butt was an old pro. And maybe someday soon, Hutch's ass would get into the spirit, too. As I promised Aguilar, no sex on school property, including the teacher parking lot. Since he also had my back at the hearing, I didn't want to disrespect him. And I really like Bryce the janitor.

"The bubonic plague is not funny," I said to my students. "And I'm not smiling. I'm just..." Having the best sex of my life with the love of my life. "Really excited about history. I love this stuff! And I want you to love it!"

"We do love it, Mr. Bright," Rosalee said. "History is my favorite subject."

She probably said that to all of her teachers.

"Is the bubonic plague going to be on the next test?" Dale asked from his corner.

"The plague that wiped out one-third of the global population? Yeah, probably," I deadpanned. "The effects of the plague were massive. Did you know that the earth's temperature dropped in the aftermath because there were so many fewer people on the planet?"

Their eyes widened in surprise. See, history was more than a bunch of dates and wars. There was also disease and famine!

"Cool," Reyansh said. He pulled out his phone.

"No phones in class. What are you doing?"

"I wanted to Google it."

"Google the thing I just told you?" I heaved out a sigh known by adults who work with kids. My students could be incredibly bright and incredibly odd.

I glanced at the back row. No more Tommy Alvarez harshing the class vibe. His parents convinced Aguilar to let him switch teachers. The joke was on him because he was switched into Mrs. Herriman's class, a seventy-year-old woman who ran her class like basic training and took no shit from students.

"The bubonic plague was a rough time for the world. Things went dormant. But the theme of history is that humans are resilient. We always bounce back stronger. Out of the darkness of the plague came our final unit of the year, the Renaissance, which gave birth to artistic beauty and scientific advancements that propelled humanity forward."

Not to be that guy who compared his love life to major historical events, but maybe Hutch and I needed our own dark ages in order to appreciate our renaissance. Or maybe I had my head up my own ass.

"Yo, do you think a plague like that could ever sweep through the world again?" Dale asked.

"With all of our medical advancements and vaccines, I strongly doubt it."

I returned to my class to check my lecture notes. Behind me, someone tapped on their desk like they were starting a drum circle. It was a soothing beat.

Tap tap-tap tap.

I spun around. The tapping stopped.

"Who was doing that?"

"Doing what?" Reyansh asked, his stab at innocence a major red flag.

"We're almost done for the day. You can hold out a little bit longer to wild out." The class went quiet. That was my cue. "All right, now what were the–"

Tap tap-tap tap.

Dammit. I didn't catch who did it that time. It echoed from somewhere in the back.

"Stop the tapping, whoever you are."

Tap tap-tap tap.

Rosalee? She was all smiles as her hands tapped on her desk. Was this a revolt? The inmates about to take over the asylum?

"What's going on?" I asked nervously, trying to maintain some semblance of order.

Dale tapped on his desk.

Then Reyansh.

I took a step back toward my desk, wishing I had those secret buttons bank tellers had.

"Someone tell me what is going on right now?" I used my firm teacher voice.

The girl in the front row left corner held up a piece of paper with a large, bold P written on it. The boy one row over held up an R. Rosalee held up the O. Then one row over from her, another student held the M. The boy in the right corner held up a question mark.

I rolled my eyes.

"What did I say? No promposals in class. Save it for after. The bell is ringing in ten minutes."

Still, they did not listen. In the second row, the five kids across held up five pieces of paper.

P-R-O-M-?

Then the third row.

And the fourth.

They were all in on it. Which meant this wasn't a promposal for a kid in my class.

But for...

Hutch strode into the classroom holding a heart-shaped poster that asked *PROM?*

"Mr. Bright," Hutch said, all clean-shaven perfection.

He handed me the poster, his metaphorical heart.

"You've been holding onto a raincheck for ten years. This time, we're going to right the wrongs of the past. Amos Bright, will you go to prom with me?"

Every single student leaned forward in their chair, hanging on my answer. If only I could get them to be this engaged with our regular lessons.

Hutch stood there, lips slightly pouted, heart in my hands.

"Yes."

The class went wild. We were going to attract the attention of all neighboring classrooms, but I'd happily tell the story of how my class was interrupted for the greatest promposal in history.

I threw my arms around Hutch's neck and kissed him softly. No making out in front of students.

The class continued to clap and cheer. Music poured from Reyansh's phone. The day couldn't get any better.

Maybe promposals weren't as corny as I thought.

———

THE NIGHT of the game against North Point was an unusually chilly spring night, but I prepared with hoodies and blankets.

Chase and Everett joined me in the bleachers to cheer on the Huskies, while Julian went to the concession stand to get us hot chocolate.

"Did they design bleachers to be as uncomfortable as possible, or is that a perk?" Everett adjusted himself with no luck.

"You should've brought a pad," Chase said.

"I prefer tampons," he deadpanned.

"No. Seat pads." Chase lifted his butt up and showed off the South Rock-branded seat cushion providing safe harbor for his tush.

"Why didn't you share this information with the rest of us?" I asked him.

"I thought you knew. And bleachers are built with the bare minimum so they can withstand temperature and weather variances. Do you think padded seats would survive the winter?"

"Chase..." Everett started. He patted him on the back hard, making his glasses jiggle on his bridge. "Never change, okay?"

Their conversation ran in my background. My eyes were glued to the field. I became an avid soccer fan now that I was openly dating the coach. Jocks hung after class to discuss Husky games and our chances of making it to the finals. And I actually had an opinion now!

"Go, go, go!" I yelled at number forty-one, barreling down the field before kicking a clean pass to his teammate and scoring. I hopped up and clapped my hands as loud as I could. "Go Huskies!"

"I'm still not used to you being butch," Everett said.

Hutch turned from his huddle with some players and gave me a wink. After his promposal, he was officially out to the entire school and happy as a clam. He preferred it this way. He didn't want to make a whole coming out announcement since straight people didn't have to do that; he just wanted people to know and go on with their lives.

He turned back around, and I admired his ass in those pants.

I loved sports.

"How are we doing?" Julian asked, returning with hot chocolate for the four of us.

"We just tied."

I gulped back a nervous lump in my throat. The players on the field moved with a graceful fluidity, weaving between opponents, sending the ball across unimaginable lengths.

Raleigh climbed the bleachers with his current girlfriend. Was she technically his girlfriend? They managed to stay together for more than three weeks, which seemed like a record for him.

They sat next to us.

"Amos, what's up?" Raleigh gave me a fist bump. "Have you met Alicia?"

"It's pronounced A-lee-see-a," she said. Alicia had small town beauty queen looks and zero interest in what was happening on the field.

"Nice to meet you."

Everett poked his head in. "You guys are a little late. The game's almost over."

"Didn't know you were so invested, Ev. We had some, uh, errands to run." Raleigh gave us an exaggerated wink. Everett audibly recoiled.

"Look at our guy." Raleigh nodded at Hutch with the affectionate gaze of a big brother. "The Huskies were already the underdog going into tonight. The fact that he managed to salvage team morale after the Tommy Alvarez debacle and make this game competitive is huge."

"Do you think Bergstrom will bring him back next year?" It was still up in the air, and Hutch said Bergstrom had stayed mum since the hearing.

"Let's see if they can pull it out tonight. Either way, Hutch has already begun studying for his certification exam. And he has a great tutor." Raleigh cracked a smile, then brushed some imaginary, not-at-all modest lint off his shoulder.

I stopped Everett from recoiling. "He's joking, Everett."

Raleigh had taken Hutch and I out to dinner a few nights ago to celebrate the soccer coach of the hour for making it to the playoffs. (Alicia couldn't make it—she had a hot yoga class.) He could be a bit of an ass at times, but he made the most wonderful toast to Hutch. There was more to this cocky jock than my friends and I gave him credit for. Hutch was lucky to have him as a friend.

"Sometimes people make jokes, Ev." Raleigh raised his eyebrows at Everett. He had the secret combination to always get a rise out of him. "How are rehearsals going for *Curious Anus*?"

"It's *Coriolanus*," Everett said through gritted teeth. I tried my hardest not to laugh. Really, really hard. "It's Shakespeare."

I was about to diffuse the situation, when the mood of the crowd shifted. Excitement built. A South Rock defense player blocked a shot, then passed it to their offensive player. He barreled down the field, the ball juggled between his ankles in perfect precision. Again, I was amazed at the coordination and poise and skill involved. He darted around opposing players while dribbling, then with what looked like graceful ease, passed the ball to his teammate who, without a single moment's hesitation, kicked it into the top corner of the goal.

The crowd leapt to its feet. I screamed and clapped so hard my hands turned red. We took the lead. Thirty seconds remained in the game, and if we held our ground, South Rock would win. On the sidelines, I found Hutch, as I always did. He was poised like he was playing, too, deadly focused on the field. His body tensed as he watched his players, and I wanted to give him a massage. Maybe I would later.

"You got this. You got this," I said under my breath.

The crowd was a mix of ravenous cheers and those watching in silence, holding their breath. My friends were on the ravenous cheer side, screaming "Go Huskies" at the top of their lungs. Including Everett. So much for thinking all sports were useless.

The buzzer went off. The bleachers exploded with noise. I screamed until my throat went raw.

Everyone got to their feet, cheering and clapping and making noise anyway they could.

The Huskies jumped for joy on the field, running into each other in a big group hug.

Hutch looked over his shoulder at me, and I wanted to remember that face forever. Pure joy radiated off him. I gave him two thumbs up. He winked back at me.

Someone was getting lucky tonight.

Before we could continue our telepathic foreplay, his players dumped the water cooler of Gatorade on his head.

Hutch's white polo shirt became see-through, so really, we all won tonight.

———

THE BUSTLING ATMOSPHERE didn't die after the game. People mingled in the bleachers and celebrated on the field. I could only imagine the parties that would be going on tonight. I hoped students were responsible!

I eventually meandered to the locker room to wait for Hutch.

I waited outside with the other family members. I'd seen Bud in the bleachers for a little bit, but he went home shortly after the game.

Hutch appeared in a fresh shirt. Streaks of Gatorade lined his pants, though. He walked my way and scooped me into a kiss.

"Congratulations! How does it feel?"

"I'm exhausted, scared shitless about regionals, and have dried

Gatorade in my hair. I'm amazing." His hands cupped my waist perfectly, as if they were manufactured explicitly for this purpose. "I saw you getting into it. Yelling from the stands."

"Guilty." I flitted my fingertips through his sticky hair. "So where's the afterparty?"

"Your bed." He growled.

"Oh?" I felt myself blush.

"For sleeping. I'm wiped."

"Oh."

"But I might get a second wind later."

"Love it."

Someone cleared their throat behind us. It was a pack of someones that I recognized from high school. Hutch's old teammates. The guys had more adult looks to them, but their faces were etched in my memory. Seth Collins stood in the back, stone faced.

I tried to pull away. Instinct kicked in, and we were back in high school and found out. But Hutch wouldn't let me go. His hands remained stubbornly in place.

"Hey guys! Blast from the past!"

"Hutch, amazing game," said Spiegelman, whose freckled face had more weight, as did his gut. "I recognized some of those plays. Holy shit, that was awesome!" The other players concurred. Except for Seth, who remained stoic as ever.

"We didn't know you were coaching. Hell, we didn't know you were back in town!" said Laken, another former teammate, whose blond locks were starting to recede.

"Yeah, it all happened pretty fast," Hutch said.

"You've been here a few months! We should hang out." Spiegelman turned to the other guys, who nodded their heads and fervently agreed. "Get the old gang back together."

"You kinda fell off the face of the earth, man," Laken said, a little hurt. "We've all wondered what you've been up to. We want to hear about Nashville and everything."

"I...I missed you guys, too," Hutch said, almost startled.

"It's getting harder now that some of us have kids, but we try to get together once a month. Us, wives and girlfriends. Amos, you're welcome to join, too." Spiegelman's eyes were on me. My throat went dry from the attention.

Hutch held me close, not letting go.

"That sounds good," he said. "We'd love to."

"We need to catch up!" Laken said.

"I'm not the player I was." Hutch looked down. "I busted my ACL."

"Shit, I'm sorry, man." Spiegelman clapped him on the shoulder. "You're still the best player I've played with. If it makes you feel better, Laken's going bald."

"It's true." Laken felt his diminishing hair. The girls at school had once gone buckwild for him because of that mane. "I'll probably be bald in a few years."

"The good thing is that you're already ugly, so it won't be much of a difference." Spiegelman broke into a laugh. Laken smacked him in the stomach.

"You're one to talk with your beer gut."

"Hey now, hey now. As captain, I won't stand for infighting among players. You're both ugly sons of bitches," Hutch said.

Hutch was easily the cutest among them, but I'll admit I was biased.

They exchanged numbers, and the guys left. Except for Seth. He stayed behind, sucking all the good vibes from the room.

"Hey," he said.

Hutch stiffened against me, his body poised for fight or flight. "Hey," he grunted.

"Hutch. Shit, I want to apologize. I remember how things went down in high school. I'm glad that you two were able to reconnect."

"No thanks to you," I said. My anger over what Seth did, the fear he instilled in Hutch that robbed him of so much. "Are you here to call us names? Threaten to chase us out of town?"

"I said I'm here to apologize."

"Then apologize," Hutch said.

"I'm sorry. I am, really." Seth rubbed at the creases in his forehead, surprisingly struggling with this. Guys like him weren't used to apologizing. "I used to believe that stuff. Straight and narrow. That's how I was raised. I think in my head, I was looking out for you and also shaming you. It's fucked up. I'm sorry."

"It's very fucked up," I interjected.

"I have three kids. Got married to my college sweetheart in a shotgun wedding. Our oldest is eight and she...they..." He was like a dam trying its hardest not to break. "They are non-binary. She–they. Shit. This is all new for me, and I'm trying to learn. What I'm trying to say is that watching them discover who they are, how they've been teased in school, it's been making me think about how I treated you. Alistar is strong, stronger than I was at their age. I keep wondering how many people like me they're going to come into contact with, how many people are going to try and 'protect' them while making them feel less than, how many people will want to break their spirit."

I never thought I'd see Seth Collins cry, and I never thought I'd care. But here we were. Tears rolled down his face, and a lump formed in my throat, too.

"So I'm truly sorry for how I acted, what I said. For keeping you two apart. I quit my job and am taking some time off. I'm reevaluating a lot about what I've believed, what I've written. Could we try and be friends again?"

I turned to Hutch, awaiting his answer. His lower lip trembled with barely contained emotion. How could we have let one person cause this much damage to our lives?

"Seth, I appreciate you coming here and apologizing. Alistar sounds like a brave, awesome kid. I wish them and your family well. And I wish I could say yes, but I can't. Not yet. There's too much water under the bridge. I'm not ready to forgive. I'm gonna need a lot more time."

"I understand." Seth held his head high, but I could see the blow of defeat in his eyes. I didn't find enjoyment in this little victory, and neither did Hutch. "I'm not proud of what I did."

"I know. It's not all your fault. I need to take responsibility for my part, too."

Seth nodded, then Hutch, then I joined in, too. We were at a weird detente. This conversation didn't go how any of us expected. We exchanged awkward goodbyes. Hutch pulled me close, and we watched Seth walk away, a hunch in his spine.

I kept thinking about what Hutch said. We couldn't blame Seth for everything. I needed to take responsibility, too. I should've fought harder for him. I was defeated by one text message!

That would not be happening again. It would take a hell of a lot more to remove Hutch Hawkins from my life.

Hutch kissed the top of my head. "Ready to get out of here?"

"Yeah. Can we stop at Remix? I need a really strong drink after that."

28

HUTCH

I looked like a penguin.

Whoever decided tuxedos were required formal attire needed to be thrown off a cliff. Because it was prom season, the tuxedo shops in the area were down to their last rentals by the time I came in. It was slim pickings between the worn out tuxes with faded cumberbunds nobody else wanted. I got one that hadn't been used since the 1970s. Not even being the coach that led the South Rock Huskies to the playoffs could score me some nice suit they had to have hidden in the back.

The man at Sourwood Tuxedo tried to get me to rent a lavender one, but I was not brave enough for that.

The simple black tux was a smidge too tight in the pants, which had flared legs, and the dress shirt had ruffles. I was a soccer coach by day, time traveler by night.

I checked myself out in my mirror once more. My phone buzzed on my bed.

Amos: What time are you coming?

Hutch: 7.

Amos: I wish we could go there together.

Hutch: This is what happens when you volunteer for shit.

Months ago, Amos had volunteered to be a prom chaperone. He had to get to the gym early to help coordinate and set up. He tried to get out of it, so that we could go together, but Aguilar held firm.

It was okay, though. We didn't need a grand entrance holding hands. The secret of our relationship was out in school. Roping his class into helping me prompose gave it away. We flirted with each other at caf duty, and kids oohed and made fun kissy faces at us, all in good spirits. We held hands in the hall. Guys on the soccer team asked me about my boyfriend Mr. B. like they would've asked about my wife. There was no pushback, no protest.

A lot had changed since we were in high school. Although, had it?

What would the reaction have been if Amos and I came out as a couple back then? Would it have been the doom and gloom I'd been projecting? My friends and teammates would've been taken aback, maybe weirded out, but what if they would've come around? What if Amos could've come with me to prom, in my friends' limo and sat at our table like we were any other couple?

There was no use in thinking about what if's, but it was hard to stop. Fear really could do a number on someone.

Amos and I didn't need to make a statement tonight. All we had to do was have a good time. We had each other. And boy, would we dance. For the past decade, I've owed Amos a slow dance. It was time to make good on that promise.

"How do I look?" I asked Pop when I came down the stairs. He was standing by the fireplace filming me on his phone.

"Pop, why are you filming me?"

"This is prom. An important milestone in my child's life."

"In a child's life. Not a grown-ass adult's life."

"You will always be my child, whether you like it or not."

I tried to block the camera, but he stepped to the side to get another angle. I did not like being documented on his shitty, old iPhone. It was going to shut down if it had to do anything more taxing than make a phone call.

"I'm helping to chaperone. I'm not attending."

"Bullshit." He smiled over the phone. "Now why don't you pose by the fireplace?"

"By myself?"

"We can photoshop Amos into the frame later."

I did the most doubly of double takes. "You know Photoshop?"

"I checked out a book on it from the library. I'm trying to learn more skills as I recover."

"You know what they say. The fastest way to become tech-savvy is to check out books from the library."

"I can't tell if that's sarcasm or not." The man was having too much fun considering he wasn't the one going to prom. "Go to the fireplace and give me a pose. Do a *Saturday Night Fever* disco pose to go with your tux."

No matter how old you were, your parents could always find a way to embarrass you. The microwave beeped in the distance. When he turned to go into the kitchen, I stuck my tongue out at his back. In a mature way.

I checked out myself in the mirror above the fireplace, verifying that every hair was in place...and that this tux wasn't too embarrassing.

My nose detected a forbidden smell. I stormed into the kitchen, where Pop was mixing around his mac n' cheese TV dinner before sticking it back in the microwave.

"What's that?"

"Dinner."

"You can't have mac n' cheese. It's filled with cholesterol and salt."

"Remember when I used to let you order a pizza when I'd go to my poker night?"

"I was thirteen, and I wasn't having heart issues." I opened the fridge and took out the Tupperware container of the meal I prepared. "I made you grilled chicken, quinoa, and cauliflower."

"Hm, mac n' cheese or edible cardboard? Tough choice."

"Pop." I heaved out a breath through my nostrils, understanding why people found raising children stressful. "Fine. Have the mac n' cheese. We'll save this for tomorrow."

I stuck the Tupperware back in the fridge.

"I'm just trying to help."

"I know, son. That's why I love you." He pulled me to him and kissed me on the forehead, and even though I was a grown-ass adult, it still filled me with love. "I wish I could be there tonight and watch you dance with Amos."

"You want to watch us dance?"

"Damn right. I want to see you two get the happy ending you never got in high school. I feel so grateful to have lived long enough that my gay son can go to the prom with the man he loves. There was a time when they wouldn't allow gay men to even teach kids."

This guy. I was two seconds away from becoming a pile of tears. Add this to the pile of what if's: what if I'd had the courage to come out to Pop in high school? The people we knew the best still had the power to surprise us.

"I love you, Pop." I pulled him into a tight hug, squeezing him so hard so a piece of him could live inside me forever. I remembered when I couldn't even reach up to his chest. I was now taller than him, but he was forever the man I was looking up to. "You want a picture by the fireplace? We're gonna get you a picture by the fireplace."

In the living room, I gave a variety of poses for Pop. I rested an arm across the mantel and winked at the camera. I hugged the air in front of me so Pop could allegedly photoshop Amos in later. I posed on the rug in front of the fireplace and made finger guns at his camera. I even did the stupid *Saturday Night Fever* disco pose–and almost ripped my pants in the process.

Pop texted me the most embarrassing shots. Or rather, I showed him how to text them to me. I ran upstairs to my phone and texted them to Amos.

Hutch: Pop is going to photoshop you into these pictures.

Hutch: He knows photoshop.

Hutch: He read a book on it from the library, so he's an expert LOL

Amos: Is it weird that I found all of these really hot? [fire emoji] Especially the one of you on the rug.

Hutch: I look like an idiot.

Amos: A sexy idiot!

I smiled at my phone, imagining his face as he came up with that expression.

Hutch: How's chaperoning going?

Amos: I already found kids drinking from a flask. And they're on the prom committee! Tonight is going to be an experience. We're going to be narcs!

Amos: You owe me a dance tonight.

Hutch: You know it.

I poked my head up at the sound of a dish and silverware clanging to the floor.

Hutch: Pop got so excited about prom he dropped his mac n' cheese. I'm heading over. I'll see you soon. [heart emoji]

I flopped my phone onto the bed and jogged downstairs, dance songs running in my head.

"Pop, are you making a mess?" I hopped into the living room. It was quiet. Too quiet. "Pop?"

From the entryway to the kitchen, I spotted his legs sprawled across the floor.

"Pop!"

I leapt over the coffee table and ran to him. I kicked away the spilled mac n' cheese.

"Pop? Pop, what's wrong?"

His face was bright red and quickly turning blue. He clutched his left arm.

"I'm okay, I'm o..." He lost consciousness, eyes fluttering closed.

"Pop!"

29

AMOS

P rom was overrated. Or so I thought. All these years, I'd been dying to know what attending prom would be like. South Rock High held their prom in the gymnasium. Even with the streamers and decorations adorning the walls, and a DJ set up on a makeshift stage, the whole thing felt like an elevated pep rally.

But that didn't stop my excitement. Maybe that was the joke of prom. Everyone knew it was corny and silly, but we all secretly loved it.

Julian and I were stationed by the front door collecting tickets and checking purses for flasks. It was a half-hearted attempt to stop covert drinking because guys could easily hide them in their jacket pockets and we weren't patting people down.

I actually loved my position because I got to see everyone.

Kids filtered into the gym and beelined for tables, then the dance floor. My students cleaned up well. It was night and day seeing them in tuxedos and fancy dresses. The night began to buzz to life. The music was pumping. Some kids went right to the dance floor.

Renaysh and Dale entered hand-in-hand, eliciting a gasp from me.

"Good evening," I said to them, my eyes shamelessly going to their hands.

"Evening, Mr. Bright," Dale said.

"And I thought Coach Hawkins and I were going to be the only same sex couple here tonight."

"What makes you think we're a couple?" Renaysh asked.

I gulped back an awkward lump. "Oh."

"We're just friends," Dale said.

I desperately wanted to break open a contraband flask and drown away my embarrassment.

"Girls can hold hands. Why can't guys?" Dale asked.

"I'm–I'm sorry. That's great. You're right. We need to show our young men that they can be affectionate without society mocking them."

He and Renaysh gave me a stern glare that told me I was so not hip with the youths today. Until they broke out laughing.

"Psych, Mr. B!" Renaysh slapped me on the shoulder. "We're totally hooking up."

He and Dale kissed in front of me and kept walking.

"What was that?" Julian asked.

"I think I just got pranked, but also gay rights, so I'm not sure."

I took out my phone to text Hutch the funny story, but I could wait to tell him in person. When he finally got here.

He had said he was on his way, yet there was no Hutch to be found.

I checked my phone. No new messages.

Amos: I just found out two of my students are in a secret gay relationship.

Amos: I don't think it was a secret.

Amos: I think I was just oblivious.

Amos: Anyway it was cute.

Amos: [Smiley face emoji] [Rainbow emoji]

I wanted to ask where the hell he was, but I held back. I didn't want to be that boyfriend. Hutch said he was on his way. He gave me his heart emoji.

He would be here.

He wouldn't bail on me like he did all those years ago. But all those years ago, he was just as excited to come to prom with me. Until he abruptly changed his mind.

"Is Hutch coming?" Julian asked.

"What's that supposed to mean?"

He lurched back. "Uh, nothing. You said he was coming, right?"

"I did, and he is. So calm down, Julian."

I made a beeline for the punch bowl before he could say anything. I filled my cup to the brim with punch and cursed under my breath when it turned out not to be spiked. Would it be conspicuous to sift through contraband for a flask?

The fruity punch streamed down my throat as I tried to get myself to relax. Hutch said he was on his way. I had to believe him. Otherwise, that would pose a major problem in our re-burgeoning relationship.

Amos: Be warned, the punch will give you an instant sugar high. [laughing emoji]

I watched my text pop into the stream of our chat. Three little dots were supposed to pop up. Any second now.

Raleigh walked the perimeter of the gym with a watchful gaze.

"Hey, Raleigh. What are you doing?" I asked him.

"I'm keeping an eye on our students. Making sure none of them try to sneak pills, drugs, alcohol, or sex into the prom."

He had the determination and seriousness of a Secret Service agent canvassing a new location. I half-expected a white wire to be coming from his ear.

"I didn't take you as such a strict guy."

"I'm doing my job." He laughed under his breath. "Sometimes being a narc can be fun."

Raleigh had layers to him I didn't have time to unravel. And how could kids sneak in sex?

"Hey, have you heard from Hutch?"

"Negative."

"Oh. Okay. You know, my phone is busted. I forgot to charge it. Could you shoot him a text? He was having car trouble, so I want to make sure he isn't having a problem getting here."

"I have a portable charger with me." He pulled from his pocket a black wire attached to a thick keychain-sized charger.

Damn. I didn't take him for the type of guy to walk around with a portable charger. He had some nerdy dad vibes to him.

"It's not a charging issue. My phone is broken. Can you just text him?"

"Yo Hutch, where you at?" Raleigh narrated as he typed. He made a whole thing about hitting send.

"Thanks."

"Excuse me." He moved me to the side and launched up to a trio of guys congregating by the wall. He stormed into the middle of their huddle and smacked a container of pills to the floor.

"And what were you planning to do with those, huh?" He towered over the meek-looking students, who cowered in his presence. Their already pale faces turned whiter. "Get high? Drug some student's drink?"

"It-it was allergy medication," said a carrot-topped student. "There's a h-h-high pollen count in the air."

Raleigh's face dropped into the core of the earth. "Oh. Well, let me help you pick those up. The nurse may also have some non-drowsy Sudafed if you need."

He got onto his hands and knees with the guys and scavenged for pills. So much for being suave like a Secret Service agent. It would've been a perfect thing to text Hutch, if only he'd text me back first.

Soon, the music picked up, and kids flooded the dance floor. My sinking feeling sank lower and lower.

Something serious might've happened to Hutch, but Occum's razor was pointing to a more logical explanation, one that already had an established precedent. Hutch got cold feet about us. We could have sex and make eyes at each other in the halls, but publicly being together was a bridge too far for him. All this openness was too much, and he wanted to run back into the closet. Or maybe I was just the kind of guy not meant to be boyfriend material.

I leaned against the wall with the other social rejects as we watched South Rock High have the times of their lives. If Hutch and I were a no-go, maybe this was the definitive sign.

When I took out my phone to check for three little dots, I got an even more definitive sign. Hutch was calling me.

"Hey," I said tentatively.

"Amos."

I immediately picked up on the stress in his voice and told all of my neuroses to take a hike.

"Hutch, what's wrong?"

"It's Pop. He's in the hospital."

"Hutch. Oh my God. What happened?"

"Heart attack."

I felt like the biggest asshole. Here I was worried he was standing me up only to find out he was dealing with his dad in the hospital. I wanted to hold him and tell him everything would be all right.

"Hutch, I'm so sorry."

"I should've texted you, but everything happened so fast."

"It's okay. It's okay. Please don't apologize."

"I wasn't standing you up."

"I never thought that." He was dealing with so much and yet still thought enough to mention our date. Why did I ever doubt what a stand-up guy he was?

Hutch exhaled like the heavy breath of someone carrying the weight of the world on his shoulders. "He's in the ER."

I curled a fist in determination. I pictured Hutch all alone in an ugly hospital waiting room. I pictured Bud all alone on a gurney. Neither deserved this fate. "I'll be right there."

"But what about the prom?"

"Fuck the prom. I'm not letting you wait it out by yourself. I'll see you in a little bit."

"What about chaperoning?"

"The kids will be alright. Hutch..."

"Yeah?"

"It's going to be okay."

"Promise?"

"Yeah." I just made a promise I couldn't keep, but I sent a mental prayer to every god in existence begging them to spare this sweet man's life. "I love you."

"I love you, too."

When I hung up, I relayed the news to Aguilar and Julian, who were understanding. I made a cameo at the dessert table and slipped a few brownies into my pockets before hightailing it out of there. Since we couldn't enjoy prom, I'd bring a little bit of prom to Hutch.

30

AMOS

Bud Hawkins fluttered his eyes open sometime after midnight. He was not the virile, jovial man I'd had breakfast with. He looked frail and pale on the hospital bed, tubes coming and going around his face and chest.

But when he fully opened his eyes, I saw that same spark that met me at breakfast for some Froot Loops.

"You're not my son." At least he had his sense of humor intact. He smiled despite all the tubes criss-crossing his face.

"He just went–"

"Pop!" Hutch raced back into the room and swooped into his seat beside his dad's bed. He couldn't figure out how to hug without messing up the hospital equipment and hurting his old man, so Hutch stretched his arms over his dad's chest like he was a straitjacket. "I just went to take a leak. I wasn't leaving."

"I know that." His dad patted him on the back, but it had a firmness to it. He would've wrapped his son in a bear hug if he had the strength.

"Pop." Even pressed into his dad's chest, I could still hear his voice break. And that caused my eyes to well up with tears. I was witnessing a private moment, the awkward observer in the corner of the room. Would it be less awkward to stay and be quiet or to try and sneak out?

"I'm okay," his dad said. "I'm okay. Just a little scare."

"It was a heart attack." Hutch smoothed a finger over a bandage on his forehead. "And another nasty fall, too."

"The fall wasn't planned. That was the free gift with purchase." Bud's voice had a raspy softness to it that came with exhaustion from fighting to live, and yet I detected the playful tone I'd heard from our previous conversation.

The doctor and nurse came in to check on Bud's vitals and welcome him back to the land of the living. Dr. Kumar was an Indian woman who managed to project professionalism despite the bags under her eyes from a long shift.

"The good news is that you only had a minor heart attack," she said.

"Hopefully it doesn't get called up to the majors," Bud said. Did I detect a hint of flirting in his voice?

"The bad news is that it sets back your existing recovery."

"Fortunately, he has multiple seasons of *The Golden Girls* he can rewatch," Hutch said. He narrowed his eyes at his dad. "If you thought I was a hard-ass before..."

"Brown rice here I come." Bud winked at him.

"Thank you, Dr. Kumar" Hutch turned to her. "How long will he have to stay here?"

"For the next two nights for monitoring at least. We'll see where we're at in forty-eight hours."

"More time for us to get to know each other," Bud said.

Did Dr. Kumar blush? I was curious enough to look down and notice she wasn't wearing a wedding ring.

"You should get some rest, Mr. Hawkins." She had a light giggle in her voice. "Same for you, too," she said to Hutch.

"I'm not going anywhere." Hutch squeezed his dad's hand.

"Hutch, you don't want to sleep on those chairs tonight. You can see me in the morning."

"I'm not leaving you."

"I'll be fine. Right, Doc?"

Did she smile again? Maybe Bud is the man I should send my friends to for flirting tips, not Charlie.

"Yes." She turned to Hutch. "It's best that you get some rest, too."

"This isn't where you two want to be spending prom night."

Bud nodded his head my way. Dr. Kumar spun around, noticing me for the first time. I gave her an awkward wave.

"Hello," I said flatly. "I'm a friend of Hutch's."

"Bullshit. You two are boyfriends." Damn, Bud was like the king of PFLAG.

Hutch cracked a smile for the first time tonight, and it filled my soul with bliss. I would help him get through this. I wanted to make him happy.

Since we were boyfriends and all, according to Mr. Hawkins.

Hutch held my hand, interlocking our fingers for strength. "We'll stay a little bit longer, then we'll be back first thing in the morning." He pointed at his dad like a parent warning his child.

"So much for sleeping in," Bud said.

The doctor and nurse left. Hutch continued to hold my hand, eyes brimming with heart. I would be his pillar.

"So, uh, Pop. This isn't the place I thought I'd be doing this, but I'd like you to meet Amos."

I waved hello, just as awkwardly as before.

"Amos and I are old friends." He raised his eyebrows knowingly.

Hutch did a double take between us. He blinked at me, wanting verification. For some reason, I decided now was a good time to have some fun.

"We're close friends, actually," I said, getting on my tiptoes.

"We go way back. We've gone out to eat together."

"Platonically, of course."

"Pop, what kind of painkillers do they have you on?" Hutch's brow adorably wrinkled in confusion. The man could make being nonplussed smoking hot. "What's going on?"

"Amos and I are breakfast buddies."

Hutch continued to master the art of cute confusion by tilting his head slightly and quirking an eyebrow.

"When has Amos been over for breakfast?" Hutch asked, and when he figured out the answer, his eyes bulged open accordingly.

"I tried sneaking out, but the man made me join him for breakfast. It was the courteous thing to do. He shared his Froot Loops with me."

"Wait a minute." He turned to his dad and crossed his arms. "You've been eating Froot Loops?"

Bud had the sweetest guilty face, as if he were trying to deny it for a second but then just gave up.

"You were having cholesterol and heart issues, and you thought sneaking sugary cereal meant for kids was a bright idea?"

"I'm a kid at heart." He shrugged, and the connected wires and tubes raised and lowered with his shoulders, giving him a puppet quality.

Hutch spun around to me. I held my hands up in defense.

"Don't blame me! I was going along with it because I was caught in an awkward position."

Hutch began cracking up, the kind of genuine belly laughter that echoed in the room. We all joined in, and nobody had ever seen a hospital room so jolly.

"Pop, what am I going to do with you? I love you, old man." He kissed his dad on the cheek. Then he tipped my chin and gave me a soft, sweet kiss that still managed to bring the heat. "And what the heck am I going to do with you, Famous Amos?"

———

WE STAYED A LITTLE BIT LONGER. Hutch and I watched TV with Bud. By luck, Bud found a Golden Girls rerun on TV with a very young (and very cute) George Clooney guest starring.

Hutch and I held hands throughout the episode. He was texting Raleigh updates with one hand, while he massaged my palm with his thumb. I kept squeezing our hands tighter together, our bond unbreakable.

Hutch left to grab a snack and take a walk around the hospital to stretch his legs. Bud looked over at me, and a wave of awkward tension filled the room. I couldn't tell if it was one-sided.

"My son's crazy about you," Bud said.

"Likewise."

"Can you grab my phone off the nightstand?"

I got up and handed it over. Bud unlocked it and swooped through until he brought up pictures.

"Hutch did a prom photo shoot. I was going to photoshop you into the pictures, or find someone who knew how to do that."

I scrolled through the series of dorky, embarrassing pictures Hutch had sent me earlier, and found them just as charming the second time around.

"I wish I could've been there."

"I have a feeling I'll get prom pictures of you two eventually." There was an interesting twinkle in his eye that I clocked.

My phone buzzed with a text from Hutch.

"Hutch wants me to go to the cafeteria." It seemed like an odd request since we were supposed to be leaving, and the cafeteria had been closed for a few hours.

"I think you should go," Bud said with another interesting eye twinkle.

I took cautious steps backward and out of his room, like maybe there was a booby trap or something. Bud seemed very invested in me meeting his son at the closed hospital cafeteria. What if I was in a horror movie and didn't know it? Just to be safe, I looked over my shoulder as I navigated through the hallways.

My curiosity and paranoia vanished as soon as I pushed open the double doors. Twinkly lights circled the room, giving this drab cafeteria an ethereal glow. Hutch stood in the center as music played, dressed in his tux that had to be fifty years old. He extended his hand to me.

"What's going on?" I took a cautious step toward my boyfriend.

Hutch pulled me against him and positioned our hands for a slow dance. "Since we couldn't go to prom together, I had prom come to us."

I followed the source of the twinkling lights to a disco ball strung up on the ceiling, hanging from an existing hook. Everett, Chase, and Julian stood at the side, shining flashlights at the ball giving the room the twinkling effect.

"I called in some help," Hutch admitted.

Streamers ran haphazardly across the cafeteria, their ends taped to the wall. It was hasty and sloppy but full of love, like a child's picture for his parents.

"You didn't have to do this," I said, gazing into his eyes and letting the world fade away. "Your dad is recovering. You have a lot on your plate."

"It was Pop's idea."

"I think Pop is my new best friend." I laughed into his shoulder. He kissed the top of my head with such tenderness, I never wanted to leave his embrace. "This explains his coy smile in the room."

"Pop's not great at keeping secrets." Hutch looked every bit the prom king. "I really wanted to go to prom with you tonight. Once again, history repeats itself."

"I like this better."

"We're not done."

Raleigh exited from the door leading to the kitchen with two plastic crowns in hand. He still had on his tux. He cleared his throat. "Hear ye, hear ye. The votes have been tallied, and I would like to announce this year's South Rock High School Prom King and King. Being a former Prom King myself, I know what a big honor this is."

I couldn't help myself and glanced over to clock Everett's inevitable eye roll.

Raleigh opened an envelope and paused for suspense.

"Your prom king and king are...Hutch Hawkins and Amos Bright."

My friends clapped for us, causing their flashlights to jumble light around in an oddly cool effect.

"Kneel so I can place your crown on," Raleigh said.

"Dude." Hutch shot him a look. "This tux is rented."

"It's a good thing I'm tall then."

In the background, I heard a very faint "barf" from the world's most opinionated drama teacher.

I knew it was a dollar store crown, and I knew nobody voted for us because I knew this wasn't prom. But the moment still gave me chills. At least in this cafeteria hospital, I was prom king with the man I loved. And damn if Hutch couldn't make a cheap crown look regal. I was totally making him wear it during future sex.

"And as is custom, our prom king and king will now partake in a traditional slow dance. Deejay..." Raleigh pointed at Julian, who switched to a new song.

One Direction's "You & I" filled the room, its melodies eliciting the same lump-in-my-throat feeling from me. Hutch held me close, swaying our bodies to the soft rhythm of the song. Every time I looked up from his shoulder, he was gazing at me like I was the Mona Lisa.

"I love this song," I said.

"This is the song you wanted us to dance to at prom. It was also on your Spotify playlist."

"Called Prom Songs." Senior year, I made him a playlist of songs we could dance to at prom. The realization smacked me in the face. "This is the playlist."

His big smile let me know I was correct.

"Hutch." I was overcome by this moment, by him. I had wanted this for so long. The more I told myself Hutch was a distant memory, the more he burned bright in my mind. Real love couldn't be ignored.

We enjoyed our slow dance, my head on his shoulder and the blissful feeling of things feeling right in my world.

"This is the best prom I've ever been to," I said.

"Is it what you imagined?"

"No." I kissed him, one in a long line of kisses I planned to give him throughout our lives. "Better."

31

HUTCH

A few weeks later, there was much celebrating to be had. It was the end of another school year, the end of my first season coaching soccer, and the (re)start of a wonderful relationship with Amos.

On the final day of exams, Aguilar had the teachers over to his house for karaoke and cocktails. He lived in a cute house with his boyfriend Clint, who had a mini apple orchard growing in his backyard, and Clint's nephew Terence who'd graduated from South Rock two years ago. Clint worked in construction and had added lots of little custom touches throughout the house, like unique moldings and a special shelf for Aguilar's cacti collection.

Chase and the science teachers played beer pong on the patio table outside, while Raleigh was double-fisting two drinks.

It wasn't only students who needed to let off steam after another school year. And here I used to think teachers dreaded the school year ending. For some reason, I pictured them solemnly returning home dreading three months without us.

I was very wrong.

"Hey Rafael, is it possible to make me a triple Rum and Coke?"

asked Marnie Washington, a seemingly mild-mannered English teacher who wore cute skirts and cat-eye glasses. It was weird hearing Aguilar called by his first name.

"I don't have a glass big enough," Aguilar said back.

"Then I'll do a Rum and Coke and two shots of rum on the side."

I raised my eyebrows. If only students knew what their teachers were like.

"Don't give me that judgmental face, Hutch Hawkins. I already have students emailing me questions about the summer reading list and parents complaining about the books I put on there. You think coaching a bunch of kids to kick a ball into a net is tough? Try getting them to read Ernest Hemingway." She downed both shots and waltzed away with her mixed drink.

I held up my beer to her back. "We're on the same team, Marnie."

She swiveled around and blew me a playful kiss, then joined her fellow English teachers.

"Maybe I should do a shot," I said to Aguilar.

"You should!" Clint swooped in to help Aguilar behind the bar, which consisted of giving the principal butterfly kisses. Clint's flannel and worn-out jeans were a sharp contrast to the shirt and tie Aguilar had on. They made a freaking adorable couple. "You deserve to celebrate!"

"I'm not sure about that."

"Don't be modest. You led the Huskies to regionals."

"We lost regionals."

"But you got there! In your first season as Coach," Aguilar chimed in. "That's very impressive."

Amos swept in next to me. "You got the team to its first regional championship game in five years despite losing your top player to an academic scandal. Your team had its highest goal average and passes per game average in two years. I'd say that was impressive."

Amos had been studying his soccer stats and regularly watching games with me, and it was such a turn on to listen to him talk sports.

He held up the shot to my lips. "You deserve this."

I supposed I did. Bergstrom officially offered me a contract to stay on as soccer coach. Even Coach Legrand called me and congratulated me on a great season. Yeah, we weren't regional or state champs, but there was always next year. Not bad for a rookie coach.

So maybe I did deserve a celebratory shot. I downed it before I could second-guess myself.

I wrapped my arms around Amos's slim waist. "I couldn't have done it without you."

"I'm not sure what I did to help besides picking off your top player, but I'll take praise where I can get it."

Amos rested his forehead against mine, and for a second, everything around us turned to glorious white noise.

"You know, I suspected there was a connection between you two." Aguilar poured himself a drink while Clint did us all a favor and loosened his tie. "I remember when I brought Hutch around that first day. There was this feeling in the air."

From what I remembered, Aguilar was one hundred percent oblivious.

"This tension," he continued.

"It was a mix of shock, awkwardness, anger, and a splash of sexual tension," Amos said.

Aguilar turned to Clint. "You know, it was my idea to put them together on caf duty."

"Where would we be without you?" I asked with a healthy hint of sarcasm.

"I was returning the favor. Did you know Amos helped me and

Clint get together?" Aguilar clinked his glass against Amos's, who blushed.

"I didn't know you were a matchmaker, Famous Amos."

"I wasn't a matchmaker. Clint and Rafael were anonymous pen pals debating whether or not to meet in person, and I gave a very crucial pep talk."

Aguilar cocked his head. "Which you ended by talking about sticking one of my cacti up your–"

"That was a misunderstanding!" Amos turned a bright red. "I was making a joke. An observation. An observation that was meant as a joke."

"About fucking a cactus?" I asked.

"The point is, I was happy to help two old men find love."

Clint brushed a loving hand through his boyfriend's hair. I hoped Amos and I were that into each other when we hit our forties.

"How's Terence doing?" Amos asked.

"Fantastic. He's kicking ass in community college. Ended his first year with all A's and one B. He's planning on applying to four-year colleges next year, may even try for Cornell." Clint and Aguilar beamed like proud surrogate papas. "He's out with friends tonight. He didn't want to party with his old teachers, which I get."

Aguilar turned to his boyfriend, a curious thought forming on his face. "Babe, do you ever notice that Terence makes himself scarce whenever I take out the karaoke machine?"

"What? Really? That's just a coincidence." Clint raised his eyebrows as he downed his drink.

Amos and I took our drinks and meandered outside. "Do you want to play cornhole?" he asked.

"You got it." Cornhole, or bags as I'd heard others call it, was a bean bag tossing game. Players had to toss bean bags onto the opposing team's board, a slanted wooden slab with a hole, the titular cornhole, in the middle. Extra points were awarded to those who got the bean in the hole. Raleigh and I had been eyeing it since we walked in.

Amos waved me over to the cornhole setup. I curled my arm around his waist like it was a natural reaction.

"It's you and me versus Raleigh and Everett," he said while sipping his beer.

"Not by choice." Everett glared at Raleigh then looked away. "I wanted to do a nerds versus jocks game, but Amos overruled me. Said it was too on the nose."

"And I wanted to team with Hutch because I wanted to win, but oh well. I guess second place is good enough," Raleigh said, cocking an eyebrow at Everett.

"Do you ever listen to yourself?" Everett asked his teammate.

"There are clips of me on YouTube, so in theory I could." Raleigh cheers'd his pint glass at his teammate.

"Can we pause the Civil War for one game?" I asked.

Everett and Raleigh shared one final acrimonious glare, then a begrudging nod.

"Good. We'll start." I slapped Amos's ass to signal his turn. He bit his lip, seemingly turned on. That could come later. First, we had to win.

Amos tossed the first bean bag. It hurtled in the air and landed an inch in front of the cornhole board.

"You can go first," Raleigh said to his teammate. "It might take you a few rounds to warm up, and that's okay."

"Thanks for the vote of confidence." Everett shook his head and shot Amos a not-so-secretive eye roll. His bean bag soared in the air and landed on the rim of the cornhole.

"Damn. I guess you're all warmed up."

I went, then Raleigh, and on and on, bean bags flying in the summer sun. Raleigh was his gym teacher self, trying to coach Everett on his toss. Everett was stubbornly having none of it.

Amos and I gave each other little touches and pats as we

passed each other to throw. It was all massive foreplay for what would come later. I didn't think I'd have energy for sex after a long day. I was ready to be proven wrong.

Everett and Raleigh gave us surprising competition. Once they put their dislike of each other to the side, they became a formidable team. Everett eventually took Raleigh's coaching to heart, and his aim improved. They started hi-fiving each other, then back pats, then acting like they were friends.

"There you go! That's how it's done!" Raleigh yelled after Everett sunk a bag into the hole.

"Just trying to pick up your slack," Everett sniped back, getting in his face with a smarmy smile.

"There is no slackage on my end. I had the perfect shot last round, but there was a gust of wind at the last second." Raleigh cocked an eyebrow to go with his sly grin.

"And I believe that story you're telling yourself is fiction."

"I think I know what I'm doing, Ev."

"Whatever you say, Ral."

Amos had the same confused look as I did. Were these guys flirting with each other? Was this a new, ahem, whole for Raleigh to explore?

Before I could make heads or tails of it, I tossed my bag way off course. It landed in a cactus pot. That was the ballgame. Everett and Raleigh hi-fived. Raleigh mussed up his hair, which made Everett's pale skin go extra red.

"See what happens when you embrace teamwork, Ev?" Raleigh said.

"I admit, being on the same team as you makes your cockiness more bearable."

"Rematch?" Amos asked them.

A familiar blonde ran over and hugged Raleigh hello before he could answer. "Hey, babe!"

Raleigh kissed Alicia—wait, no, he was onto Svetlana now—and grabbed her ass as he lifted her up. "You're here early."

"I left work early. It's so nice out and the store was slow."

"Did you tell your manager?" Raleigh asked her. "I thought you were working at the store solo today."

"I texted him and left a note on the window that we had a power outage and had to close early. He'll understand. Let's go for a drive!" She had the bounce of a girl who never left her sorority. Her hair swished into Amos's face.

"Let's do it!" Raleigh gave her a sloppy kiss on the mouth and another ass grab. Did all opposite sex couples look like that when they made out? "I'm gonna head out," he said to me.

"Cool." We fist-pumped.

"We'll do a study session this week. Get you certified by the end of summer."

"Deal." I was looking forward to Raleigh helping me get my teaching certification.

He fist-bumped Amos and then Everett, who seemed not into the whole thing.

"Nice work, teammate," Raleigh said.

"Let's never tell anyone this happened," Everett shot back.

Raleigh and Svetlana left. Everett watched them go, lingering on the door for an extra moment after they were long gone.

———

ALTHOUGH IT WASN'T my graduation, I got surprisingly emotional watching my students step onto the podium to receive their diplomas. Even my gym students, who could barely take golfing seriously, made me get a lump in my throat. They'd made gym class fun, and I was probably never going to see most of them again after tonight.

Man, that got bleak fast.

Summer got off to a fantastic start. Amos took on a job at For Goodness Cakes, a bakery in downtown Sourwood. It added money to his travel fund. He brought home a cupcake or brownie for us to share on his patio while we watched the sun set over the river and mountains.

I picked up extra cash teaching soccer camps and being a ref for summer leagues. The rest of my time was spent studying, going to Remix and Musical Mondays with friends, grabbing beers with Raleigh, and taking care of Pop. I had more of a social life six months after moving back home than I had through my entire professional soccer career.

"You and Amos should move in together."

Pop grilled out for the Fourth of July, and his suggestion landed like the fireworks we'd be watching later tonight.

Amos looked up from his corn on the cob. A few seconds ago, we'd been talking about the best walking trails in town now that Pop had regained some of his strength. He was not one for segues.

"Pop, you really want me gone, huh?"

"You spend enough time over there. Have you guys talked about it?"

The truth was...we hadn't. Which was crazy now that he mentioned it. I'd been spending three or four nights a week over at Amos's place. His bed could fit both of us, and we didn't have to be worried about being quiet. Aside from sex, though, it was nice to have a place that wasn't decked out in my old high school glory.

His condo felt like a home to me. But it wasn't mine.

I waited for Amos to say something. What if I was spending too much time over there and he felt awkward saying something?

"Pop, I don't want to leave you alone. You're still recovering."

"I'm doing great. I'm going back to work in mid-July. Finally!"

I leapt out of my lawn chair. "You are?"

News to me.

"I just got it cleared with the MacArthur Center and Sarita. I finished all of *The Golden Girls, The Golden Palace,* and the spinoff *Empty Nest.* The timing is perfect!"

"Pop, are you sure? I mean, I can stay here, make sure you're okay."

"Hutch, I'll be fine. Have a hot dog." He literally handed me a hot dog in a bun. "And speaking of hot dogs, you haven't answered my question about co-habitating."

Amos choked on his corn. I went Hawaiian Punch red. I prayed Pop never tried to tell anyone a gay joke. I'd never be able to look at a hot dog the same way again.

"We'll think about it," I said and gave Amos a grateful grin for putting up with my probably senile father.

"I don't need to think about it. I'm for it." Amos shrugged his shoulders as if it were clear as day. "You're over at my place a lot already. Might as well pay some rent and use the extra closet."

For a guy who could be neurotic and opposed to making a clear decision, his confidence unnerved me.

"Are you sure about this?" I asked.

"Are you?"

Living with Amos sounded like the dream. And not gonna lie, so did the extra closet.

"Hell yeah." I bit into my hot dog.

"Make sure he cleans."

I turned around and glared at Pop. "Since when do I not clean?"

"Just saying..."

Amos grabbed me by the shirt and pulled me to him for a kiss that rivaled all the fireworks lighting up the sky.

"Wait." I removed myself from my darling boyfriend and turned back to Pop. "Who's Sarita?"

"My doctor." He had a coy smile on.

"Dr. Kumar from the hospital who you were blatantly flirting with an hour after having a heart attack?"

"Having a near death experience showed me I had to start living."

"With your doctor?"

"We can't choose who we love. Love is love is love, according to Manuel Lin-Miranda."

"It's Lin-Manuel Miranda."

"She's a lovely woman. And now that Bud doesn't need to troll Milkman to find you a boyfriend, he can focus on his own love life." Amos reached over and gave Pop a fist bump.

"What's this?" I waved my finger between them. "Since when are you two friends?"

And since when did Amos fist bump?

"Now that it's summer, I stop by for Breakfast with Bud on Fridays."

"Breakfast with Bud is a thing?" I asked.

"He brings me Froot Loops." Pop had the happiest grin. Apparently watching his son go insane with confusion was a parental highlight.

"Sarita and I have a date scheduled for this week." Pop raised his eyebrows. "And I already cleared it with my doctor that I can take Viagra."

"Dr. Kumar *is* your doctor!"

"And she very much approves." Pop broke into a hearty laugh.

"Gross." That was one pill I would not be monitoring for him.

The backyard filled with the laughter of Pop and Amos, my two favorite people in the world. I pinched myself for how great things had turned out with my life. When I got cut from the Troubadours, it was like falling into a hole that I thought I'd never be able to climb out of. But thanks to the love of Amos, and the support of Pop and my new friends, I'd not only escaped that hole, but I'd soared to unimaginable heights.

And so long as I didn't have to keep hearing about my elderly father's sex life, the best was yet to come.

32

HUTCH
THREE MONTHS LATER

T he alarm clock blared at full blast. I reached my hand out from spooning my boyfriend to slap it quiet. I kept missing, though, hitting every other object on my nightstand until finally I knocked the clock to the floor, where it continued to blare and beep like we were under imminent nuclear attack.

"Nice job," Amos said in his growly sleepy voice. He shoved a pillow over his head to block out the blaring noise.

I hobbled out of bed and dug out the clock, which had managed to fall into the wastebasket and tip it behind the floor-length curtains. This thing was like the girl who fell down a well.

I pulled it from the trash and raised it high over my head, yanking the cord from the outlet and vanquishing the beast.

"I rule."

Amos leaned onto an elbow to take in the sight of his stark naked boyfriend hoisting an alarm clock radio into the air. Mostly, he was taking in the stark nakedness, his eyes stopping at crotch level.

"Happy first day of school to me."

Living with Amos had really been the dream, no doubt. We

managed to spend more time together without being on top of each other. I got to wake up to his beautiful face, make dinner together, and cuddle on the couch as we watched TV programming not from the 1990s. Amos was also chill about my stuff being everywhere. He really wanted the place to be for both of us.

Amos began making breakfast. I sat on the foot of the empty bed, wiping the last bits of sleep from my eyes. There were pieces of me throughout the bedroom. Old posters, soccer memorabilia, an old jersey, my teaching books. I was originally nervous about moving in because this was Amos's place. I didn't want to feel like a roommate.

At first, I was extra careful about using appliances and asking for permission before eating things in the fridge. But soon, the weirdness faded away. We were a couple, one cohesive unit, and it didn't matter about the technicalities of who owned what.

After brushing my teeth and putting on underwear, I stumbled into the kitchen where Amos was whipping us up omelets. The smell of savory vegetables on a hot skillet and bread crisping in the toaster sent my stomach into overdrive.

"You are amazing," I said to Amos while leaning over the breakfast nook and swiping an orange from his fruit bowl.

"This is a special first day of school breakfast. Believe me, most days, we'll be lucky to race out of here with a breakfast bar." Amos methodically stirred the egg yolk as it hardened, then mixed in the sautéed onions and mushrooms.

"Are you nervous?"

"Are you?" he cocked a curious eyebrow my way.

"Yeah. There are butterflies in my stomach. I always get a little nervous on the first day of school. Just the newness of it." I tried peeling my orange in one continuous loop, but the skin refused to cooperate.

"You know that you're not the one attending classes this time around."

"Funny."

"It's your first day as a full-fledged teacher." Amos slid the omelet onto a clean plate. We brought the plates to the dining table, which was covered in books I'd used to pass my certification exam.

"I never thought I'd be a gym teacher. We always made fun of them, like who'd want to be a gym teacher? But it's cool. I can help kids with their physical fitness."

"I hated gym. It felt as useless as..."

"Learning history?" I bit into my omelet and moaned in delight.

We ate our breakfast fast since the clock was ticking. At least it wasn't blaring anymore! I dug into the eggs and toast like I was dying of hunger. Pro tip: find a man who can cook. A great cook is better than a big cock. I should put that on a bumper sticker.

Was it weird that I found Amos cute while he ate, his cheeks bunching up and eyes rolling back in culinary pleasure? It was weird. But it was still cute.

Amos wiped off his mouth and went back into the kitchen. He came back a moment later with a kid's soccer-themed lunchbox. Soccer balls dotted the blue plastic.

"I got this for you for your first official first day of school." He opened the lunchbox, which was full of lunch. "There's a turkey sandwich, a fresh apple, and a thermos of La Croix. The La Croix might be flat by the time you drink it."

My heart swelled to even bigger sizes for this guy. "Amos, I am the luckiest man on earth."

"It's literally just a sandwich and chips."

I rolled my eyes at his modesty. I clutched the lunchbox against my chest. "This is going to be the greatest lunch I've even eaten in my life."

I pecked him on the lips. "Thank you." I pecked him again. "I love you." And again. "Best boyfriend ever." And now I slipped in some tongue.

Oops.

Amos massaged my tongue with his.

Or not oops.

"When do we have to leave for school?" I asked while our lips were pressed together.

"Twenty minutes." He slid his tongue into my mouth, then back out, sending a jolt of lust through my body. "But we need to get showered and dressed."

"We can multitask." I picked Amos up and carried him down the hall into the bathroom.

"Wait. Don't put too much weight on your knee."

I'd had a good summer of my knee not acting up, save one time when I stupidly said yes to playing frisbee with Raleigh. It was a gorgeous summer day, which I then had to spend recuperating on the couch.

Once in the bathroom, I stripped off his clothes with one hand while turning on the shower with the other. My dexterity was A-plus.

Goosebumps crested across his lithe, firm body as I ran my hands up and down his torso, taking in the creamy soft skin. My dick poked into his thigh. He followed me into the shower where the water slicked our skin. I pushed him against the wall as I devoured his body, planting rough kisses on his neck and down his chest. Amos let out groan after groan as I took him in my mouth.

His thick rod sent heat pulsating through every nerve ending. Bitter pre-come hit my throat and I bobbed up and down on his dick. Amos dug his fingers into my hair and pushed me further, forcing me to take more of him. Water cascaded down my face as I sucked him off, unleashing glorious sounds from my man above.

I cupped his sack in my hand, flicking my tongue over his nuts.

Feeling him quiver under my touch made my dick super hard, like need-a-permit-to-carry hard. I drifted a sneaky finger down his taint and brushed it over his ass. He put up a leg on the edge of the tub as if we were mindreading, giving me full access to his pink hole. I brushed my tongue over his opening, the skin clenching at my touch.

"We're going to be late," he breathed out. "Traffic. Parking space." He could barely string together a coherent thought.

"If you want me to stop..." I went to stand up, but he pushed me back down.

"Make it fast and furious. I want to come and be punctual."

So much for not being able to spit out a coherent thought.

"One Vin Diesel, coming right up." I forcibly moved his legs apart. He hoisted one of them onto the edge of the tub, giving me a clear shot to that beautiful hole. I swirled my tongue around his opening, eliciting more pants and grunts from above. I gave his ass cheeks a few hard slaps, the sound echoing loudly in the shower. My cock leaked down my leg. Heat built in my core.

I picked Amos up, his legs finding their familiar spot around my waist. My feet slid on the tub floor, and even though I was hard and brushing against his hole and ready to combust, this whole thing felt like a broken neck waiting to happen.

"I can't get balanced."

I could push him against the wall and fuck him from behind, but I wanted to look at him. Watching his eyes go glassy with ecstasy was a necessary component.

"We can leave the shower and come back," he said.

"Is that still shower sex, though?"

"Let's not get caught up on semantics."

Right. The clock was ticking, and I couldn't go to my first day of school with blue balls.

I lay down on the bathroom rug. My eyes rolled back into my head as he lubed me up and let me impale him. Since we were exclusive, we eschewed condoms. More money to put toward Rome.

But back to fucking. What a perfect start to the morning. Amos bounced atop me, his dick flopping on my stomach as heat and desire choked his breath. His eyes were heavy-lidded and over-flowing with lust.

"Come for me," I growled.

He held onto my chest for dear life as waves of release shot across my chest. I lifted my hips to fill him completely, giving jack-hammer thrusts until the orgasm drew my balls up. I pulled out and came on his ass.

After catching our breaths, Amos leaned down to kiss me. I could've held him against me and made out all day.

"Let's go. We're going to be late."

"Can't we say we missed the bus? Or the dog ate my home-work? Or maybe there was a power outage and our alarm clock didn't go off?"

Amos stood up and hoisted me standing. We got into the shower, cleaned ourselves off, and made our way to a new school year.

33

AMOS

TWO YEARS LATER

I n the spot where I was standing, ancient Romans conducted regular market activities thousands of years ago. There was a whole civilization doing the same things we did today: running errands, going to market. Gladiatorial fights were essentially ancient football games with extra blood splatter.

I walked around the ruins, eroded blocks of tan rocks that had once housed advanced structures. Patches of grass grew around stone pathways. Tourists milled about around me, headphones in on their audio tours, taking picture after picture. I didn't need pictures. I just wanted to experience being here.

I closed my eyes and imagined being a Roman back then conducting business at the market. What kind of conversations did they have? Did ancient Romans smalltalk and have petty grievances with each other like us modern folk did? What would they think about us treating the crumbling remnants of their market as a historical landmark?

Warm, assured hands massaged my shoulders.

"Whatcha thinking?"

"Just wondering about our ancestors."

"And if they really used bathhouses as gay sex joints?"

I spun around and kissed Hutch quiet. The man had gone full tourist with a Rome T-shirt and fanny pack. Bud had insisted he wear one since wallets could easily be pickpocketed.

Yes, somehow, by the grace of God, Hutch made a fanny pack sexy.

"So what is the official word on Romans having gay sex like it was nothing?"

"You are obsessed with Roman bathhouses."

"I'm a curious learner."

This guy. I wasn't much better, though. When we watched sports on TV, ninety-nine percent of my comments were about the players' asses.

"Roman men were allowed to have same-sex sex without being ostracized from society but only if they took on a dominant role. So basically, Romans were bottom shamers."

"Nothing to be ashamed about." Hutch gave my ass a surreptitious squeeze.

From his fanny pack, he pulled out a bag of Skittles and poured candies into his hand. He picked out the greens and yellows and handed over the rest to me.

"You can eat any color you want," I said. "You don't have to keep doing this."

"I know I don't." He smiled as he popped a green Skittle into his mouth.

Once the bag was empty, and we washed the sugar residue off our hands, we continued ambling through the market ruins as I continued to explain what market life was like in ancient Rome. He did his usual thing of spinning my wedding ring around my finger while caressing my palm. Sweet and sensual. We got married three months ago in Aguilar and Clint's backyard amid blooming, fragrant apple trees.

When I first decided to save up money for a trip to Rome, I

never thought I'd be coming here on my honeymoon. We waited until the school year was over to visit.

"Speaking of bathhouses, did you know that the town Bath in England got its name because Romans had built bathhouses there? They also built over 55,000 miles of road that still exist in the UK."

Hutch had gotten used to me droning on during this trip. I was his own personal tour guide whether he liked it or not. He pretended to act interested and never tried to shut me up.

"Please tell me if I'm rambling," I said self-consciously.

"I love when you ramble. You're passionate about this stuff, and I love seeing you in your element."

That was how I felt listening to Hutch talk about soccer and watching him on the sidelines at games. I wasn't a sports guy, and I'd never seek it out on my own accord, but Hutch's passion rubbed off on me.

"I can't believe I'm here." I craned my neck around, still pinching myself that I'm in Rome. "I couldn't have done it without you."

Quite literally. Hutch contributed to the travel fund, helping us get here faster.

"Where to next?" he asked.

"You mean for lunch?"

"Now that you've crossed Rome off your travel bucket list, where should we take our next vacation to? We can refill our travel fund for more adventures."

I wanted to travel the world with Hutch. I could be anywhere as long as I was with him.

"Australia?" I threw out. "I want to see the Sydney Opera House and go snorkeling in the Great Barrier Reef."

"Let's do it! I can try surfing."

Hutch tanned and glistening on a surfboard? Yes, please.

"Well, technically our next trip is to New Orleans."

"Yes! I'm looking forward to it. You know, your niece has strong legs. I think she could play soccer."

"You said that about my nephew, too. Your mission is to turn my whole family pro."

"I think there are some soccer genes in your family that need to be explored. Also, how good was that bottle of champagne your parents sent to our room?" Hutch did the Italian kiss of his thumb and fingers. He'd been doing that a lot on this trip.

"I can't believe my parents sent me a bottle of champagne on our honeymoon. I can't believe we're excited to visit my family again. It's wild. Somebody pinch me."

Hutch pinched my nipple. Fortunately, my fanny pack was situated over my crotch.

But truly, it was a miracle. The Miracle of Hutch. When we got more serious, he'd encouraged us to visit my family in New Orleans. He hit it off with my parents and sister's family, bonding over sports. He didn't have the awkward history that I had with my family. His clean slate made it easier for him to chat and find ways for us all to spend time together. He was the bridge I needed to reconnect with them.

Honestly, after Hutch and I got together, I was ready to write them off. I had Bud and Hutch and my friends. But after Seth and Hutch managed to make amends, it inspired Hutch to help me. *Don't give up on them*, he'd told me. *Let people surprise you.*

He rubbed his stomach. "Maybe first we should plan for lunch. I'm getting hungry."

Sightseeing was just a nicer word for "walking aimlessly for hours." My stomach rumbled as well. The scent of pizza was never far in Rome.

We walked up a hill from the market that overlooked more ruins and the Colosseum in the distance. I found shade under some trees, a welcome relief from the hot July sun.

"Question." Hutch sat down on a rock, a rock that might've

been where ancient Romans sat millennia ago. "Did they have history teachers back then?"

"In ancient Rome?"

"There were schools, right?"

"Wealthy kids had private tutors."

"Did those tutors teach history?"

I took a large sip from my South Rock High water bottle. "What are you getting at?"

"Like at what point did humans start studying history? Ancient Rome is history. What would their history be? Dinosaurs? Cavemen?"

Hutch...managed to stump me with a really interesting question.

"My guess is they didn't know about dinosaurs or cavemen. I think they assumed the gods created everything and that was that. They didn't seem like people who looked backwards."

"They're missing out, because history is my favorite subject. But maybe it's because I'm hot for teacher." Hutch winked at me, and we continued our dream vacation.

Thanks for reading!

What happens when mortal enemies Everett and Raleigh are forced to be fake boyfriends? Find out in *Drama!*, an enemies-to-lovers, fake boyfriend, nerd/jock romance and Book 2 in the South Rock High series. Grab your copy today.

Want to learn more about Charlie the bartender and his hot, bear husband Mitch? Their love story can be found in the Single Dads Club series, which is also set in Sourwood. Their book is The Barkeep and the Bro, which also features lots more Amos.

To read the whole story about Principal Aguilar got together with his boyfriend Clint, join my mailing list *The Outsiders* and receive the free story, *Getting Schooled*. It's filled with humor, heat, heart, and cacti.

Rafael

As principal, my schedule is chock full of mentoring students, coffee (obviously), and butting heads with construction worker Clint.

His laid-back parenting style for his detention-prone nephew is making my job extra difficult. And it doesn't help that whenever he comes in for a meeting, I imagine him grinding me like a pencil sharpener.

The highlight of my day is talking to Mr. Appleseed, my email pen pal. With each message, he worms his way closer to my heart. Is this a one-sided love connection destined for another heartbreak?

Clint
One day, I'm chugging along as a lifelong bachelor. The next, I'm an instant parent to my nephew after my sister unexpectedly dies. He's hurting, and I can't do anything right.

The last thing I need is for some fancy-pants principal to remind me that I'm floundering in my new role.

At least I have CactiGuy. He's the one person in this world I can truly confide in, the one person who makes me believe I can do this dad thing.

But now he wants to meet. Will he like the man behind Mr. Appleseed?

Getting Schooled is a sexy, sweet novella containing all your enemies-to-lovers, single dad, anonymous pen pal vibes...plus a karaoke machine to keep things interesting. It's a prequel to the South Rock High series, but can be enjoyed on its own.

Join today at www.ajtruman.com/outsiders

Please consider leaving a review on the book's Amazon page or on Goodreads. Reviews are crucial in helping other readers find new books.

Join the party in my Facebook Group and on Instagram

@ajtruman_author. Follow me at Bookbub to be alerted to new releases.

And then there's email. I love hearing from readers! Send me a note anytime at info@ajtruman.com. I always respond.

ALSO BY A.J. TRUMAN

You Got Scrooged

Written with M.A. Wardell

Marshmallow Mountain

ABOUT THE AUTHOR

A.J. Truman writes books with **humor, heart, and hot guys.** What else does a story need? He lives in a very full house in Indiana with his husband, son, and cats.. He loves happily ever afters and sneaking off for an afternoon movie.

www.ajtruman.com
info@ajtruman.com
The Outsiders - Facebook Group

Printed in Great Britain
by Amazon